Awakening Desires

I was dreaming . . . someone lay beside me on the hard, narrow bed . . . rough, strong hands were caressing my body, touching me intimately as I had never been touched before . . . my thin gown was being pulled down past my shoulders and breasts, while the strong hands cupped my breasts, squeezing them roughly. . . .

Suddenly I was wide awake, my eyes open and staring into the dense blackness of my room.

"Here now, Antonia, love, what is this gown for? Surely, we know each other better than this . . ." a deep male voice spoke wryly, his lips brushing my ear—and then he looked at me.

"My pardon, ma'am," he continued easily in a gentle Scots accent. "It seems I've stumbled into the wrong room, quite by mistake, I assure you."

His eyes, as black as the night itself, traveled down past my face to my breasts. With one swift movement, the stranger reached down and drew my gown back over my shoulders. Once more I felt the strange sensation of rough hands on my bare skin; my body responded as if trained to his touch.

As he bent over me in that brief moment, his face only inches from mine, he stared at me intently, then said gently, "Why, yer just a wee lass."

Then, with a wry, mocking smile, he bowed elaborately, grabbed his shirt and coat from the floor where he had dropped them, and left the room.

The Fires of Beltane

Pamela Wallace

PINNACLE BOOKS • LOS ANGELES

THE FIRES OF BELTANE

Copyright © 1978 by Pamela Wallace

All rights reserved, including the right to
reproduce this book or portions thereof
in any form.

An original Pinnacle Books edition,
published for the first time anywhere.

First printing, September 1978

ISBN: 0-523-40376-3

Cover illustration by Bill Maughan

Printed in the United States of America

PINNACLE BOOKS, INC.
2029 Century Park East
Los Angeles, California 90067

FOR EARL

We hear the merry pibrochs play,
  We see the streamers' silken band.
What Chieftain's praise these pibrochs swell,
  What crest is on these banners wove,
The harp, the minstrel, dare not tell—
  The riddle must be read by Love.

SIR WALTER SCOTT
Lord of the Isles
Canto First, IV.

Prologue:

On Culloden Moor in the wild, rugged Highlands of western Scotland where the tragic battle between the Scots and the English was fought in April, 1746, there stands a simple gravestone. It reads:

CONAL MACLAREN, BELOVED
OF BRENNA BREAC.   OUR
LOVE SHALL DEFY TIME.

THE FIRES OF BELTANE

CHAPTER 1

Lord of the isles, whose lofty name
A thousand bards have given to fame
LORD OF THE ISLES
Canto First, VIII

I had been sleeping soundly, deep in a dream filled with the summer-brown plains of the San Joaquin, when I was abruptly awakened by the sound of the driver shouting hoarsely, "Fort William in ten minutes!" Opening my eyes slowly, reluctantly leaving the memory of the dream, I uncurled my body from the corner of the cramped, dingy coach. My legs had fallen asleep and my left arm ached from leaning on it while I slept. As I rubbed my arm and shook my legs, I looked at the other passengers. There were two, besides myself; a young man with bright red hair, a handlebar mustache, and a rakish air; and an older man in dirty, ragged clothing, with white hair and the face of an apostle. The young man sat opposite me, occasionally giving me a surreptitious glance out of keen blue eyes, while the older man sat next to me, his face in profile. He had sat that way, stiff and unmoving, for the entire six hours of the journey.

In profile, the old man's spirituality was startling; a long, fine nose and firm chin half concealed by a white beard; the face of a saint. Then suddenly he turned to pick up his pack from the floor of the coach, and I saw him full-face for the first time. It took all of my self-control not to gasp. The lid of one eye was permanently closed and the other stared at me with startling penetration.

The old man lifted his pack, which was covered with oil-cloth and had a strap for his shoulder, and placed it on the seat between us. In it I could see a strange assortment of pins, needles, tape, buttons, ribbons, combs, and brushes. Leaning back in the seat, his face once more in profile, he straightened his faded green tartan waistcoat.

I looked out of the window, embarrassed at having stared so obviously at the man's distorted face. The window was lowered halfway and the rushing wind whipped the two thick braids that hung to my waist. Strands of hair that had escaped from the braids blew softly across my face. The closer we came to Fort William, the faster the driver urged on the horses. As we rounded a bend, I caught a glimpse of the team, their gleaming brown coats covered with white lather. Outside, also, I could see the heather-covered hills of western Scotland. In the distance, the woods were stained with autumn colors, and I could see a flash of water, probably from a small loch, between the trees.

When I first arrived in England and took the train from London to Edinburgh, I thought surely there could be nothing greener or lovelier than the English countryside. And then the train passed through Carter Bar and into Scotland. Heathery moors sloped down to distant valleys, autumn mists crept from wood to wood, and the sea pounded savagely against sheer cliffs. In the foreground rose the tall peaks of the Eildon Hills, blue as grapes, and quite beautiful. But I thought, with a sudden sharp pang of homesickness, that these mountains were not as tall and majestic as the Sierra Nevada back home. This land wasn't neat and well-tended as England, or my own San Joaquin Valley in California, but wild and harsh and almost uninhabited. Nature ruled here, not man.

As I looked at the overpowering landscape, I felt my body stir and I knew that somehow I belonged here. Though this strange, wild land was completely alien to me, I felt that, in some inexplicable way, I was coming home ...

I was brought out of my reverie by the young man opposite me who began singing. Looking at me out of the corner of a bright blue eye, he sang boldly:

"As I went down to Overgate, a lassie passed me by, she winked at me wi' the tail o' her eye, but mind ye I was fly. Ricky do dum day, do dum day, ricky, dicky do dum . . ."

Just then the coach rounded a sharp bend and I interrupted the young man's song by falling headlong into his lap. Laughing good-naturedly, he helped me up, leaving his hands around my waist for just a moment longer than was necessary.

"I'm very sorry," I apologized, after I had returned to my corner of the coach. Outside I heard the driver curse the horses, then whip them on.

"Quite all right," the young man responded lightly in the soft, lilting accent of the Scot. "They call that turn 'The Devil's Elbow' because it is so sharp. By the way, I am Garth Farren, originally of Lochalsh, now living in Glasgow and bound for Inverness. And yourself? I can tell from yer accent yer no' Scottish nor a Sassenach neither."

"Sassenach?" I asked, confused.

"A rather impolite term for Englishman," Mr. Farrén explained with a wry grin.

"I'm from the United States," I answered hesitantly, remembering Aunt Mercedes's stern warning about talking to strangers, especially men. But I had gone against my naturally friendly nature for three weeks, playing the prim and proper young lady, and now I rebelled.

"My name is Carissa Rey, but everyone calls me Chrissa."

"Rey is a Spanish name, am I right?" Mr. Farren asked easily.

"Yes," I responded happily, enjoying the first real conversation I had known since my journey began. "My father was a Californio, a descendent of the original Spanish settlers in California. But my mother was from Scotland."

"California . . ." Mr. Farren pronounced the strange name awkwardly. "Ye're a long way from home, Chrissa Rey. May I ask what such a pretty Californian is doing in a draughty old coach in Scotland all alone?"

"I'm on my way to the Isle of Skye to live with my mother's former guardian, Sir Duncan MacLaren."

I saw Mr. Farren's expression sober for a brief moment before he carefully replaced it with a smile, and the old man sucked in his breath in a shocked gasp. I knew that something I said had surprised them both.

"Is anything wrong?" I asked Mr. Farren frankly.

"O' course not," he answered lightly.

But the old man said harshly, "The world an' all that is in it stands on the brink o' hellfire! The MacLaren would do well to mind that!"

He turned his one piercing brown eye on me, seeming to look into my very soul. In spite of myself, I shivered.

"Dunna pay any attention to the bodach," Mr. Farren whispered to me as the old man turned away. "He's only a packman, a bit daft from wandering alone through the hills."

"But what did he mean, 'The MacLaren'?"

"That is how we refer to the chief of the Clan MacLaren. Sir Duncan is the chief."

Then he added, clearly trying to change the subject, "The MacLarens are an ancient clan, descended from Somerled, Lord of the Isles. But then, I imagine ye ken all about the history of the MacLarens."

"No," I admitted, rather embarrassed. "I know very little about them. Who was the Lord of the Isles?"

"He ruled the islands off Scotland's western coast, including Skye, and recognized no king above him," Mr. Farren answered proudly. "For centuries the chief of the MacLarens was Lord of the Isles. He was a powerful king in his own right . . . until the Sassenachs came to power, o' course."

I wondered how he knew so much about the MacLarens, and as if reading my mind, he continued easily, "Kyle of Lochalsh, where I am from, is separated from Skye by only a few hundred yards of water. We know everything that happens on the Misty Isle, as 'tis called."

"The Misty Isle," I repeated softly. "What is it like?"

"Ach, well, it must be seen, no' described," Mr. Farren said firmly. "But I can tell ye 'tis a very special place, no' like any other."

And then he added, in an almost reverent tone, " 'Tis the mountains that make it seem so magical . . . the Black Cuillins. In the old days, when the folk of Skye lived in stone huts, they worshipped the mountains. An' even today there are powerful superstitions surroundin' them."

Just then the coach came to a screeching halt outside an inn in the village of Fort William. The driver called down that passengers bound for Inverness must leave to board another coach, and the strange old man

6

left quickly, without looking back. Mr. Farren stepped outside, then suddenly turned back to me and said through the open window, in a voice grown suddenly grave, "Take care, Chrissa Rey. Terrible things ha' been known to happen to bonnie lassies like yoursel' on Skye."

I started to ask what he meant by such a strange remark, but he walked away hurriedly and in a moment disappeared into a crowd of people.

After tossing down some baggage from the top of the coach the driver returned to his seat and whipped on the new team of horses that had been quickly harnessed. I caught a glimpse of pristine white houses with clean, simple lines, before we were once again in the country.

The road stretched on in bleak solitude, with only an occasional windowless crofter's cottage, built of turf and roofed with thatch, to break the desolation of the darkening countryside. I saw only one person, a young girl in a black dress with a white scarf on her head. On her back she was carrying a large basket filled with peat, the basket held by a rope slung across her chest.

A mist came up, making the countryside grow mysterious and veiling the mountains. Now the beautiful scenery seemed chilling and fearful, and in the cold coach I wrapped my thin black cloak more tightly around me. I looked outside to find that what had once been huge rocks were now cloudy shadows. There was the sound of distant thunder rolling angrily around the hills. Suddenly there was a flash in the mist, then more thunder.

The mist turned to rain, coming in, thin, slanting, and cold, through the half-open window. Closing the window, I curled up in a corner of the coach, trying to stay warm and not dwell on Mr. Farren's ominous parting warning. And there also was the harsh admonishment of the strange, white-haired old man . . .

For the first time I began to have serious doubts about the family I was about to meet, a family I knew almost nothing about.

The coach rocked back and forth over the bumpy, uneven road, and gradually I was rocked to sleep like a baby, curled in the fetal position, my head resting against the cold leather of the seat. I dreamt again of the San Joaquin Valley, a tough little Indian pony named Lindo, and a large adobe house with a huge fireplace in the living room. There were people in the dream, a woman with fiery red hair and a soft face, and a tall, dark-haired man. And then a strange face appeared. At first pale and saintly, it gradually turned satanic, the features distorting. A voice came from it, spitting viciously, "Beware the MacLaren!"

A sound, at first far off and muffled, but slowly growing to a mind-shaking roar, brought me out of the nightmare. The roar grew louder, almost overwhelming, and I looked quickly out of the window, fully expecting to find an avalanche of boulders bearing down on us. I saw that the road had narrowed through a rocky gorge. On one side was the mountain, on the other a sheer drop to a river far below. Ahead I could clearly see the Falls of Measach, shining pale silver in the moonlight, that the driver had earlier told me to expect. They roared over two hundred feet down into the boiling waters of a river. "The devil's cauldron," the driver had called it.

This then was the Corrieshalloch Gorge, and that meant that we were near Mallaig where I would board a boat for Skye. I was fully awake now, and filled with a great sense of expectation as I thought of soon meeting the man who had raised my mother.

The rain had stopped but the wind blew hard and as the coach picked up speed rushing down the mountain, I could hear the wind's high-pitched scream. Then I saw the lights of Mallaig and moments later the town itself.

Mallaig lay on the Sound of Sleat, its harbor tucked away in a shelter of hills and rocky headlands. Boats of all sizes and shapes bobbed up and down in the rough water and wind-spawned whitecaps shone in the moonlight. The driver pulled up in front of an inn situated only a few yards from the waterfront. A sign swung back and forth crazily in the wind, and I could just make out the words, "Cock 'n Crow."

As the driver opened the door for me, he said in a voice grown hoarse from shouting at the horses, "Ye'll be comfortable here, miss. The innkeeper, Mrs. MacGregor, will tell ye how to catch the ferry to Skye."

He then climbed to the top of the coach and handed down my one worn suitcase to an old servant who appeared out of the inn. I followed the thin, wizened little man inside to the first warmth and light I had known in hours.

9

The inn was plainly furnished and obviously visited mostly by hunters and fishermen. The narrow hall leading into the main room was lined with glass cases containing mounted salmon; over the large stone fireplace in the middle of the room were two stags' heads looking down with glassy stares. The reception office itself formed a kind of cage for Mrs. MacGregor, who looked distinctly like a bird, plump, tiny, and sharp-featured, with eyes that darted about nervously. She was thin-lipped and clearly suspicious of a young girl traveling alone.

When I asked about the boat to Skye, Mrs. MacGregor replied curtly, "Leaves at eight o'clock in the mornin'. *Precisely*. Ye can tak' breakfast afore ye leave."

Then she motioned to the man who had brought in my bag to take it up to my room, and I followed him quietly. After climbing two flights of low stairs and walking down a long, dark hallway lit only by one pale lamp, we came to my room. I noticed when we entered that there was no lock on the door, but when I mentioned this, the little man assured me simply that there was no need for locks in Mallaig. I was too tired to really care, to do more than give the room a cursory glance. It was small but clean and comfortable, with a window overlooking the harbor. In a corner stood a washstand and small, round mirror.

The servant left and I quickly shed my wet, dirty traveling clothes and slipped into a thin cotton nightgown that I had long since realized was far better suited to mild California nights than chilly Scottish ones. Walking to the window I looked out, wondering if the vague black outline I saw in the distance, far beyond the harbor, was Skye. Then I went to bed, crawling happily under the thick blankets, and, exhausted, fell immediately into a deep sleep.

I was dreaming . . . someone lay beside me on the hard, narrow bed . . . rough, strong hands were caressing my body, touching me intimately as I had never been touched before . . . my thin gown was being pulled down past my shoulders and breasts, while the strong hands cupped my breasts, squeezing them roughly . . . they slid down past my waist and hips to my thighs, caressing them lightly . . . teeth bit into the soft flesh of my neck sending shivers of pleasure and pain through my body . . . within me something was awakened, something deep and mysterious, while, instinctively, my body responded to the caressing hands in crosscurrents of growing pleasure . . . I was pulled against a hard body, and I could feel a broad chest and strong arms, and below, where his body narrowed, a growing hardness thrust against the small of my back . . . then the hands spread my legs open and reached up . . .

Suddenly I was wide awake, my eyes open and staring into the dense blackness of my room.

"Here now, Antonia, love, what is this gown for? Surely we know each other better than this . . ." a deep male voice spoke wryly, his lips brushing my ear.

Pulling away from his firm grasp, I whirled around and came face to face with a man,

11

hardly more than a vague shadow in the utter darkness.

"What the hell do you think you're doing!" I lashed out angrily, consciously imitating the harsh tone I had often heard the ranchhands use, hoping my bravado would somehow frighten off my attacker.

There was a stunned silence, the roving hands stopped abruptly, then the man said slowly, "I'm afraid there's been a mistake. I thought . . . you were someone else, ma'am."

He stood shakily and I realized suddenly that he was drunk, that in his drunken state he had stumbled into my room instead of this Antonia's. At that moment the moon, which must have been obscured by clouds, came out and the black room was flooded with moonlight. I could see the man clearly now, standing in front of me, tall and dark-haired and naked to the waist.

It was the first time I had ever seen a man's bare chest, and I could not stop myself from staring with wonder and frank curiosity. His chest was broad and dark, covered with black hair tipped with silver. It was a powerful, muscular, completely masculine body, and I shivered again when I remembered that my own body had been pressed against it.

To my surprise, the man smiled, betraying a secret amusement at this embarrassing and awkward situation.

"My pardon, ma'am," he continued easily in the gentle Scots accent that sounded almost like some great cat purring. "It seems I've stumbled into the wrong room, quite by mistake, I assure you."

12

His eyes, as black as the night itself, traveled down past my face to my breasts, and I realized with sudden mortification that they were still uncovered. With one swift movement, the stranger reached down and drew my gown back over my shoulders. Once more I felt the strange sensation of rough hands on my bare skin, and my body responded as if it had been trained to his touch.

As he bent over me in that brief moment, his face only inches from mine, he stared at me intently, then said gently, "Why, ye're just a wee lass."

I hesitated, then answered firmly, "I'm old enough to know how to scream when someone barges into my room and behaves as inexcusably as you have. If you're not gone by the time I count to three, that's just what I'll do."

He looked at me for a moment, with that same wry, mocking smile, then bowed elaborately, grabbed his shirt and coat from the floor where he had dropped them, and stumbled out of the room, gone before I could even begin to count.

I lay trembling from fear and something else that I couldn't name. Why hadn't I screamed, I asked myself angrily, dismayed at my behavior. But I knew the answer. When I had turned and looked into those black eyes, I felt a shock of recognition. They were very familiar, as if I had looked into them many times before. It was like a vague memory, deeply buried, that won't quite come clear. I felt strongly that I had gazed longingly into those eyes before, and yet ... I couldn't have.

I awoke early the next morning, tired from a fitful night's sleep. The memory of what had occurred hours earlier remained strong, and I felt a vague disquiet. I dressed slowly, with fumbling fingers, then stood in front of the window overlooking the harbor. As I was standing there, a coach pulled up beneath my window, and I was surprised to see that it was the same coach that had brought me to the hotel the night before. The driver, looking tired and dirty still, jumped down and began talking to a tall, bearded man who had just walked out of the inn. Even though the wind was high, I could hear what they were saying.

"What are ye doin' here at this time o' mornin', John?" the bearded man asked in a thick accent.

" 'Tis himsel' wantin' to go to Fort William," the driver replied, "an' payin' me twice the fare for a coach full o' passengers. It seems Sir Duncan isna' so sick after all an' he's off as soon as he came."

"Aye, an' good riddance, I say," the bearded man spoke forcefully. "We dunna need *his* kind here."

"And what kind is that?" a harsh voice asked sardonically from out of sight.

Almost immediately, a man as tall as the bearded man, but broader in the shoulders, stepped into view. I realized with a shock that it was the same man who had come to my room during the night. Next to him stood a petite, slender woman whose head barely came to his shoulders, her face hidden by the hooded cloak she wore; the infamous Antonia, I thought wryly. The man's brown hair was whipping

14

about his face, his black eyes were blazing, and his mouth was set in a thin, hard line. There was something almost evil about him, and I saw the driver step back, obviously afraid.

But the bearded man stood his ground, though I saw his eyes flinch.

"Ye ken what kind I mean, MacLaren!" the bearded man responded defiantly. "Ye ha' the deaths of two innocent people on yer hands. Yer no' a man but the devil himsel' . . ."

He had not quite finished when the man called MacLaren hit him, a hard, staggering blow that sent him reeling to the ground, his nose flattened and spurting blood. Then MacLaren shouted at the driver to be off, and helping the woman quickly inside the coach, he followed, slamming the door behind him.

The driver gave the bearded man a long look, saw that he was getting to his feet, and climbed back onto his seat. Untying the reins and taking the long black whip into his left hand, he shouted at the horses, who lunged off. In a moment the coach was out of sight.

The bearded man disappeared back into the inn, one hand cupped over his bleeding nose, cursing MacLaren.

Backing away from the window, I stood in the center of the room, trembling. The man who had come to my room in the middle of the night was a MacLaren, a relative of Sir Duncan . . . and an accused murderer.

The stone floor is bitterly cold and filthy, thinly strewn with old, damp rushes. I have wrapped the thick red and black MacLaren tartan tightly around my shivering body, but it does little good. Still, I am alive and will remain so. Lorn does not intend that I should die, merely that my will be broken.

There is a pale shaft of light filtering down through the hole in the ceiling of the tiny room. It is morning, another night gone. I cannot remember how many nights I have lain in this dank, wretched place, but it seems that I have been here forever. My memories of the outside world . . . of Conal and that last terrible day . . . are like vague dreams. But no dream could be so painful to remember.

Soon, I know, Lorn will come and, peering down through the small opening, ask if I remain obstinate. I wonder that he can still want me, for I know that by now I must look dirty and haggard, deathly pale from a complete absence of sun, a far cry from the proud girl whom Conal once loved so passionately.

When I was very young I was taught that I had been blessed with great beauty. Megan, the ugly old hag they called a witch, foretold my future, saying that my pleasing countenance would attract a great and wealthy man. But when I rushed back to the cell that my mother and I shared outside the monks' quarters at the chapel to St. Columbia and related what Megan had foretold, my mother beat me. Later, when I bathed my bruised shoulders in the burn that

16

ran near the chapel, I knew that it had been a mistake to talk of such things to my mother. She had been banished to the lonely, desolate retreat when I was still merely a stirring in her womb, accused of infidelity.

I never knew my father, but heard my mother rant against him bitterly every day for the fourteen years that we lived on the small, bleak island to the north of Skye. It was a relief to leave our cell for my lessons with the monks. Those grim, black-garbed figures were the only men I saw, save for a rare fisherman, come to place water on the blue altar stone in the hope that the Saint might vouchsafe him a fair wind. The monks, my mother, and Megan, banished to the island for using witchcraft to steal her neighbors' milk, were the only inhabitants of my narrow world until I was past fourteen. And then an ironic fate placed me in Conal's path . . . and therein lay my fulfillment and my destruction.

CHAPTER 2

Now nearer yet, through mist and storm,
Dimly arose the Castle's form.
LORD OF THE ISLES
Canto First, XXIII

An hour later I was leaning over the deck of the Stornoway boat, "The Glencoe," feeling full of adventure. As I turned from the misty headlands, grey in the drizzle, and gazed down at the clear, bottle-green depths of the Atlantic Ocean, the strange, disturbing feelings concerning the man called MacLaren were put behind me.

The deck of the boat was full of people; an older man in tweeds, leading a bright-eyed black and white sheep dog on a leash; a young, harried-looking governess sitting out of the

19

wind with four small boys, all in new suits; and a fat-faced young man in a black velour hat and dove-grey gloves. Mustachioed men in unpolished black boots and worn tweeds walked about, leaning on tall sticks, talking in Gaelic.

The ship steamed up the Sound of Sleat, between mountains vague in the increasing rain. Occasionally the sun would find its way through the clouds and light up a valley, a patch of heather, or a small, white farmhouse.

Hours later, the rain stopped and the clouds began to lift just as the sun was setting. It was then that I first saw the strange, grotesque mountains of Skye, blue-black and forbidding in the distance. I had read their names in a book I purchased in Mallaig—Blaven, Sgurr nan Gillean, Marsco, Beinn Dearg. They rose, tall and barren, surrounded by an eerie stillness, bathed in the clear, luminous northern light. As I looked at them, I felt the strange atmosphere that evokes what the Scots call the "wave in the heart." I was overwhelmed by these beautiful, awesome mountains, and I easily understood how people could once have feared them so much that they worshipped them. As the boat drew closer to them, I felt that I was heading toward the end of the world.

Suddenly I heard a splash near the boat and looked down to see a grey seal jump out of the water; not up and down playfully, but in a low, forward parabola, clearly trying to escape something behind him. The next moment I saw what was pursuing the little seal—a huge, dark whale, its rough, glistening back arching out of the water, rapidly closing in on its terrified prey. My hands gripped the railing tightly as I stared in horrified fascination. In a matter of seconds the seal and the whale had disappeared behind the boat to finish their grim chase out of sight.

I stood frozen to the railing, my new-found confidence shaken badly. Something in me had responded to the terrified seal, my own inarticulated fear connecting with his. I felt a surge of homesickness deeper than anything I had experienced during the long weeks of my journey, an intense longing for the familiar landscape and people of my home. In a moment, tears were mingling with the salt spray on my face.

The rain shook me out of my depression. It was starting to come down hard again and I moved to stand under an awning. The boat was steaming in between the mainland of Scotland and the island of Scalpay, and to the west loomed the giant mountains of Skye. Lights shone infrequently on the shore and there was no sound but the thrust of the steamer through the quiet sea. I felt the salt spray diminish as the boat slowed to enter the harbor of Portree.

The ship turned into the quiet harbor and sailors made it fast to the dock. I could smell the sweet reek of peat and see lights shining on the hillsides that sloped down to the edge of the village. People were standing on the jetty waiting to receive mail and other deliveries from the mainland. Among them was a short, red-bearded young man of about thirty standing next to an elegant carriage pulled by two well-matched greys. His eyes searched the deck

21

of the ship, went past me, then came back. He continued to stare at me rather hesitantly as I made my way down the gangplank and over to the luggage unloading area. A porter had just handed me my dufflebag when the young man walked up, doffed a worn green cap, and inquired politely in a thick, soft accent, "Pardon me, miss, but would ye be Miss Carissa Rey?"

I nodded, and his plain, freckled face broke into a broad grin.

"I knew it! There was somethin' aboot yer face, in yer pretty grey eyes mainly, that reminded me o' yer mither, tho' yer hair be black an' hers was red as a hot poker if I remember right."

"You knew my mother?" I asked eagerly.

"*Och*, aye, tho' I was only a mere lad when she left. But here I stand a bletherin' in the rain an' ye no' ken who I am. My name is Willie Fraser an' I am Sir Duncan's chief groom. I was sent to tak' ye to Castle Stalker."

With that he picked up my bag and led me to the carriage, quickly helping me inside out of the rain. I settled comfortably back in the seat as we took off, and surveyed my surroundings. This coach was a far cry from the one I had taken to Mallaig. The seats were well-cushioned and covered with red velvet. Red velvet curtains hid the windows. And there was a black and red traveling rug to keep my legs and feet warm. Judging from the opulence of the carriage and the fact that Sir Duncan had been so generous with my travel expenses, I decided that he must be a very wealthy man.

Pulling back the curtains, I looked out through the rain at the small village of

22

Portree. Few lights were shining and the streets were almost deserted, though it was only nine o'clock. There was a row of single-story shops along each side of the main street, then houses climbing up the hillsides around the small village.

We were quickly out into the countryside where the landscape changed abruptly to stark moorlands and bulky mountains. Aside from Portree, it was a desolate area, devoid of other villages or even isolated cottages. Once, lightning flashed over the far mountains and for an instant they were illuminated. The tall, jagged peaks were outlined against the dark sky, drenched in mystery and terrors. For one strange, mad moment I felt like flying from them as from the devil himself.

Closing the curtain quickly, I settled back in the seat, drawing the rug tightly around me. I wondered what it must be like to live always in the shadow of those awesome mountains. I could easily understand how people could be affected by them, as Mr. Farren had said, for even I felt strange stirrings and wild fears when I looked up at them.

And then I saw Castle Stalker.

At first it was nothing more than a dark outline through the rain—massive towers and hoary battlements rising above the surrounding countryside. As we grew closer, I saw that it rose sheer from the almost perpendicular edges of a rocky promontory, surrounded on three sides by the sea.

We were rapidly drawing closer to the castle, and I could see it clearly now. It was built of grey stone blocks, three stories tall, with a round tower on the right rising two more stories. A narrow bridge spanned what must once have been the moat, leading to the broad steps of the front entrance. Everything I had ever read of enchanted castles, captured princesses, and victims being tortured in dungeons, came true as I looked at the turrets of Castle Stalker lifted high in the dark above the trees. The very name, Castle Stalker, when spoken in a whisper on a black, stormy night seemed to conjure up blood, fire, and things done long ago in the dark.

As the carriage drove noisily over the rough stone bridge, I saw a light shining dully over the tall oaken doors. But all of the windows of the castle were dark. It was past ten o'clock and I knew that in a quiet place like Skye everyone would long since have retired to bed.

The carriage stopped abruptly and seconds later Willie opened the carriage door, extending his hand to help me alight. As I stepped down, the tall doors of the castle opened, and out stepped a thin, gaunt-faced woman holding an iron lamp in front of her. Wearing a white lace cap over greying brown hair pulled back in a severe bun, she looked altogether stern and forbidding.

She stared at me silently for a long moment, and I realized with intense embarrassment that I must look a sight with my hair hanging limply in the rain and my plain brown dress wrinkled and dirty. Looking me up and down critically, the old woman said in a hollow voice, completely lacking in warmth, "Welcome to Castle Stalker, Miss Rey. I am Rose MacBean,

24

the housekeeper. Ye best hurry in out o' the rain."

With that she turned and disappeared back into the castle. I followed quickly, then suddenly hesitated as I stood on the worn moonlit steps, staring into the empty blackness of the castle. I felt a wave of fear so great that I clenched my hands till the knuckles turned white and I could feel the nails biting into the soft palms of my hands. My breath came in short, quick gasps, as I was overwhelmed by a sudden, unreasoning terror. What could be in there to frighten me so, I wondered, horribly confused.

"This way, miss," Mrs. MacBean called to me from the black interior of the castle.

With tremendous effort I forced myself to pass through the doorway and into the castle.

Mrs. MacBean walked quickly through what I later learned was the Great Hall, a large entrance room with a ceiling that rose two stories. In the middle of the room a spacious oaken stairway led to a balcony overlooking the hall. Hunting trophies of old MacLaren chiefs were hung on the walls, along with old Moorish ironwork in strange, intricate designs. I stood staring at the Great Hall until Mrs. MacBean, who had mounted the stairs, called back impatiently, "Yer room is this way, miss."

As I hurried to catch up with her, I heard Willie behind me, carrying my bag up the stairs. From the pale light shed by the small lamp that Mrs. MacBean carried, I could see little of the surroundings. Then, as we walked down a long, wide hallway on the third floor of the castle, I felt my skin crawl and I sensed that in the darkness around me eyes were staring at me. Looking closer at the walls on either side of me, I caught glimpses of portraits— MacLaren ancestors in gilt frames, men in old uniforms and older tartans, elegant women in high bodices. Despite the different periods of time represented, all had the same insolent air of pride.

Suddenly Mrs. MacBean turned into an open doorway to the right and moments later I was standing in what was to be my room. The grim-faced housekeeper lit a lamp on a table near the huge canopied bed, then bent to stoke the dying fire in the marble fireplace. The room was large and well-furnished, with three tall windows that looked out onto the rear of the castle. There was a desk and chair, a tall oak dresser, vanity table, wardrobe closet, green velvet settee, and in a corner behind an ornate Chinese silk screen, a hip bath made of smooth, gleaming Skye marble.

While Mrs. MacBean hurriedly checked the room to make sure everything was as it should be, I stood at one of the windows and stared out at the mountains in the distance, on the other side of Stalker Bay. The Black Cuillins . . . tall and barren and overwhelming.

Willie arrived with my bag and after depositing it near the bed, he doffed his cap and bade me goodnight. Mrs. MacBean also turned to go. But as she walked through the doorway, she stopped, said brusquely, "This was yer mither's room," then vanished into the dark hall.

I was touched by the fact that she had given me my mother's old room, if indeed it had been her decision. Quickly I looked in the closet and in the drawers of the dresser for any signs that my mother had once lived here, but there were none. Finally, I gave up, overcome with exhaustion from the long journey. I had planned to unpack my things immediately, but I was so tired that I simply pulled out my nightgown and left the rest of the unpacking for the morning.

After turning out the light, I lay down on the huge, soft bed. Flames from the fire cast a soft glow about the room, and I could hear the gentle, soothing sound of the waves lapping the beach only yards away. As I lay in the darkness, I felt the heavy, slumbering quiet of the castle. It seemed strangely like a living thing, a great huge beast, motionless in sleep, which when awake would have a mood and will of its own. And yet I no longer felt the terror that had overwhelmed me as I stood in front of the castle earlier. It was as if the act of entering this formidable, ancient place had broken a spell. I was here, and what would happen, would happen.

Brenna
April, 1746

Megan lived in the ruins of Dunscaith, the "fort of gloom" in the ancient language. The ruins sat moodily on the summit of an isolated rock on the southern shore of a long, narrow, nameless loch. There was a ravine between the ruined castle and the mainland crossed by two arched walls which once, so Megan said, were bridged over with wood. But that was long since gone, and the narrow, high passage was a

27

fearsome thing to walk over. During the many long, eventless years that I secretly went to Dunscaith to visit Megan, I saw the castle gradually fall into greater and greater decay. As the mortar disintegrated under the influence of the sea, air, and wind, the stones at the foundations loosened and fell away, and the upper courses then collapsed under their own weight. Each time I went there I half expected to find Megan buried under a mound of freshly fallen rubble. But when I finally left the island, she was still there, living in the castle and managing somehow to elude the falling stones.

I asked her once how such a strange, gloomy, isolated place came to be and she answered in her half-mad, sing-song way, "All night the witch sang, and the castle grew up from the rock, with tower and turrets crowned; all night she sang—when fell the morning dew 'twas finished round and round . . ."

She told me wondrous tales of the castle, when it was heavily fortifed and holding many soldiers. During one battle, she said the seven ramparts' palisades of iron were spiked by human heads. And in the fastnesses of Dunscaith was a pit guarded by ten snakes. But my favorite story was that of Sgathach, a queen in the days of Fingal, who possessed a magical three-stringed harp, one string of which when plucked caused singing and merriment. Having only heard the heavy drone of the monks' chants, I had no idea what singing and merriment were like, but I imagined they must be quite wonderful.

Thinking back on it now from this grim

prison, remembering how little I had during all those years, is it any wonder that I was willing to sacrifice everything—honor, pride, the very future of the Bonnie Prince himself—for my one chance of happiness?

CHAPTER 3

Proud was his tone but calm; his eye
Had that compelling dignity,
His mien that bearing haught and high, . . .
LORD OF THE ISLES
Canto First, XXXI

When I awoke the next morning, the sun was already high and the room was bright with light. The storm had passed and left behind a beautiful, clear day. Slipping on my robe, I walked over to the tall windows and looked out, eager to see what the view was like in the daylight. I discovered that the windows overlooked the gardens in the back of the castle. They were neatly manicured and bright with a variety of flowers, some of which I recognized as broom, or genesta, the deep golden flower that grows in huge bushes all over Scotland. The gardens sloped down to the very edge of the short cliff, and beyond that the sea shone bright blue and calm. In the distance were the low-lying, mist-shrouded forms of other islands. As I looked at them, I became filled with a sense of loneliness and sorrow, and I quickly turned away from the bay toward the mountains in the distance. As the sun rose higher in the sky, the pale clouds above the mountains seemed to catch fire, burning red and gold above the jagged spires of the Sgurr-nan-Gillean. The mountains changed colors—first blue, then grey, then silver, and as the sunlight and shadows danced on their craggy slopes, the mountains themselves almost seemed to move, coming nearer and then retreating. The enchanted silence of this strange morning was broken only by the distant cries of birds in marsh and heather, and by the silver music of a nearby stream running over smooth pebbles.

In that moment I understood what Mr. Farren had meant when he spoke of the spell of Skye. It was, indeed, a haunted place. . . . For some reason I couldn't dispel the sadness that had crept up on me while looking at the islands in the distance. For the second time in two days my eyes were filled with tears,

I hadn't cried, at least not in front of anyone, since my parents died when I was seven years old. A fever swept through the small village of San Luis Obispo on the central California coast where we lived. I was too young to know what the illness was called. I only knew that people sickened and died, that homes which had once been full of talk and laughter, were boarded up, to become empty and silent.

My father died first, his death coming so quickly that his body was burned and buried before I knew that he was gone. My mother lingered for a short while longer. I wasn't allowed to go into her room until the third day of her illness. Then, minutes before she slipped into the delirium that preceded death, the doctor, looking old and dirty and utterly exhausted, took me in to her.

I almost didn't recognize her. Her face was pale and drawn, covered with perspiration; her bright red hair clung limply to her forehead and cheeks. She held my shaking hands as her grey eyes stared urgently into my frightened ones. For a moment it was so quiet that I could hear the ticking of the grandfather clock in the next room.

And then she spoke in a hoarse, painful whisper.

"Your father had to leave ye, child, and I must join him. But ye will be fine. The doctor will take ye to your Aunt Mercedes and Uncle Randolph. They will care for ye and ye will survive. *You* are a survivor, Chrissa. Never forget that."

There was more that I didn't understand. I didn't even understand what she meant when she said that I was a survivor. But later I understood. There were many times in the following years when I would wake in the middle of the night and know that I was alone, that there was no one standing between me and the nameless, shapeless horrors of the darkness.

And I would bury my head in my pillow and cry deep, muffled sobs that wracked my small body. But when the sun rose and I joined Aunt Mercedes and Uncle Randolph at breakfast, my eyes were dry.

That was being a survivor.

Aunt Mercedes and Uncle Randolph were not unkind to me. They took me into their home without comment, as a matter of course, fulfilling their obligation to their orphaned niece completely. I was fed and clothed and eventually given my own pony to ride over the hundreds of acres of the Wyngate Ranch. That they were entirely lacking in affection toward me was due to the tremendous bitterness that consumed them both. If they had no love for me, it was equally true that they had no love for each other.

They never explained their feelings to me, of course, but I learned enough from Milky, the ranch foreman and my best friend, to understand their bitterness. Milky had been with them for nearly fifteen years, since before Mercedes Rey had married Randolph Wyngate out of financial necessity. As a member of a Californio family that had once been wealthy and powerful, she considered herself far above the coarse, crude American. But the Rey family had fallen on hard times, as had most others after the United States took over California, and she had been forced to put aside her pride. Uncle Randolph, Milky insisted, was deeply in love with the beautiful Mercedes Rey and was blinded to her true feelings toward him.

The marriage was an unhappy one. But

eventually there was a son, Andy, whom they both adored, and it looked as if a truce would prevail between them. Then, in the year before I came to live with them, Andy died. Milky would never tell me exactly what happened, but it was clear that my aunt and uncle each blamed the other for their son's death. The atmosphere of their home grew cold and grim, and they were barely civil to each other.

There were times when it seemed that Uncle Randolph wanted to reach out to me to establish some kind of close relationship. A short, stocky man with reddish-brown hair and a ruddy complexion, he was not without a sense of humor. And occasionally he would tease me in a fatherly way as we sat over the dinner table. One such time, when I was eight and had only been living at the ranch for a few months, Uncle Randolph said to me, "Chrissa, I watched you trying to ride old Rosie today. I imagine you're pretty sore from falling off her."

"It didn't hurt," I lied quickly, embarrassed to discover that someone had been watching me.

"Well, I always did say that girls ain't good riders," he continued easily, his brown eyes twinkling. "Especially when they're so small their feet don't reach the stirrups."

He concluded, grinning openly now, "Guess we'll just have to get you something a little more your size. Like that chestnut pony in the small corral."

My eyes grew big with astonishment and pleasure. I had wanted the beautiful little pony since I had first seen it, but I had never expected to be allowed to ride it for I knew that it had belonged to Andy.

Before I could say a heartfelt "Thank you," Aunt Mercedes interrupted quickly, "I don't think that would be a good idea, Randolph. That pony isn't right for Carissa. I suggest that you find *another* pony for her."

I looked at her, sitting regally at one end of the long mahogany dining table opposite Uncle Randolph. She was tall and slim and elegant, still a beauty though she was past forty, with her black hair piled high on her head, secured by a tortoiseshell comb. Her dark eyes looked back at me coldly, without emotion, and I knew that the pony was lost.

Later that night as I was passing the parlor on my way to bed, I saw Aunt Mercedes standing inside, staring at the portrait of Andy that hung over the fireplace. And though I couldn't put it into words, somehow I understood Aunt Mercedes. She would never let another child take Andy's place—in any way.

But aside from the strained relationship between my aunt and uncle, and my aunt's consistent coldness toward me, the ranch was a wonderful place for a child to grow up. I gradually became an accomplished rider and eventually Uncle Randolph gave me a small pinto, whom I named Lindo, to take the place of the pony I had wanted so badly.

In the winter I rode recklessly through the tall, emerald-green grass that grew thickly everywhere, leaving a trampled path behind me. And in the summer I always came in covered with dust from the plains that by June were dry and barren. By the time I was twelve I was pestering Milky to let me help break the green horses. He always refused saying, "Yuh may not act like it most of the time, but yuh *are* a girl—and girls ain't s'posed to be bronc busters."

I was an almost complete disappointment to Aunt Mercedes, refusing to conform to her ideas of how a young lady should behave. I was a tomboy, headstrong, independent, and much more comfortable in men's Levis than thick petticoats and full skirts. But Aunt Mercedes never gave up trying to mold me into a model of feminine grace and deportment. She forced me to spend endless unhappy hours learning to sew, embroider, and play the piano. I eventually became surprisingly adept at these feminine pursuits, though I never ceased to dislike them intensely.

I was only really happy when I was riding over the fields on Lindo, attired in faded Levis and an old flannel shirt. In the summer, when the temperature often rose above a hundred degrees, I would ride Lindo to a nearby stream where I could strip to my bloomers and go swimming. Later, I would sit on the bank, drying off, and look at the heat haze shimmering above the flat, parched brown fields.

During the quiet times like these I often thought of my parents. Though I had heard a great deal about my father from Aunt Mercedes, who was extremely proud of her family's history, my mother was a mystery. Aunt Mercedes, who clearly disapproved of her brother's marriage, would only say that Diego Rey had married beneath himself when he wed

Catherine MacLaren, for it seemed she had no dowry.

Other than that I had only my own memories to go on. My memories were of a kind, loving woman who sang songs in a strange language called Gaelic. I wondered about my mother's background, what part of Scotland she had come from, what her family was like. With my vivid imagination, I wove romantic fantasies about her. In some she was the daughter of a wealthy but cruel man who disinherited her when she married my father. In others she was a simple milkmaid who captured my father's heart with her sterling virtue and great beauty.

I thought I would never know the truth about my mother until that hot July day in 1899, three months after my seventeenth birthday, when the letter with the strange seal came.

The letter was lying upside down on top of a stack of mail on a silver platter that sat on a table in the hallway. Normally I paid little attention to the mail for none of the letters that came were ever for me. But that letter intrigued me. The seal on the back was stamped with something that looked like a family crest—two lions guarding a castle.

I looked at the seal for a long moment, then turned over the envelope to see who had sent the letter. There was no return address, but the stamp showed that the letter had been mailed in Portree, the Isle of Skye, Scotland.

The Isle of Skye . . . somehow it seemed that I had heard the strange, beautiful name before, but I couldn't remember where or when. I wondered if this was where my mother came from, and suddenly I was filled with intense curiosity and excitement. Clutching the letter tightly in my hand, I ran to Aunt Mercedes's room. Since the letter was addressed to her, only she could open it.

I knocked loudly, then waited impatiently for a long moment until I heard Aunt Mercedes's irritated "¡Venga!" Quickly I opened the door and entered, and found my aunt sitting in a rocking chair near the window, mending clothes. Rushing over to her, I thrust the letter into her hands, announcing dramatically, "It's from Scotland!"

She betrayed no emotion other than a mild surprise, but merely sat stiffly for a while, staring out the window, making no move to open the letter. Finally, after what seemed like a very long time, she carefully slit the envelope with a pair of scissors lying in her sewing basket. Inside was one sheet of paper with a few brief lines of writing on it.

I waited expectantly and momentarily Aunt Mercedes said softly, "It is from the man who was your mother's guardian, Sir Duncan MacLaren. He is ill and wishes to see you before he dies. If you are willing to make the journey to Castle Stalker, his home, then I am to write him immediately. He will send instructions and money for the journey."

She looked up at me and the confusion I was feeling must have shown for she explained quickly, "When your mother came down with the fever, she left a letter that she asked me to mail to this Sir Duncan. I understood that she informed him of her imminent death and advised him that she was leaving behind a child. I mailed the letter, including my name and address, but I never heard from him. You should keep that in mind when deciding whether or not to accept his offer."

I understood precisely what she meant. The MacLarens had known about me for ten years and yet they had never shown any interest in my welfare. But in spite of that, I felt that I must go to Castle Stalker on the Isle of Skye. It was an opportunity to learn the truth about my mother's background, and I wanted desperately to do that. Already from the brief letter I had learned that my mother had been orphaned, like myself, and raised by a guardian who probably was a relative since his name was the same as hers.

Looking directly at Aunt Mercedes, I said firmly, "I want to go."

After a tense silence she said curtly, "Very well, I shall make the arrangements."

One month later I stood on the platform outside the train station in the small village of Tulare, waiting for the train that would take me to San Francisco and from there to New York. Beside me was my one worn dufflebag carrying the few items I cared to take with me. In a corner of the bag, under my clothes, was a faded photograph of my mother and father, taken when they were married.

At the station that day my aunt was her usual cool, aloof self, but my uncle was openly affectionate. As the train whistle blew and I prepared to board, he hugged me tightly, whispering in a trembling voice, "Take care of yourself, Chrissa. I'll miss you."

A minute later I was sitting in a private compartment as the train slowly pulled away from the station, watching the receding figures of my aunt and uncle standing alone on the small wooden platform. Ahead of me lay a lonely journey of several thousand miles to a mysterious castle on a remote island . . .

I was so deep in my memories that I didn't at first hear the knock on my door. Then it came louder, bringing me back to the present with a jolt. Turning, I called "Come in," and the door opened to admit a young maid, carrying a tray heavy with covered dishes and a silver teapot in a knitted blue cozy.

She walked awkwardly across the room, depositing the tray carefully on a small table near the windows. Then, turning back toward me, she curtsied, her hazel eyes lowered demurely. She had orange-red hair that escaped in curling tendrils from a black cap, and was dressed primly in a black dress and white apron. With full red lips and a voluptuous figure that the severe dress couldn't hide, she was actually quite attractive, though Aunt Mercedes would have called her looks "shameless."

She seemed rather ill at ease, so I said encouragingly, "Good morning. I'm Chrissa Rey, what's your name?"

"Lucy, miss," she replied shyly, adding, almost as an afterthought, "I've brought ye yer breakfast. The rest o' the family ate an hour ago. I would ha' awakened ye but Mrs. MacBean said we should let ye sleep since ye arrived so late."

41

Pointing at the tray, she recited, "There's scones, oatmeal, ham, and tea."

I was surprised at how hungry I suddenly felt. Throughout the trip I had been so excited that I hadn't eaten much, but now I was famished. I sat down at the table and began to eat with relish. The hot scones, a sort of sweet biscuit topped with melted butter and jam, were especially delicious. Momentarily, however, I looked up to see Lucy still standing over me awkwardly, peering at me curiously out of the corner of an eye.

"Is something wrong?" I asked finally, thinking that my manners, which I knew were far from perfect, might have offended her.

"Och, no, miss," she responded quickly. " 'Tis just that, well, Morag, the cook, told us that ye were half Spaniard and we didna' ken what to expect. We, some of us, that is, thought ye might be verra dark an' gaudy, wi' a comb in yer hair an' a red shawl over yer shoulders, like the gypsies who come 'round sometimes."

I burst into laughter, the first time I had really laughed in a long time.

"Don't worry," I finally managed to say to the distraught looking Lucy. "I'm really very American and not at all exotic. In fact, I think everyone will probably be quite disappointed in me. Perhaps I should dress up as you describe so they won't find me too dull."

Lucy's guileless, open countenance broke into a wide grin, as she said easily, "Och, miss, ye're teasin' me," and we both laughed together.

She continued, " 'Tis just that there was so

42

much excitment aboot ye comin'. Sir Duncan sent Willie doon to the dock every day for the past week on the chance ye had come."

Suddenly Lucy's hands shot up to her mouth, her eyes went big and round, and she said nervously, "Oh, crivens, I forgot to tell ye, Sir Duncan is expectin' ye in the library at ten and 'tis nearly that now."

At this announcement all the excitement I had felt throughout the journey came flooding back and I felt my body tense as I stood and walked over to my dufflebag. "Well, I'd better hurry and dress, then," I said, trying to sound casual and confident.

"Oh, miss, ye must let me help ye," Lucy insisted, following me eagerly. "I'm to be yer maid, ye know, an' anythin' ye need, just ask."

She stopped abruptly, bit her lower lip worriedly, then added uncertainly, "Unless, o' course, ye're no' happy wi' me. I must tell ye that I am new at this, bein' a personal maid, that is. I've always worked in the kitchen wi' Morag 'till now. 'Twas Mrs. MacLaren's idea that I be yer maid. But I've been talkin' to her girl, Yvette. French she is, and knows all aboot the latest fashions an' hairstyles an' all. She's teachin' me all aboot sich things an' I will try to be acceptable to ye."

I was discovering rapidly that Lucy was a nonstop talker when she felt relaxed and comfortable, in sharp contrast to the shy person she had first appeared to be. Finally I simply interrupted her monologue, insisting, "I'm very happy that you're to be my maid. And I'm sure you'll be much more than acceptable. Don't worry about being new at it. I've never had a personal maid before, so I'm new at it, too."

"Never had a maid!" Lucy exclaimed incredulously. "But who dresses ye then?"

"I do," I answered simply. "I've been dressing myself since I was seven, so you see, I'm used to it. At seventeen I doubt that I will be needing help."

"Seventeen?" Lucy asked, clearly surprised. "Why, miss, I should ha' thought ye were no more than Miss Betheny's age, an' she's barely fifteen. 'Tis the way ye wear yer hair, in those long braids that makes ye look so much younger. Ye must let me fix it in a more mature style. Ye know . . ."

Before she could continue indefinitely, I interrupted, "Who is Miss Betheny? And Mrs. MacLaren? Is she the wife of Sir Duncan?"

"Ach, no," Lucy replied. "Mrs. Antonia MacLaren is the widow of Sir Duncan's older son, Robert. He died five years ago on their honeymoon. She was his *second* wife."

Lucy looked at me slyly, clearly trying to decide how frankly she could talk to me. Finally she said slowly, "There are those who think she wasna' too bereaved." And then she continued quickly, "Anyway, Master Robert left a daughter, Miss Betheny, and a son, Master Jonathan, from his first marriage."

I realized that my new family was larger than I had expected, and somehow the news was encouraging. Instead of a lonely castle with one unknown old man, as I had feared, there was a whole houseful of people, including a girl near my own age.

"Do they all live here?" I asked, when it occurred to me that Mrs. MacLaren and her step-children might have their own home.

"Aye," Lucy responded. "Except for Master Alex, o' course."

"Master Alex?"

"He is Sir Duncan's younger son, the only living one now," Lucy explained with a trace of nervousness in her voice. "He was here for awhile, but he left the day before yesterday. Mostly he's gone."

I realized immediately that Alex MacLaren must be the man I had met at the inn, the man who had been called "worse than the devil himself"; the man who had touched me as no other man ever had. I still shivered uncontrollably when I remembered the feel of his hands on my bare skin, his eyes staring frankly at my uncovered breasts...

I couldn't resist asking, "What is Alex MacLaren like?"

"Oh . . . tall an' black-eyed, no' more than thirty-two or thirty-three, I should imagine. Rather handsome, some think."

And then Lucy gave me a sidelong glance, adding casually, "Has quite a way wi' lassies."

Inexperienced as I was, even I understood her tone and the slight blush in her cheeks. She was attracted to this Alex MacLaren, had even perhaps been his mistress. My suspicions of him were confirmed. He was a lecherous rake-hell who took advantage of any woman he fancied, including the servants in his father's house.

Just then Lucy spoke urgently, "Och, miss, 'tis nearly ten. We must hurry!"

I let her button my dress, then sat quietly at

45

the dressing table as she quickly brushed my hair. I knew that if I refused to allow her to help me she would feel I was rejecting her because of her inexperience as a lady's maid. And though I had only known her for a brief while, I instinctively liked her and wanted her to be my friend.

As I sat in front of the mirror, feeling Lucy gently pull the stiff bristles of the brush through my long hair, I studied my appearance. Lucy's comments regarding the wild speculations among the staff made me wonder what kind of impression I would make on Sir Duncan. The Spaniard in me was obvious, in my black hair and olive complexion. But there was Scottish, too, in my grey eyes and turned-up, freckled nose. I decided that aside from the fact that my mouth was a bit too full and I was taller than a girl should be, Sir Duncan shouldn't be too disappointed in me.

Lucy interrupted my critical self-appraisal, saying happily, "Yer lucky to hae such pretty black hair, so fine an' soft, no' course an' curly like mine. But some day when we hae more time, ye must let me fix it in a fancier style."

She braided my hair quickly, with surprising expertise, and we left immediately. As we walked hurriedly along the wide hallway, I saw that the castle looked quite different during the day than it had the night before. The portraits that had seemed so menacing earlier, were now merely interesting.

There was one in particular that especially intrigued me. Hung in an inconspicuous corner where it would easily escape attention, it was poorly cared for and covered with a thick coating of dust and grime. The fact that it was unfinished, everything beneath the faded face only blank canvas, added to an air of neglect and unimportance.

All of this I noticed hurriedly as Lucy led me down the hallway. The face itself—a young woman with tousled hair that could have been blonde or light brown, and pale eyes—was a blur. And yet, this dirty, incomplete painting interested me as none of the others did. I found myself wondering who the girl had been and why her portrait was incomplete. Perhaps, I thought sadly, she had died while sitting for the painter.

We were passing through the Great Hall now and in the bright sunlight it was even more impressive than it had appeared the night before. The flat, panelled ceiling rose at least twenty-five feet and on the walls I could see more clearly the Moorish ironwork that I had only glimpsed earlier. It was shiny black iron, with numerous curling tendrils and crestings, carrying sconces or brackets for lights. And on either side of the tall oaken doors leading outside were iron eagles with extended wings. I could easily imagine the fierce-looking eagles mounted on a wall in a castle in Spain.

As we walked across the Great Hall toward a door in a corner, Lucy said softly, "The library is right there, miss."

Stopping in front of the door she continued in a low voice, "Dinna be afraid."

I couldn't help smiling to think that my nervousness was so apparent.

Lucy opened the door, stepped just over the

threshhold, and announced coolly, "Miss Rey, Sir Duncan."

Then she stepped aside for me to enter.

Gathering my courage, I boldly walked through the doorway, chin held high, into the library. Whatever I had expected, however, it wasn't this. In the middle of the small, book-lined room, sat the man who had been my mother's guardian—in a wheelchair. A red and black tartan rug was thrown over his legs and in his right hand was a cane. I saw his back straighten as I entered and he made a tremendous effort to raise his grey head proudly. His face was pale and lined, his lower lip quivered, and the wrinkled, bony hand that held the cane shook uncontrollably.

But though he was old and feeble, and clearly very ill, there was still an arrogance about him, the air of one who is accustomed to being in command. There were traces of the bold, proud, even hard man he had once been, in the black eyes that looked directly at me, and in the firm, stubborn chin that jutted out almost angrily.

I walked up to him, then stopped, not knowing what to do next. There was a long pause as he stared at me, then he spoke in a weak, rasping voice.

"So, ye're Catherine's daughter. There's no' much of her about ye. Except in the eyes, perhaps. Take after that thievin' papist father of yours, I see."

I reacted as I usually did to criticism, immediately and hotly, without thinking, forgetting that this was an obviously sick old man who should not be argued with.

"My father was not a thief! He was a God-fearing man who believed in the Catholic faith. And I'm proud to look like him."

To my surprise, Sir Duncan laughed weakly. "I suppose ye do take after Catherine after all," he responded in his low, unsteady voice. "Ye've got her temper." Then he added soberly, "I haven't long to live, as ye can plainly see, child. I wanted my affairs to be in order before I go to meet God. I thought of what the Bible says . . . the sins of the father shall not be visited on the child. And that is why I asked ye here. This was yer mother's home for most of her life, till she ran off with that Spaniard. She was a MacLaren, and you are also. This shall be yer home for as long as ye want, and what would have been hers upon my death, will be yours. We MacLarens take care of our own."

As I stood there listening to the speech that was clearly tiring Sir Duncan a great deal, I realized that he expected me to accept everything he was saying without question. He was not used to being defied, the MacLaren of MacLaren, a man everyone would take orders from. I wondered how he and his tempestuous son, Alex, got along.

It occurred to me that it must have been terribly hard for my mother to have gone against his wishes and run off with my father. I wondered again what her relationship had been to Sir Duncan, but somehow I didn't feel I could ask him. He seemed accustomed to asking questions, not answering them.

Suddenly he started to cough violently and in an instant a woman had rushed to his side. I had been so absorbed with Sir Duncan that I hadn't noticed her standing in a nearby corner. Plainly dressed, wearing a nurse's cap, she had a pinched, grim demeanor. She handed Sir Duncan a pill, then put a glass of water to his lips.

"It's too much for you," she said tightly in an English accent that seemed somehow incongruous in the surroundings. "You'd best go to your room and rest now."

"All right, woman," Sir Duncan responded in a barely audible whisper.

She started to wheel him toward the door, but he stopped her with an imperious wave of his gnarled hand, and turned back to me.

"Just one question," he said, and his voice was so weak that I had to strain to hear him. "Was it worth it? Was she ... happy?"

I knew that my mother had run away from her family to marry my father, so I understood immediately what Sir Duncan meant. But I didn't know what to say. I had never thought about whether my mother, who had died so young, had been happy. Quickly I tried to remember her, and all the memories were the same—a laughing, singing, loving woman. For the first time in many years, I remembered what she had said to me as she lay dying: "Love is all that matters, child."

Looking at Sir Duncan, this frail shell of a man with death written plainly on his pale face, I answered honestly, "Yes, sir. She was very happy."

His eyes filled with tears and he nodded vaguely, before the nurse wheeled him out of the room.

I stood in the center of the room, alone, feeling somehow sad and disappointed. In the back of my mind throughout the long journey had been the thought that perhaps Sir Duncan would turn out to be a kindly father figure, someone loving and protective. It had been a very long time since I had felt that I had anyone to turn to, anyone to rely on other than myself. But after my short meeting with him, I knew that this wasn't to be. Sir Duncan was as cold and proud as Aunt Mercedes. In spite of his obvious affection for my mother, he had never forgiven her for running away. Only imminent death and a strong sense of duty had persuaded him to bend enough to send for me.

I was as alone as ever.

Brenna
April, 1746

It was when I grew from a child to a woman, when my body bled and I knew I could bear a child, that Megan prophesied my future. I remember that day well. I arose early, before my mother, and hurried away from the chapel toward Dunscaith. It was so early that the autumnal mists lay over the fields in long, waist-high streaks of silver. Thin grey veils were queerly twisted in hollow places, lying above old watercourses like the ghosts of other streams that once ran there. As the sun rose, the mists fell away, like spectral armies in retreat, curling off or streaming upwards from the earth. The air came sweet from the sea, ice-cold and scented with the pungent earthiness of autumn, and all the land smiled like a baby suckling at his mother's breast.

51

Megan was bent over the fire that burned continually in a small anteroom just inside the castle. She looked up at me slowly when I came running in, and in that instant I knew that this was to be a very special day. She did not smile as usual, but said tersely, "Sit, child."

I sat on a dirty rug on the far side of the fire from Megan, and waited for the pronouncement that I sensed would come. Through the ever-changing flames of the fire I saw Megan's deeply lined, weathered face watching me carefully. Finally she spoke.

"Ye're no longer a child."

It was not a question. I nodded, and I felt my excitement fade, replaced by a growing sense of uneasiness. I had never seen Megan look so grim and foreboding.

And then the prophecy came, in a short, rapid burst of words that seemed to be torn from Megan's very soul.

"Ye're a beauty . . . many men will want ye, but only one will truly hae ye . . . a great an' wealthy man."

And then it was over. Megan's catlike green eyes blinked once, as if she were coming out of a trance, and she sighed deeply.

I sat there, stunned, for a long moment. It was not terrible, as I had feared, but wonderful!

"But, Megan, 'tis a good fate you portend for me," I said finally, confused by her deadly silence.

She answered enigmatically, "To hae the sight, as I do, is a mixed blessin'."

"Is there more, then?" I asked anxiously.

52

But she shook her head heavily and said firmly, "Go, child."

There was no disobeying her. I left immediately, but as I made my way back to the chapel, I thought of what she had said, and even her strange sadness could not destroy my happiness. To attract a great and wealthy man—what more could a girl hope for?

CHAPTER 4

In distant lands, by the rough West reproved,
Still live some relics of the ancient lay.
LORD OF THE ISLES
Canto First

As I was standing in the middle of the library, forcing myself to accept the sad reality of the situation, I had the strange sensation that I was being watched. There was no sound or movement, but *something* told me that I was not alone. Whirling around to face the open French windows that led to the gardens, I came face to face with a young girl who was standing just outside. My abrupt movement startled her and she jumped nervously. She looked to be about fourteen or fifteen, with light brown hair pulled back from a face that would have been plain had it not been for her eyes, large and round and black as night. I knew immediately that this must be Betheny.

"Hello," I said politely.

"H-hello," she stammered nervously in response.

When she said nothing further, I volunteered, "I'm Chrissa Rey. Are you Betheny?"

"Yes," she answered with a hesitant smile. After a moment's pause, she continued, "I'm s-sorry. I didn't mean to spy on you. Lucy told me you were here and I came to meet you."

"I wanted to meet you, too," I responded easily.

There was another awkward silence and it became apparent that Betheny was painfully shy. She reminded me somehow of a small, wounded animal, afraid of the world, all its defenses up. She was several inches shorter than I, probably not even five feet tall, I guessed, and very thin. Her tininess added to her air of fragility, and I found myself feeling protective toward her, though I had no idea why she would need protection.

"I was very glad when Lucy told me about you," I began, smiling. "It will be so nice to have a friend here who is near my own age."

Betheny smiled tentatively, then spoke shyly, "Lucy s-said you are terribly nice. She was right."

She hesitated, then continued, "I was very much looking forward to your coming. It gets rather lonely here."

"But don't you have a brother?" I asked impulsively.

"Oh, Jonathan's mean, he teases me about

my s-stammer," she answered, blushing furiously.

I could see that Betheny's speech problem was an intense embarrassment to her.

"A stammer is nothing to be ashamed of," I said immediately, trying to assuage her embarrassment. "We all have problems. and I'm sure Jonathan has his share. I know I do."

Betheny's beautiful black eyes widened as she asked frankly, "What problems do you have?"

I was taken aback by her straightforwardness, but after a moment I answered honestly, "I have a terrible temper. I don't like taking orders from anyone. I've been rather used to being on my own and now when someone tries to tell me what to do, I don't take it very well."

"Everyone tells me what to do," Betheny said ruefully, looking downcast.

Before I could think what response to make to her pathetic statement, she continued more confidently, "Have you s-seen the castle yet?"

I shook my head no, and she asked eagerly, "Would you like to s-see it? I'm a very good guide, I know absolutely everything about it."

"I would love it," I answered happily.

Leaving the library we walked through the Great Hall to the rooms on the other side of the ground floor of the castle. These were mostly the servants' quarters and the kitchen, and they were all deserted. Betheny explained that nearly everyone had gone to the wedding of the head gardener and the upstairs maid.

She showed me where additions had been made to the castle throughout its long history, and as she talked I thought what a difference

57

there was in her cultured speech compared to the thick accents of the servants. Whereas Willie and Lucy spoke so thickly that at times I could barely understand them, Betheny and Sir Duncan almost sounded like upper-class English. When I asked Betheny about this she explained simply, "Jonathan and I were educated in England, and grandfather had an English tutor when he was young. It's the fashionable thing to do. Most everyone in the upper class is educated in an English s-school."

And then she added proudly, "Except that Uncle Alex refused to do it. Grandfather s-sent him to a school in England, but he ran off. He hated it, you see. Grandfather kept s-sending him back and he kept running off."

Betheny clearly admired her uncle's rebelliousness, probably, I thought, because it was a quality she seemed to lack. I suspected that she would like to be more like her adventurous, defiant uncle.

We had returned to the Great Hall now, and Betheny continued with her guided tour. She spoke knowingly of the castle's history, and I could tell that this place meant a great deal to her.

"The keep, this s-section that is five stories tall, is over a thousand years old, and the rest of the castle was built around it. Down through the centuries different chiefs added on to it and when grandmother came, s-she had the entire interior renovated."

After walking up the broad flight of stairs leading to the first story Betheny led me into the drawing room. She explained that it had once been the banqueting hall when the keep was all that existed of Castle Stalker. The room was beautifully furnished with a crystal chandelier, a gleaming black grand piano on a raised platform, and ornate furniture reflecting the varying tastes of different mistresses of the castle. But the huge stone fireplace with massive chimney breasts emblazoned with the MacLaren coat of arms, and the enormous thickness of the walls revealed in four deep window bays, indicated the tremendous age of the room. `

"It's only been for the past hundred years or s-so that the decoration has been so elegant," Betheny explained. "Till then, it was rather a rough existence."

Her soft, tentative voice droned on and on, and I found myself daydreaming, imagining the room as it must once have been when it was the baronial hall of a powerful island chief: the ceiling a massive oaken covering of heavy beams and boards stained black by the smoke driven down the chimney by the raving Skye winds . . . the fireplace a cavernous arch filled with a huge fire of peats . . . on the walls, tapestries, stands of arms, plumed helmets, and shirts of chain mail . . . the stone floor strewn with rushes, filthy with the remnants of many feasts, amidst which dogs quarrel fiercely for the bones . . . at the upper end of the hall, next to the fire, a low raised platform supporting the lord's table . . . and sitting there, overlooking his clan, the Lord of the Isles, the black-eyed MacLaren of MacLaren, watching me closely, obsessed with desire for me, his very eyes seeming to impel me toward him . . . "Brenna, come here, lass . . ."

I fainted.

My head was swimming and when I looked around, everything was blurred. Gradually my vision cleared, and I could see that I was sitting on the floor, my head propped against a chair, and Betheny leaning over me, her face pale and anxious.

"Chrissa!" she shouted. "Are you all right?"

"Yes," I finally managed to say, surprised at the dryness in my mouth.

"What happened?" Betheny asked, near tears.

"I believe I fainted," I said slowly, embarrassed to admit it, though it was rather obvious. I had never fainted before, and had no idea why it should have happened now.

"I'll ring for Lucy," Betheny said immediately, and before I could stop her, she pulled the velvet bellpull in the corner.

"I'm quite all right," I insisted, trying to stand. Though my legs felt weak, I managed to rise, and stood leaning against the chair.

In a moment Lucy arrived and Betheny asked her to bring some tea immediately. Lucy left wondering, I'm sure, why we wanted tea only an hour after breakfast. I sat down heavily in the chair, with Betheny hovering anxiously over me.

"Are you s-sure you're all right?" she asked nervously. "Perhaps we should send for the doctor."

"No, please," I insisted. "I really am much better now. It was just a temporary dizziness. I don't know why it came on me like that."

Betheny bit her lip, then said hesitantly, "Morag s-says there are things here we don't understand, things not of this world. Especially in a place as old as Castle Stalker, that has seen s-so much of death and tragedy."

Normally I would have vehemently denied such supernatural ideas, but now I remained silent. Something inexplicable *had* just occurred. For a brief period I had clearly seen the past. Not only seen it, but been a part of it.

Or was it just a vivid hallucination brought on by fatigue from my long and strenuous journey from California? And if it *was* merely a hallucination, why did it leave me with a name . . . Brenna . . . so strongly in my mind?

Lucy entered then with the tea, and after dutifully drinking a strong, hot cup, I insisted that Betheny continue the tour of the castle. I was more fascinated by it than ever, and determined to find out as much about it as I could.

A door at one end of the drawing room led into the large, elegantly furnished dining room. A brightly polished oak table capable of seating twenty people stood in the center of the room. And against one wall was a huge, ornately carved sideboard that Betheny said had been brought from London over two centuries earlier. It was an attractive room, filled with sunlight from four tall windows that looked out onto the rear of the castle.

Betheny walked toward a wide double-door at the far end of the dining room, saying, "Now I'll show you the best room of all. It's terribly grand, really."

She opened one of the doors and I looked in at a huge, ornately decorated ballroom. As I walked into it, I thought to myself that it was indeed "grand." I had never seen anything so magnificent in my life. Several giant mirrors reflected the marble-panelled walls and the huge crystal chandelier hanging in the center of the room. Tall windows along the wall overlooking the sea were draped in heavy red velvet, and at the far end of the room a raised platform was provided for the musicians.

"You s-should see it when it's filled with people!" Betheny exclaimed excitedly. "When the candles in the chandelier are lit and people are waltzing around the room. Many of the gentlemen wear the traditional kilt and the ladies are all in silk and satin and fabulous jewels."

She sighed, continuing softly, "There hasn't been a ball in years, not s-since father died. Grandfather frowns on them, you see."

"Will there ever be another ball?" I asked.

"Yes," Betheny answered hesitantly, suddenly looking shy and nervous again. "On Beltane. That is the first day of May and it is always celebrated with bonfires. I shall turn sixteen that day and it is family tradition that I must have a debut. Grandfather has already s-said it shall be."

"You don't seem very excited about it," I observed gently.

"Oh, I like Beltane," she responded quickly. "The bonfires are quite exciting, but . . ." her voice trailed off as she looked down at her feet dejectedly. Finally she finished softly, "I s-shall be the center of attention. Everyone will be looking at me, talking about me. And it would be s-so awfully embarrassing to be a wallflower."

She stood there with her head hung, looking so miserable that I felt intensely sorry for her. Poor child, she was frightened of everything, including things that should have been exciting and enjoyable. I thought how in a way she and I were alike, only I had learned to hide my fears from the world, while hers were plain to see. The protective feeling I had immediately felt toward her when I first saw her in the library was stronger than ever. All my life I had not only wanted someone to love me, I had just as strongly wanted someone I could love and care for—someone who could make me feel needed. I felt that Betheny needed me and I wanted desperately to help her.

Putting my arm around her shoulder, I said confidently, "Don't be ridiculous. You won't be a wallflower, you'll be quite a success!"

"You really think so?" Betheny asked hesitantly.

"Of course," I responded with forced enthusiasm, inwardly determined to make my promise come true. Between now and Beltane, nine short months, I would teach Betheny to have more confidence in herself. I realized that I was trying to play Pygmalion, and I couldn't help smiling inwardly at the thought, aware that I could stand some improvement myself. I had spent most of my life in Levis and a man's shirt, and even now I felt uncomfortable in a dress. And as for other articles of feminine attire, especially stays and corsets, I simply refused to wear the uncomfortable, restraining things. All in all, I was hardly a likely candidate to make Betheny a ballroom success, but I intended to do my best.

Betheny interrupted my thoughts with a suggestion to continue the tour in the portrait gallery, and we left the beautiful, empty ballroom.

The portrait gallery was the wide hallway on the third floor where the family bedrooms were located. As we walked along the hallway, I was again surrounded by the faces of MacLaren ancestors.

"This is a portrait of the tenth chief," Betheny began, pointing to a very old painting. "He died in 1497. He's my favorite of all the old ones. While in Portree one day he saw a beautiful peasant girl and immediately fell in love with her. He pretended he was a poor landscape painter and wooed and won her. But when they were married he brought her back to the castle and told her the truth. Instead of being happy she was very s-sad because she felt she wasn't well-bred enough to be the mistress of Castle Stalker. She grew ill and died very young, leaving one son. The chief was heartbroken and never remarried. Isn't it romantic?" she sighed.

I couldn't help smiling at Betheny's romanticism, realizing that for her it was an escape from the unhappiness of her life.

Then we were standing in front of the relatively recent portrait of a stern-faced man with dark blue eyes and reddish blond hair, and Betheny grew suddenly sad.

"That was my father," she said softly.

As I looked at the picture of Robert MacLaren, I could see no resemblance between him and Betheny. Where he was fair, she was dark; and where he had the hard arrogance of his father, Betheny had an appealing softness.

"Lucy told me that he died several years ago. I'm very sorry."

"It's all right," Betheny responded quietly. "It happened a long time ago. That was when Uncle Alex returned for the first time. He had left when I was just a baby, and travelled all over the world, even to India. He and grandfather never got along, you s-see. But when father died, he had to come back for awhile. Though he is away quite a lot, he generally returns every few months at least, to supervise the running of the estate. Grandfather can no longer manage it. When Jonathan comes of age next year and takes over the estate, I imagine he will go away again for a long while. I shan't like that."

"You like your uncle quite a lot, don't you?"

"Oh, yes! He's very different from father. Father was terribly serious, much like grandfather, and awfully religious. But Uncle Alex just likes to enjoy life and have adventures. I love to hear him talk about the places he's been and the exciting things he's done."

Though I disagreed with Betheny's adoration of her uncle, I said nothing. I could understand how, being an orphan, she could be so attached to him.

Pointing to a nearby portrait of a young boy about ten years old, Betheny continued, "That's a portrait of Uncle Alex when he was a child. He refused to s-sit for another when he grew up."

The boy in the picture had pink cheeks and

wide-set, innocent dark eyes. Dressed in a kilt, holding a bow and arrow, he looked every inch the young Scottish gentleman. But there was something rather sad and lost in his expression, and the stubborness of the firmly set chin foreshadowed the harsh man he would become.

"We'd best hurry if we are to have time to see the grounds before lunchtime," Betheny said suddenly.

We left, and as we walked down the hallway toward the stairway I glanced back quickly at the portrait of Alex MacLaren, wondering if he had been as unhappy as he looked in that picture.

Then, near the stairs, I again noticed the unfinished portrait of the blonde girl, and I stopped Betheny.

"Who is that?" I asked, pointing to the painting.

Walking closer to it Betheny stared at it for a long moment. Finally, shaking her head, she said, "I'm not really sure. I think when I was a little girl father told me a story about it . . . something about the girl being betrothed to a MacLaren. Perhaps the painting was intended as a wedding gift from her to him."

"But why was it never finished?"

"I don't know. Perhaps s-she died," Betheny replied matter-of-factly.

"Do you know her name?"

"No, I don't think s-so . . . wait a minute, I think father did tell me. Now, what was it? Something unusual, I remember, not a common name. In fact, it was rather like your name . . . short and s-soft . . . I remember! It was Brenna . . . Brenna something or other. I can't remember the last name; in fact, I'm not even s-sure father knew it."

"Brenna . . ." I repeated the name slowly, under my breath.

"It's not a very good painting, though," Betheny said, dismissing it immediately. "Most of the others are much better, and some are quite valuable. Well, we'd best hurry, or we'll never finish the tour before lunch."

I said nothing, but followed her quietly, lost in thoughts that I couldn't explain to myself, let alone Betheny.

Outside I saw Castle Stalker in daylight for the first time. Although the interior had been greatly remodeled, the exterior was just as it had been for centuries, the blocks of grey stone worn rough and uneven. If anything, the castle was even more imposing in the bright light of day than it had been in the darkness. There was a permanence about it, a feeling that it had stood here forever, untouched by the passage of time. As I looked up at it towering above me, I felt a deep emotion that was hard to articulate. Here, the MacLaren of MacLaren called together his clan in war and in peace throughout Scotland's long, stubborn independence. Here, the clan gathered for the last time in 1745 to fight the English. They had lost, most had died, and with them went the power of the clans as England began its harsh rule of Scotland. Now, for over a hundred and fifty years, Castle Stalker had stood as a silent reminder of the glory that once was.

Standing here on a cool autumn day, looking at the castle, I felt a tremendous sadness. There was no honor in defeat, no dignity for a people who lived under the control of their conquerors.

Betheny looked at me intently, then said softly, "You look s-so sad and faraway."

"I was just thinking of all the things that must have happened here over a thousand years."

"I know. It *is* a s-strange feeling."

Walking on around the castle, we crossed a stone bridge spanning the castle water, a shallow stream cascading down to the sea in a small waterfall. From the rear, Castle Stalker looked even more fantastically picturesque, almost like one of the bizarre castles in Albrecht Dürer's engravings. I could easily imagine it as a fairy stronghold, suddenly rising from its rocky foundations and floating away, like the enchanted palace of a spellbound princess, to disappear in a magic mist.

And then we came to the sea-gate, once the only entrance to the castle when the Keep was all that existed of Castle Stalker. The side-post of the original gate still stood there, two long stones set up on end, one on top of the other, in the primitive Celtic manner. As Betheny and I stood looking through the ancient gate to the worn steps that led up to the castle, I thought of the poetic description of the mystic castle of King Pelleas:

"Behold the enchanted towers of Carbonek
A castle like a rock upon a rock,
With chasm-like portals open to the sea
And steps that meet the breaker."

"I imagine this must have been the scene of many battles," I said to Betheny who was picking bluebells a few feet away.

"Oh, yes," she said brightly, straightening up and looking at the gate. "Once an especially wicked MacLaren trapped his own brother and nephew here and killed them, assuring his accession to the title and land."

I grimaced and Betheny laughed, a soft, girlish giggle that transformed her plain face, making her look rather pretty.

"It's true," she insisted. "More than one man has committed murder for Castle Stalker. Uncles have killed nephews, brothers have killed brothers. The old MacLarens were quite ruthless, actually, and the vast lands belonging to Castle Stalker were considered quite a prize."

As she talked, she glanced down at the small gold watch pinned to her dress and said quickly, "It's nearly lunchtime. We'd best hurry in or grandfather will be furious."

We walked quickly round to the front of the castle and hurried up the stairs to the dining room. Sir Duncan was already seated at the head of the table, still in his wheelchair, his nurse standing in a corner looking, as usual, vaguely disapproving. Glaring at us as we sat down, he said gruffly, "Betheny, ye know I cannot abide tardiness."

"Yes, grandfather," Betheny spoke softly, looking down at her plate.

Before I could insist that it was my fault that we were late, Sir Duncan turned to me and said curtly, "Carissa, this is my grandson, Jonathan."

He motioned to a pale, weak-chinned young man with bright red-gold hair sitting opposite me, and I immediately recognized a strong re-

69

semblance to Robert MacLaren. Jonathan was rather tall and gangling, and still enough of an adolescent to betray a certain awkwardness when meeting a young woman near his own age.

"How do you do?" I said politely.

He nodded coolly in response, then said arrogantly, "I'm told you come from California. A rather rude and uncultured place, surely."

"Perhaps not as cultured as Europe," I replied curtly, "but at least the people there are well-mannered toward strangers, which is more than you can say for yourself."

Jonathan was obviously taken aback at my bluntness, and even blushed furiously when Betheny giggled and said, "A bit of your own medicine, Jon."

Jonathan looked as if he was about to retort sharply when Sir Duncan interrupted angrily, "Betheny! Jonathan! Enough! I won't have any arguments at the table. I send ye to England to get a decent education, to learn how to behave, and ye act like crofter's ill-mannered brats."

Betheny hung her head abjectly, and even Jonathan accepted Sir Duncan's verbal whipping silently. Feeling embarrassed and ill at ease, I concentrated on my plate of food. But when I looked down at it, I saw that there were three forks and an equal number of spoons, not to mention two knives. I had no idea which utensil to use, for back in California I had never been presented with more than one fork, one knife, and one spoon. I looked up at Betheny and my confusion must have been apparent, for she silently pointed to the fork on the outside, then with an exaggerated movement, picked it up and started eating. I did the same, and for the rest of the meal, I looked to Betheny to guide me in my choice of utensils. Clearly, I thought, I had a great deal to learn.

The rest of the meal passed quietly, though Jonathan occasionally managed to tease Betheny without Sir Duncan hearing him. Instead of responding in kind to Jonathan's teasing, which I sensed came more from an overdeveloped arrogance than a genuine wish to hurt, Betheny sat in silent agony.

It became apparent that Jonathan was spoiled and rather too aware of his position as heir to the title. He obviously needed a lesson in good manners.

At one point during the conversation, Betheny began to describe the stables to me, offering to show them to me that afternoon. I was excited to hear that there were stables, and I said brightly, "I would love to see them. Back home, I rode every day. Perhaps tomorrow we could go for a ride and you could show me the countryside."

"Tomorrow is the Sabbath," Sir Duncan admonished immediately. "There will no' be ridin' on the Sabbath!"

I felt stunned and unfairly rebuked, but didn't know what to say. I couldn't understand what could possibly be wrong with riding on Sunday. Even if the morning was spent in church, as I expected, there was still the long afternoon with nothing to do. But I knew that I had a great deal to learn about the ways of this country, and I said nothing.

As I sat there quietly, Jonathan said casually, but with a mischievous twinkle in his dark blue eyes, "Don't expect Beth to show you around. At least not on horseback. She's afraid of horses and has never learned to ride, I, of course, am an accomplished rider."

I turned to Betheny to ask if this were true, but she shot back angrily, glaring at Jonathan, "You can't ride Charger!"

"That's only because Uncle Alex won't allow me to, *yet*," Jonathan responded defensively.

I interrupted what promised to become a full-fledged argument by asking Betheny if it was true that she didn't know how to ride.

"Yes," she answered sullenly, looking away.

"Then I will have to teach you," I said firmly. At her shocked look, I added gently, "It's all right, it's really not so difficult. And once you become used to horses, you'll realize there's nothing to be afraid of."

"Do you really think I could learn to ride?" Betheny asked shyly, clearly dismayed by the thought.

"Definitely. We'll start your lessons tomorrow. I mean Monday," I added quickly, glancing nervously at Sir Duncan, who, fortunately, was deep in a private conversation with his nurse. And I added meaningfully, "I think we can both teach each other things."

Betheny understood and smiled broadly.

Luncheon ended then, before Jonathan could comment on my proposal to give Betheny riding lessons. Sir Duncan bade good afternoon to the three of us, and his nurse quickly wheeled him away.

As Betheny and I also rose to leave, I heard

a noise directly behind me. Turning quickly, I caught a face, with a glaring scar on one cheek, disappearing rapidly behind a door. Someone had been watching me and had not wanted to be seen.

Brenna,
April, 1746

'Twas in the autumn, when the heather bloomed again after lying dry and brown all summer, that I learned of my father's death. Brother Thomas came to the small, grim cell that my mother and I shared, and said that a sailor had come with news for my mother. When my mother heard this a strange expression crossed her face. I had never seen her look quite that way before. Her eyes brightened and her mouth, always set in a tight frown of barely suppressed fury, relaxed. With a great sense of surprise, I realized that for the first time in my memory, my mother looked hopeful.

She bade Brother Thomas bring in the sailor, and a moment later the stranger appeared. He was not a man but a lad, hardly older than I, with a soft, beardless face and a nervous manner. He stood in the narrow doorway and spoke haltingly, as if reciting a poorly memorized poem.

"Mistress Rhoda Gowrie bid me tell ye that yer husband, Alisdair Breac, is dead, an' his house an' lands ha' passed on to ye. She bids ye come home."

There was no more to the message. The young sailor stood quietly, waiting for my mother's response. It came like a gust of wind down a narrow glen, sudden and forceful.

"I have waited fourteen long years to hear those words! The words that will finally set me free forever."

She laughed shrilly, then stopped abruptly and finished coldly, "So Alisdair Breac is dead at last. May his black soul rot in hell for all eternity!"

Both Brother Thomas and the lad were shocked, but not I. I knew my mother and the depth of her hatred for my father, too well.

The young sailor's boat lay over in the bay that night, and early the next morning the three fishermen on board made ready to leave. They had agreed to take us back to Portree with them, and we waited impatiently on the sand while they loaded our few belongings onto the small boat.

I felt someone staring at me and when I turned around, I was surprised to see Megan standing at the crest of the small hill that overlooked the bay. How she knew that I would be here was a mystery, for I had not told her that we were leaving. My mother had been so consumed by excitement that she had slept fitfully and risen before the sun. I had no opportunity to slip away from her to visit Megan one last time.

But now as I looked at Megan standing barely a hundred yards away, I was determined to speak with her. My mother was absorbed in the sailor's movements and did not see me as I ran softly over the sand and up the gently sloping hill.

I stopped just in front of Megan, breathless

from running uphill. She looked down at me silently, her arms folded across her thin bosom, tightly clutching a worn black shawl that barely covered her bony shoulders.

"Ye're leavin' at last," she said softly.

"Yes!" I responded eagerly, fully aware for the first time of how happy I was to leave that accursed island.

"Brenna . . ." she began slowly, then stopped. "Take care, child," she finished simply, with a long sigh.

"The boat is ready to leave. Go now," she ordered curtly.

I looked back down the hill and saw one of the sailors, a big, burly man, helping my mother into the boat. Turning back to Megan, I searched frantically for words to express what I was feeling, but the words would not come. Finally, I said quickly, "Good-by," and hurried back down the hill and across the beach to the boat.

Minutes later as the boat slowly sailed out of the bay, I sat in the stern watching Megan's small black figure recede in the distance. She remained on the hill, motionless and somehow very grim, like a strange sentinel. And I thought, confused, there was something she wanted to tell me. She had come to see me for the last time with a message . . . or a warning . . . but instead she merely said, "Take care, child."

CHAPTER 5

For if a hope of safety rest,
'Tis on the sacred name of guest,
Who seeks for shelter, storm-distress'd
Within a chieftain's hall.
LORD OF THE ISLES
Canto First, XX

Lucy woke me Sunday morning, but it was a different Lucy than the boisterous girl who had laughed with me the day before. Wearing a neat skirt and coat, and a discreet black hat, she looked positively demure.

"I'm sorry to wake ye so early," she apologized, "but the family leaves early for the kirk an' I was afraid ye might oversleep." And then she added, "Mr. MacLean's preachin' the day an' he's a grand preacher."

77

After helping me dress, she left to ride with the other servants to the kirk, or church. When I went downstairs to the dining room I discovered Sir Duncan, Betheny, and Jonathan already seated. Sir Duncan looked even more grim than before, in a black cutaway coat, a waistcoat that showed almost as much boiled shirt as an evening waistcoat, punctuated by two gold studs. Inside his stiff, pristine white collar was a small black tie. One gnarled hand rested on the Bible sitting next to his plate as he regarded me with a steely grimness. The pale, haggard look of his face added to the silent rebuke in his eyes.

Finally he said coldly, "Ye must take care to rise earlier on the Sabbath, Carissa."

I nodded, saying nothing.

Then he continued, "We observe the Sabbath strictly. No work is done that is not absolutely necessary. When we return from the kirk we occupy ouselves reading improving works. There is no riding, nor singing, nor anything frivolous."

I thought, what a stern God it must be that Sir Duncan worships. And later, as I sat on a hard wooden pew in the church in Portree, listening to Mr. MacLean preach a long and terrifying sermon, I understood exactly how stern the Scottish God was. He was much like Sir Duncan, someone to be feared and obeyed without question.

There was one light note, however. I had wondered why Lucy, who had neither a stern nor especially religious nature, should be so eager to hear the Rev. MacLean. But when I met him after the service and discovered him to be young and quite unmarried, I understood her excitement. The preceding evening as Lucy had helped me get ready for bed, she had confided to me that she was desperate to get married. And as I watched her during the service, her hands folded primly in her lap, her hazel eyes gazing up adoringly at the young minister, I realized that she had set her sights on him.

Sunday afternoon and evening were interminably boring, and I was immensely relieved when Monday morning finally came. By nine o'clock, Betheny and I were out at the stables, watching a fine-looking bay gelding being shod, when Willie walked up.

Smiling broadly, he doffed his cap and asked politely, "How do ye do, young lassies?"

"Fine, thank you, Willie," I answered cheerfully. "Betheny is showing me the stables. I'm very impressed with your horses—you obviously take good care of them."

"Why, thank ye, miss," Willie responded happily, pleased by the compliment. "I can see ye know somethin' o' horses. Perhaps ye could teach Miss Betheny to appreciate them."

"That's just what I would like to talk to you about," I said quickly. "I'm going to start giving Betheny riding lessons and I thought you might select a docile mount for her."

"I know just the horse. A fine little mare wi' a bit o' spirit but easy to handle."

"That sounds perfect. And as for myself, I think that bay gelding there will do."

Betheny turned to me with a startled expression on her face, while Willie looked suddenly cold and withdrawn.

79

"That is Charger, miss," he said coolly. "He belongs to Master Alex."

The way he said "Master Alex," tightly, his voice carefully controlled, sounded as if he didn't like Alex MacLaren. In fact, it sounded as if he disliked him a great deal.

I said politely, "If you think he would not want someone else to ride his horse . . ."

Betheny interrupted quickly, "It isn't that, Chrissa. I'm sure Uncle Alex wouldn't mind; in fact, he's hardly ever here to ride Charger. It's just that he's a very difficult horse to ride and you might be hurt."

" 'Tis true, miss," Willie added. "Charger is a fine animal, but spirited an' stubborn as they come. Very few people can handle him."

"Well, if that's the only problem, don't worry," I said confidently. "I'm a very experienced rider and I'm sure I can handle Charger. Get him saddled and I'll show you."

Willie looked far from pleased but nodded reluctantly. Betheny, too, looked worried, but said nothing as we started back for the castle to change into riding clothes.

Fifteen mintues later I returned to the stables to find Willie standing next to two saddled horses, Charger and a small, grey mare. Beside him, Betheny was waiting patiently, dressed in a black hat, black coat, and full black skirt. As I walked up to them, Betheny gasped, "Chrissa! What on earth are you wearing?"

I was in my usual riding attire of Levis and shirt, and I realized that to Betheny I must look a sight.

"This is what I always wear," I explained simply.

Willie was obviously trying to conceal his amusement at the situation, but he couldn't resist smiling broadly when I added, "But Betheny, you can't wear that ridiculous skirt. No wonder you have trouble riding."

"But this is a proper habit," Betheny responded defensively.

Suddenly something else occurred to me and I asked, "I suppose you ride sidesaddle, too?"

"Of course. All young ladies do."

"Well, *I* don't," I said firmly. "And neither will you. That is a ridiculous way of sitting a horse. Riding astride is much more natural. That way your legs can grip the horse's sides, to help you stay on."

"Oh!" Betheny gasped, her hand flying to her mouth, and her face turning crimson.

Willie coughed nervously then said quickly, "Uh, er, I'd best go see to somethin'," and hurriedly left.

"What's wrong?" I asked, turning to Betheny.

"Well," Betheny began slowly, obviously terribly embarrassed. "You s-said legs."

"Is that bad?"

"Actually, yes. Young ladies never mention their limbs in mixed company. We always refer to them as limbs, never . . . legs," she finished hesitantly.

"But that doesn't make any sense!" I said hotly. Then I realized that Betheny was only trying to help me, to explain the prevailing etiquette, and I apologized.

"I'm sorry. I shouldn't be angry with you. It's just that it seems so unimportant to me whether you call legs limbs or legs. And I don't see why it should matter if you discuss them in mixed company. After all, men must know that woman have legs. Oh, well . . . I'll try to remember so that I won't embarrass you again."

Betheny smiled, clearly relieved. However, while I was willing to give in on the matter of semantics, I was adamant about her riding attire. I knew it would be impossible to teach her to ride, and to enjoy it, if she had to wear a heavy, cumbersome skirt and sit sidesaddle. She refused to wear trousers such as mine, so we compromised by returning to her room and doing a bit of work on her skirt. I slit it up the middle, then sewed the two sections to form very wide trouser legs. It still looked like a skirt when she stood in it, but she could ride astride.

An hour later we were back at the stables and I began the first lesson. Though the little mare Willie had selected for Betheny was obviously very gentle, Betheny was at first afraid to even touch her. I explained carefully that Betheny must not be nervous for her nervousness would be communicated to the animal, making it hard to handle. After a few minutes of talking gently to the horse, and stroking its neck, Betheny began to be less afraid. When the little mare gave her a friendly nuzzle in return, she was positively delighted.

I briefly explained the rudiments of riding—mounting and holding the reins—then said calmly, "We might as well try the real thing now."

"You mean actually get up on the horse?" Betheny asked worriedly.

"Yes," I answered firmly, and asked Willie to help her mount.

When I saw that she was sitting correctly in the saddle, I quickly mounted Charger who immediately began prancing around nervously. I knew that it would take all of my attention to control him, and I immediately regretted insisting on riding him, when I would necessarily have to give so much of my attention to Betheny.

But I wasn't about to admit that I had been wrong and ask for another horse.

We left the stableyard at a sedate walk. Fortunately the mare showed no inclination to run off with Betheny, and I was managing, though with a great deal of difficulty, to keep Charger under control. He clearly hadn't been ridden in a very long time and was eager to take off in a full gallop.

As we headed out onto the road leading away from the castle, Willie called after us, "Remember, miss, he's an unpredictable, stubborn horse." And then he added mischievously, "Like some lassies I know."

Betheny looked at me and laughed, and I couldn't help laughing also. So far, everything was going well, and I felt very confident.

It was a clear, sunny day, perfect for riding. We took a path off the road that ran parallel to the sea, on one side of us were the moors, covered with white heather, and on the other side was the glistening blue ocean. I talked to Betheny as we rode, correcting her whenever necessary and complimenting her often. Though she was so nervous at first that she sat rigidly in the saddle, gradually she began to relax and enjoy the ride.

When we had been riding for over half an hour, we stopped at the edge of the cliff to rest and look at the view, which was breathtaking. Bright yellow broom grew in huge clumps at the very edge of the cliff, and beyond was the ocean, serene and deep blue. In the distance were rocks where seals raised their young, and beyond them, lying low in the hazy distance, were the vague forms of other islands.

Nowhere was there any sign of human habitation, and for a moment I felt a sharp sense of the loneliness that is so much an intrinsic part of Skye.

While Betheny and I stood there, neither of us speaking, the sky began to grow cloudy and dark. In a matter of minutes, the sun was obscured by a large storm cloud, suddenly turning the bright day dismal. I knew that we would have to hurry to reach the castle before the storm broke, so I quickly helped Betheny mount, and we set out at a canter toward the castle. The joy had gone out of the ride now, for dark shadows from the storm clouds slid noiselessly across the ground, frightening the horses. Betheny was again nervous, clearly anxious to reach the safety of the stableyard.

We were about half a mile from the castle when the thunderstorm struck. Rain poured down in heavy drops, lightning flashed, and thunder rolled heavily over the distant hills. Betheny's mare remained calm, but Charger became even more difficult to control. When a bolt of lightning struck within a few hundred yards of us, the big gelding bolted, running off the path, tearing wildly through the rain. I tried to pull him back but it was useless. He was terrified and oblivious to my desperate tugging on the reins.

Then, unexpectedly, there was a stone wall in front of us. With a powerful lunge, Charger gathered his legs beneath him and cleared the wall easily. I felt myself slipping, and the last thing I remember is seeing the ground rushing toward me . . .

I awoke some time later. The first thing I was conscious of was a terrific pain in my head. Then I realized that I was lying on something soft, and when I opened my eyes I saw that I was in a huge, canopied bed with warm blankets pulled up to my chin. My riding clothes were gone and I was wearing a lace-edged woolen nightgown.

The room was totally unlike any at Castle Stalker—large and elegantly furnished with modern furniture and impressionist paintings on the walls. Spread over the polished hardwood floor were several blue and red Persian rugs that obviously were of fine quality and very expensive. Whoever owned this house was not only wealthy but possessed an eye for beauty.

I tried to sit up but immediately fell back against the plump goosedown pillows, my head spinning painfully. After a few seconds, I tried again, more slowly, finally managing to sit erect with one hand gripping the bedpost firmly. Slowly I pulled my legs from under the heavy blankets and swung them over the side of the bed. But my legs were wobbly and when I tried to stand, I nearly collapsed. As I leaned against the bed, the door across the room opened and a slender, almost gaunt, blond young man entered, carrying a tray with a beautiful pastel-colored porcelain teapot and cup on it.

He stopped when he saw me standing by the bed, flashed a captivating smile and admonished in a cultured voice with only the slightest hint of a Scottish burr, "You should *not* try to stand, you know. You could be more hurt than you realize."

Setting down the tray on a nearby table, he walked over to me and gently helped me back into bed.

As he pulled the blankets over me, I looked up at him intently. I guessed that he was about thirty years old. He was very tall, well over six feet, his thinness adding to the impression of exceptional height. His eyes were pale ice-blue and his hair was that light, almost white-blond that one sees in Scandinavian countries. There was a softness, a gentleness about him that was somehow not at all effeminate. But there was something else, too, something I couldn't quite understand. I had the strong feeling that his gentleness wasn't all there was to him . . .

I must have looked very wary as I scrutinized him, for he said quickly, "I'm sure you're wondering where you are and what sort of rascal you've gotten yourself involved with. Well, to explain, my name is Christopher MacKenzie, affectionately known as Kit. I found you lying unconscious next to the wall that surrounds my property and brought you back here to my house. I've sent a boy for the doctor and he should be here soon."

He smiled reassuringly, then turned and walked over to the table where the tray with the teapot was sitting. After pouring a cup, he brought it over to me and waited until I had taken a sip of the hot, strong liquid, before continuing easily, "Now that I've introduced myself, may I ask your name? Or are you, perhaps, the Queen of Elfland come to dare me to kiss you and join you in fairyland? Being the reckless ne'er-do-well that I am, I may just do that!"

I couldn't help smiling at his good-natured teasing, and responded shyly, "My name is Chrissa Rey. I've just come to live at Castle Stalker with the MacLarens."

For a fleeting moment I thought I saw his expression harden, but almost immediately he flashed that beguiling smile and I felt sure I must have imagined it. He said merrily, "Well, that is certainly a coincidence. You see, Alex MacLaren and I are great friends. How did you come to stay at the castle?"

"Sir Duncan was my mother's guardian. He invited me to live with him."

Briefly I explained my background, including the recent trip from California to Skye. When I finished, Mr. MacKenzie asked unexpectedly, "And what do you think of your new family?"

"I can't say . . . actually, I hardly know

them. In fact, I've only met Alex MacLaren once—briefly."

"Well, you'll be in for a surprise there," he laughed. "Alex and I are much alike, carefree and something of black sheep. We have drunk together and caroused together since we were frustrated, pimply youths. Of course, you know what they say—the true Scot is at least on nodding terms with the devil, an uproarious, dissolute rogue who loves wild parties."

Ever since Mr. MacKenzie had entered the room I had wanted to ask him what became of my clothes and how I got into the nightgown I was wearing. Finally, I said bluntly, "Mr. MacKenzie..."

"Please call me Kit," he interrupted. "After all, though you arrived in an unorthodox fashion, you are nevertheless a guest in my home and we should be on friendly terms, I think. And may I say, *ceud mile failte*, which in Gaelic means, 'A hundred thousand welcomes.' That is the traditional welcome of a highlander to a guest."

"Well, Kit, then," I continued, acutely embarrassed. Finally I plunged ahead, "I've been wondering how I got into this nightgown."

Kit responded easily, "I imagine you have. Your clothes were soaked through, quite muddy, in fact, and I thought it best to get you into something dry."

"*Who* changed my clothes?"

"I must admit I did," he answered with that disarming smile. "You see, my housekeeper is the only female servant here and she's gone today to the christening of her first grandchild. There are only myself and a groom here.

88

Though I'm sure the groom would have enjoyed the chore, I thought it best that I do it."

He finished, grinning openly, "I tried to do it with my eyes closed but you were as wet and slippery as a seal pup!"

Kit and I laughed together, and the awkward moment was over, I realized that I was being silly about the whole thing. It was perfectly natural that he would have gotten me out of my wet clothes and into dry ones. But when I thought of him undressing me I was reminded of that other time, when another man had looked at my uncovered body. My reaction then had been so different . . . so acutely aware of my sex . . .

Just then the distant sound of a bell ringing came through the open bedroom door.

"That must be the doctor," Kit said immediately, and left. In less than a minute he returned with Dr. Ross, a short, stout, balding man.

Setting his bulky black bag on the table next to the bed, Dr. Ross turned to me with a kindly smile and asked in a thick accent, "How are ye feelin', lass?"

"I think I'm quite all right, aside from a headache," I answered.

"Well, let's hae a look an' be certain. A fall from a horse can be a verra serious matter."

Looking over the top of the glasses that were perched precariously on the end of his broad, flat nose, he said to Kit, "This is no' a public examination, Kit."

Laughing, Kit responded, "Oh, yes, of course. I rather thought you might take that attitude, doctor."

And he left the room, carefully closing the door behind him.

A half hour later, Dr. Ross was satisfied that I had sustained no injuries other than a few bruises and a temporary headache and dizziness. After giving me some pills for the headache, he told me that I could get dressed and return to Castle Stalker. I was about to explain that I had no dry clothes to change into when there was a knock on the door and Kit entered.

Turning to me, Dr. Ross said with a sly grin, " 'Tis no' a safe place here for any attractive female whether she be fifteen or fifty, an' the sooner ye leave here the better."

Kit retorted in mock indignation, "But, doctor, you know I draw the line at forty," and they both laughed heartily.

Dr. Ross took his leave of us then, saying that he would find his own way out. When he had gone, Kit walked to a wardrobe in a corner of the room and took out a beautifully tailored brown merino dress and a pair of matching brown boots.

"I think these should fit well enough to get you back to Castle Stalker," he said easily, laying them on a nearby chair. "I'll wait for you in the drawing room downstairs. It's easy to find—just turn right down the hallway outside this door, and go down the stairway. It's on the left."

And then he was gone.

I dressed quickly. The boots were a bit tight but the dress was almost perfect. The woman it had been made for must be as slender as I and only an inch or two shorter, I thought. I couldn't resist glancing in the wardrobe and was amazed at what I saw. There were at least three dozen dresses, beautifully tailored and made of the finest materials; ballgowns of velvet and silk, and day dresses of every fashionable material. On a shelf above the dresses were two rows of hat boxes, and on the floor of the wardrobe were a dozen pair of shoes stacked in a neat row.

I had never seen such clothes before, and was frankly curious about their owner. Kit had not mentioned a wife or sister, and these were not the sort of dresses to be worn by a mature woman such as a mother or aunt. But I knew I couldn't satisfy my curiosity for it would be extremely rude to pry into the personal life of a man I had only just met.

Leaving the bedroom, I walked down the short hallway and descended the curving stairway. MacKenzie House was small compared to Castle Stalker, and quite modern. When I entered the drawing room, I saw that it, too, was furnished with elegance, good taste, and a seeming disregard for expense. Here, as in the bedroom, Persian rugs covered the polished hardwood floors, and green velvet drapes hung at the tall windows. But what caught my eye and held it was a portrait hanging above the marble fireplace.

It was nearly life-size, about five feet tall, and dominated the room. The subject was a young woman, probably no more than twenty or so, who bore an uncanny resemblance to Kit. She had the same white-blonde hair, piercing blue eyes, and pale complexion. Dressed in a light blue silk gown cut low to accentuate a dazzling diamond necklace, she was incredibly beautiful. She was like a Dresden china doll, utterly perfect in every respect.

But it wasn't her fragile, unflawed beauty that made me stare mesmerized at her portrait. There was something about her eyes, an expression of deep and compelling sadness, and a hint of something else . . . madness. This, I thought soberly, is what Ophelia would have looked like had she been real.

Kit had been standing in the room near a French window. When he spoke suddenly, I realized with a guilty start that I had been staring fixedly at the portrait.

"God, look at the time! The MacLarens must be wondering what has become of you. I sent a servant over to tell them you were all right and would be returning immediately, and here I've kept you for another hour. I hope at least it's been a pleasant stay for you."

"Oh, yes," I answered honestly. "Your house is so beautiful."

"I appreciate beauty. I like to be surrounded by it. There is so much ugliness in the world that it is an incomparable joy to find a thing of perfect beauty—to have the good fortune to keep it all to yourself and cherish it."

It was obvious that Kit meant what he was saying. This house was full of priceless beautiful things, all perfectly arranged. It was almost like a carefully guarded retreat from an imperfect world. And the girl in the portrait was the penultimate example of this—a creature of perfect symmetry, seemingly untouched by anything base or ugly. I wondered if she was even a part of the real world, or simply remained outside it.

"I'd best get you to the carriage," Kit said suddenly.

He led me outside and I realized with a surprisingly sharp sense of disappointment that he wasn't going to tell me who the girl in the picture was.

It was still raining hard outside as Kit hurriedly helped me into his waiting carriage. While he stood outside the door, I leaned through the open window and said quickly, before the driver could whip up the horses, "Kit, I want to thank you . . ."

But he interrupted me immediately with a wry, "It was my pleasure. You are a charming young lady, Chrissa Rey, and I look forward to seeing you again."

Then he ordered the driver to be off and a moment later the carriage was rolling bumpily down the gravel drive. At the end of the long, curving drive I looked back at MacKenzie House and saw Kit still standing in the rain, his arms folded across his chest, his expression thoughtful.

> *Brenna*
> *April, 1746*

It rained heavily on the journey to Skye, but just before we sailed into Portree Harbor the skies cleared and the sun shone brightly. As we entered the small, perfect half-circle of a bay, a rainbow was shining over the tall white houses in a scene lovelier than my fondest dreams. Everywhere I looked were houses and people and fine carriages hurrying along gravelled roads.

It was all bustle and excitement, talk and laughter, as I stood at the helm of the boat, taking it all in like a poor dumb thing. My eyes and ears were full of sights and sounds such as I had never even imagined. I loved it . . . I loved all of it, the blessed noise after years of silence.

There was a woman standing on the dock, looking out to sea. As our boat came closer to her, she shouted and waved, at the same time holding a handkerchief to her eyes. This was my mother's sister, Rhoda Gowrie. As soon as our boat was made fast to the dock, my mother ran to her and they embraced tearfully, both too overcome to speak for several minutes.

That first night we slept in my aunt's small house. It seemed like a grand castle to me, full of wonders—sweet-smelling linens on the soft beds and food such as I had never imagined, treacle scones, fresh herrings in oatmeal, delicious cakes, and tea from China and India.

It was a wonderful night, full of new experiences and undreamt-of pleasures. Throughout it all there was not a mention of my father. The next morning as my mother and I prepared to leave to go to our own house, my aunt mentioned my father for the only time.

"Alisdair Breac left ye little, Mairi," my aunt said simply.

"No matter," my mother answered curtly, "I have outlived him, as I swore I would."

We left then, in a straw-filled wooden cart pulled by a tired old pony borrowed from my aunt. I looked back over my shoulder at Portree as it disappeared behind us, filled with longing for it before it was even out of sight.

The journey took several hours, for our house was far from Portree and the pony was slow. I looked at Skye, the island I had heard so much about from my mother and Megan. It seemed to me to be just like the island we had recently left. Butterflies flew around brightly colored wildflowers, then disappeared as a wind came down from the mountains, pressing down the heather and the grass.

And then I saw the Black Cuillins, and they were utterly unlike anything on that other island. I shivered as I looked up at them, standing grape-blue and still in the morning sunshine. It seemed as if God, when he pulled their massive bulk from the bowels of the earth into the light of the sun, said, "These mountains shall be the essence of all that is terrible in mountains. They will have all the mystery of high places, carved into a thousand jagged, towering shapes. Their scarred ravines will remain forever barren, never to nurture life."

I swore silently that I would never go into the mountains' deep, dark depths, but would stay on the moor, far from their dangerous magic.

My mother shouted suddenly above the roar of the wind, "There is our home, child."

I saw a small stone house in a state of great disrepair, sitting alone in a rocky field on the edge of the dirt road. The timbered roof was full of gaping holes and the door sagged crookedly on one rusted hinge. Looking around me, as far as the eye could see, there was no sign of life.

I was to be alone once more.

CHAPTER 6

For look on sea, or look on land,
Or yon dark sky—on every hand
Despair and death are near . . .
LORD OF THE ISLES
Canto First, XIX

The ride from MacKenzie House to Castle
Stalker took only twenty minutes, and for most
of that time I thought about Kit. He was
pleasant and amusing, and I found myself looking forward to seeing him again, though I still
had the feeling that there was more to him
than the carefree, joking man he appeared to
be. At any rate, I concluded, it would be interesting to get to know him better.

As we drew near the castle, I began to feel
apprehensive about the reception I would receive. I knew my accident and absence had

97

probably caused quite a stir, and I felt intensely uncomfortable about that. I wasn't worried about Betheny, for I knew that if she hadn't made it back to the castle Kit would have heard and told me. What bothered me most was the thought that Willie would think me a fool for insisting I could handle Charger and then being thrown. But anyone, even the best rider, falls sometimes, I insisted stubbornly to myself. Somehow I would have to persuade Willie to let me ride Charger again to prove that I could do it. And I would have to talk to Betheny immediately to dispel any fears that my accident might have caused her.

As the carriage pulled to a stop at the front entrance of the castle, I was surprised to see Dr. Ross entering the huge oaken doors. As I was wondering what the doctor was doing here, Willie suddenly appeared and helped me out of the carriage.

"Are ye all right, lass?" he asked anxiously.

I assured him that I was fine and apologized for worrying them all. "Did Charger come back?" I asked.

"O' course," Willie responded derisively. "That one knows where home is."

"And Betheny?" I asked guiltily.

"She's fine," Willie assured me. "She was a wee wet an' worried aboot ye, but 'twas all."

"I want to ride Charger again," I insisted firmly.

"We'll hae to talk aboot that later, miss," Willie protested, then added in a whisper, "Ye'd best go to yer room now. There's trouble in the castle."

"What is it?" I asked quickly. "Does it have to do with Dr. Ross?"

wi' him outside o' MacKenzie House. 'Tis Sir

"Aye. I went after him meself, an' caught up Duncan. He's taken sick again. But I think Miss Betheny is waitin' for ye in yer room. Ye'd best go now."

I nodded silently and did as he suggested. When I entered my room a few minutes later, I found Betheny there, still in her riding clothes. As I walked in, she ran toward me and asked worriedly, "Are you all right? Oh, Chrissa, I was s-so worried! I came back right away and we were forming a search party when one of Kit's servants came to tell us he'd found you."

"I'm sorry I worried you. I'm perfectly fine, really. And I'm *very* sorry about running off and leaving you alone like that. I'm afraid your first riding lesson didn't go very well. But believe me, that *won't* happen again."

"Don't worry about me," Betheny said with surprising confidence. "I was all right. You should have s-seen the look on Jonathan's face when I came riding back alone. He won't be able to say I'm afraid to ride *now*."

Her voice was full of pride and I realized that though this experience had been frightening, it had taught Betheny that she could handle things better than she thought she could. Then I remembered about Sir Duncan and said gravely, "Willie told me Sir Duncan is ill. Is it serious?"

"Yes," Betheny responded with a long sigh. "I'm afraid it is very bad this time. I don't think he'll recover. He's quite old, you know, and for the past few months he's gotten worse

99

and worse. He used to be s-so strong, he never seemed old at all. But lately . . ."

Her voice trailed off and I could see that she was extremely upset. After losing her father and mother, it would be hard on her to lose her grandfather now, even though he was not exactly a kind, loving, old man.

She continued, "With grandfather ill, Uncle Alex will have to return. Grandfather can't run the estate at all now."

She brightened at the thought of her uncle's return, and it was obvious that she was eager to see him. But my feelings were just the opposite. I felt strangely afraid of once more seeing the man who evoked such disturbing feelings in me.

Dr. Ross remained at Castle Stalker far into the night. When he finally left, just past midnight, he merely said, "It doesna' look good. I'll be back tomorrow."

The next morning Betheny and I were walking on the grounds near the front drive when Kit came riding up. Though the rain that had continued throughout the night had stopped earlier, there were huge puddles of water everywhere, and Kit's horse splashed through them, spraying tiny flicks of mud onto his grey trousers. Other than the mud on his trousers, Kit was dressed immaculately in a black jacket and white cravat secured by a gold pin. He was really quite elegant looking, and I realized with a jolt that he was an extremely attractive man. Dr. Ross had probably only been half-joking when he had accused Kit of seducing many women.

Pulling his horse to a halt just in front of us, Kit called out cheerfully, "Good morning, lassies. How are you today?"

"Quite well, thank you," I replied, feeling strangely embarrassed and shy. "What brings you to Castle Stalker?"

"I've come to pay my respects to Sir Duncan," Kit answered simply. "I understand he's not feeling well."

"I'm afraid grandfather can't receive visitors, Kit," Betheny said softly. "He's really gravely ill."

Kit's expression sobered and he answered quietly, "I'm sorry to hear that, Betheny. I hope he makes a swift and complete recovery."

Turning to me, he asked solicitously, "I hope you are feeling better today, Chrissa?"

"Oh, yes, much better, thank you," I replied, flustered. Kit's blue eyes were twinkling and I knew he was amused by my embarrassment.

After a few minutes of polite small talk, Kit bade us good day and rode off. As soon as he was out of earshot, Betheny turned to me and said excitedly, "I think he likes you!"

Laughing, I responded skeptically, "Oh, Betheny, that's ridiculous. What on earth makes you think that?"

"Word travels quickly round here. I'm sure Kit knew that grandfather is far too ill to receive visitors. And, besides, he and grandfather have never been friendly. I think he just used that as an excuse to come and s-see *you*. Oh, how romantic to think that he would s-save your life and then fall in love with you!"

Betheny's wild speculations were so ludicrous that I found myself laughing, and somehow the awkwardness I had felt earlier disappeared. I told Betheny that her romanticism was getting the best of her good sense, and that ended the conversation.

Our walk was cut short at that point by the rain that began again and we returned quickly to the castle.

All of that dark and stormy day a pall hung over the castle. Servants went about their business quietly, their faces grim and worried. Even Jonathan, who was usually boisterous, was silent and well-behaved. No one pretended that Sir Duncan was well-loved, but he *was* the laird and if he died it would be a momentous thing for everyone in the castle.

Dr. Ross returned that afternoon and Mrs. MacBean took him immediately up to Sir Duncan's room. A half hour later they both walked slowly down the stairs, talking in low tones, their faces drawn. Betheny and I were in the drawing room where she was teaching me to play chess. When we saw the doctor, we both rose and hurried over to him.

"Is there any change?" I asked softly.

Dr. Ross slowly shook his head no, gazing at us sadly through his thick glasses.

"Will ye stay to tea, doctor?" Mrs. MacBean asked with a good deal more cordiality in her voice than was usual.

"No, thank ye kindly," Dr. Ross declined quickly. "Molly Taggart's bairn is due and I must be hurryin' over there."

He said goodby to us then, promising to return again the next day, and Mrs. MacBean escorted him to the door. As they left, Betheny turned to me and said quietly, sounding utterly forlorn, "Oh, Chrissa, I'm s-so frightened of death."

I didn't know what to say. In her short life, Betheny had seen most of her family die, and I knew no words to ease her sense of abandonment. I understood the depth of such a loss all too well. I had never been openly affectionate, for shows of affection were not encouraged in my aunt and uncle's house. But now I impulsively put my arm around Betheny's slender shoulder and hugged her tightly for a moment. It was the only thing I could think to do.

I went to bed early that night, but could not sleep. Finally, after three hours of staring at the slowly dying fire, I decided to go down to the kitchen to brew a cup of tea. I slipped on my robe, then walked quietly through the dark hallway, my way lit by a cruisie, a small iron lamp with a handle and a crucible for oil that I held in front of me. The castle was dark and still, the only sound the low roar of the storm outside. The atmosphere seemed full of foreboding, and I found myself hurrying faster toward the relative warmth of the kitchen.

As I came to the end of the hallway, the pale light shed by the cruisie illuminated the half-finished portrait of the girl named Brenna. Walking closer to it, I held the cruisie next to it, only inches from the girl's face. Her hair was long and golden, falling in thick waves around her face. Her eyes were a light, tawny brown, flecked with gold, and almond shaped. They reminded me of the eyes of a lioness I had seen when a small circus came to Tulare one summer. There was something half-wild in

103

the expression they held. Her lips were full and sensuous, the sort of mouth that would appeal greatly to men, I guessed.

What sort of woman had she been? Hardly older than I, I thought, and yet I suspected that she knew a great deal more about men than I did. Hers was not an innocent face. As I looked at the portrait, my face pressed close to the face of the girl named Brenna, I felt my body stir, as if old memories, long buried, were awaking. This girl touched something deep inside me, something that was vaguely frightening. I wasn't sure I wanted to understand what I felt.

Pulling away abruptly, I turned and fairly ran down the stairs to the kitchen.

When Betheny had taken me on a tour of the castle, she hadn't actually shown me the kitchen, and I was now surprised to see how large it was. It was at least thirty feet square, with a huge fireplace at one end and a long trestle table along one wall. A teakettle was sitting on the large iron stove, with steam coming from the spout. For some reason, the fire had been left on underneath it. After looking in several cupboards I finally found a cup and saucer and a tin of *Earl Grey* tea. I was preparing to pour water from the kettle into the cup when suddenly I heard a sound behind me. Whirling around, I came face to face with an old woman holding a cruisie.

The woman, who was short and plump and wearing a shawl thrown over a heavy woolen nightgown, had a long, ugly scar down one side of her wrinkled face. She looked as surprised to see me as I was to see her.

"You startled me," I said finally after a tense moment of mutual appraisal.

"I'm sorry. I heard somethin' an' wondered who would be here this time o' night. I'm Morag, the cook." And then, holding her cruisie up to cast more light on me, she peered closely into my face and said intently, "Ye're Chrissa Rey?"

I nodded, feeling sure that I had seen her somewhere before. Then I realized with a start that it was *her* scarred face I had seen briefly behind the door at luncheon my first day at the castle.

"Why were you watching me the other day?" I burst out.

Looking embarrassed and ill at ease, she answered awkwardly, "I knew the laird wouldna' want me to come to the dinin' room. But I was that anxious to see ye. I had to find out if ye were the one in the dream. But come, child, 'tis cold standin' here. Let's go into my room an' we'll talk."

I wondered what dream she was referring to, but I said nothing. As with most elderly people, I suspected that it would be better to let her explain herself in her own good time.

She led me into her room which was directly off the kitchen. It was small and plainly furnished, but warm and comfortable, with a small stone fireplace in a corner. As Morag poured me a cup of tea from a teapot on a table near the fire, she motioned to me to sit in an old worn chair opposite her.

"I've been here at the castle for nearly fifty years," she began easily. "An' I knew yer mither from the time she were a wee bairn.

105

There was never a sweeter, more beautiful babe, an' she grew up the same. But then, ye must ken all this."

"No," I answered quietly. "She died when I was seven. I know almost nothing about her."

"Ach, my poor, wee Cathy," Morag said sadly. Then she asked, "Would ye like me to tell ye aboot her?"

"Oh, yes!" I replied eagerly, beginning somehow to like old Morag and feel comfortable with her, despite the strange appearance the scar gave her.

"'Tis a long story," Morag began, settling back in her chair. "When the laird, Sir Duncan, was young, he fell in love wi' a lassie named Alison. Alison was a great beauty an' many young men were courtin' her, includin' Sir Duncan's second cousin, a lad named Jamie MacLaren. Well, Jamie won Alison's heart an' hand. Sir Duncan was fair broken-hearted but he hid it well an' continued to be a great friend to both Jamie an' Alison. In due time Alison bore a bairn, yer mither, an' Sir Duncan was named godfather to the child. Soon thereafter Sir Duncan married a rich widow, slightly older than himself, who bore him two sons, the poor dead Robert an' Master Alex.

"Then, on a trip to Edinburgh, Alison an' Jamie were killed in a terrible train accident, leavin' their young daughter an orphan. Sir Duncan took her in an' raised her as his own. He loved her dearly, for she was all that was left of his dear Alison."

Morag smiled lovingly as she remembered my mother, and I could see tears in her narrow brown eyes. She continued, her voice trembling, "She grew up to be a beauty like her mither, o' course. She were quite a handful, though. So good-hearted, but always gettin' into mischief because she *would* hae her own way. She an' Sir Duncan would argue somethin' fierce, for neither liked to give in. But he loved her all the same, 'twas plain to see. The lads hereabouts liked her, too, an' even some gentlemen from the mainland were after her. But she would ha' nary a one o' them. Sir Duncan didna' mind, for he was no' anxious for her to marry an' leave him.

"An' then Cathy met yer feyther, who was travellin' hereabouts, an' he was more a man than any o' the dandies she had known. Sir Duncan invited him to stay one weekend, an' by Sunday night Cathy an' yer feyther were deep in love. Sir Duncan was so angry when he found out! He ordered yer feyther to leave, an' he did. But Cathy said, 'I'll marry that man, an' you nor no one can stop me!' She was stubborn, that one. That night yer feyther came back for her an' they escaped together. I helped them an' watched as they rode off together in the night. 'Twas the last time I saw her."

Morag stopped to wipe the tears from her eyes with a coarse grey woolen handkerchief. Then she continued matter-of-factly, "The next mornin' when Sir Duncan found out he went into sic a rage. But 'twas no use. She was gone an' we never heard from her again until yer aunt's letter came a month ago an' Sir Duncan said ye would be comin'."

Looking at me kindly, she smiled gently, then continued, "Ye've no idea how excited I was to hear Cathy's bairn was comin'."

She sighed deeply and was silent for a long moment, clearly tired from the lengthy speech. After studying me carefully for a few moments, she concluded, "Ye're like her, ye know. No' in looks so much, tho' yer eyes be as soft an' grey as a dove, just like hers. But in spirit ye're like her. Ye're no' a one to be told what to do."

"Thank you for telling me about her. I feel I know her better now."

I thought I must be tiring Morag, letting her speak for so long so late at night, and I offered to leave. But she stopped me, saying heavily, "No, there is somethin' else I must tell ye. The *dream*."

I waited and in a moment she began to explain slowly, "On the night ye came to the castle, a vision appeared to me while I was sleepin'. 'Twas the spirit of a lass, an' I knew what that meant. That person is in deadly danger. Perhaps no' now, but sometime . . . Still, I didna' ken whose spirit it was till I saw ye at luncheon that day, an' then I knew."

She stopped, looked at me intently, and finished, " 'Twas yer spirit, Chrissa."

I said nothing, merely staring at her in disbelief. It was clear that she firmly believed what she was saying. On an island like Skye, so remote and isolated, with traditions going back to the Norse settlers who worshipped pagan gods, it was easy to understand how superstitions could remain so entrenched in people's minds.

Morag looked at me closely, then said good-naturedly, "Ye think I'm a daft old woman, but I ken what I'm sayin'. I'm the seventh child of

108

a seventh child, an' have the sight. I see what others canna."

She paused, then began, "I'll tell ye a story. 'Twas several years ago on Beltane, the night that witches come out, an' it was verra late. I was in my room when suddenly I heard a terrible noise. An unearthly sound, it was, the clash o' metal on metal an' the hoarse shoutin' o' men. An' over all was the wild high skirl o' the pipes. I went outside an' the sound was clearer, comin' from that small hill near the castle. Then the sounds stopped an' the night was silent save for the sound o' waves lappin' at the beach. An' then the sounds began again, but wi' a difference; now it was the clatter o' hangin' platforms bein' built, an' the screams o' men dyin'. The sounds came nearer, the sounds o' men marchin' over heather an' bog, but all unreal, like the sound o' surf beatin' on a distant shore. An' among the talkin', shoutin' men was the occasional scream o' a woman."

Morag stopped, then finished in a whisper, "That hill is called Cnoc a' Chatha, the hill o' battle, an' has been called so since my grandmother was a wee lass."

I didn't know what to say to this. As I sat there, watching the dim light of the fire casting strange shadows over the small room, I wondered if Morag might be right. I remembered the inexplicable feeling I had experienced when I had fainted earlier, and Betheny's frightened voice saying, "There are things we don't understand here, things not of this world."

Perhaps Morag was right . . . perhaps I *was* in danger.

No, I couldn't accept that. I told myself I was being ridiculous. Morag was entitled to her superstitious beliefs, but that didn't mean that *I* had to accept them. I stood up abruptly, saying quickly, "It's very late and I must go to bed. Thank you for telling me about my mother."

Tears came to Morag's eyes again, and she brushed them away with a shaking hand. " 'Twas nothin'. Off to bed wi' ye, child."

But as I left the room, Morag called after me urgently, with real fear in her voice, "Mind what I say. Ye're in danger an' ye must be careful!"

When I awoke the next morning, the sky was grey and cloudy and it was clear that the storm would be back. My room, which had been so bright and cheerful, was dark and gloomy, and it only added to the depression I felt when I remembered Morag's grave warning from the night before.

First the strange old man on the coach had warned, "Beware the MacLaren," then Mr. Farren had said that "terrible things happen to pretty lassies on Skye." And now a mystical old woman claiming to have special powers was telling me that I was in danger. It seemed that almost from the first moment I had arrived in Scotland, frightening things had begun to happen.

But it was more than that. I had been overwhelmed by inexplicable feelings that were unlike anything I had ever felt before. At times it was almost as if I was two people, with conflicting feelings and emotions . . .

My grim thoughts were interrupted by Lucy, who came in with my regular morning cup of tea. She was more quiet and subdued than usual and I suspected that the news about Sir Duncan must be bad. Then I remembered that Lucy had worked with Morag in the kitchen before becoming my maid.

"Lucy," I began quickly, "last night I met Morag."

"Did ye now," Lucy responded easily. "I'm glad, for I know she was anxious to meet ye."

I didn't know how to ask what I wanted to ask, so I said instead, "That scar is strange—do you know how she got it?"

"Aye," Lucy answered immediately, perking up a bit. " 'Twas in the Battle o' the Braes twenty years ago. Women an' children fought the sheriff an' his men who were enforcin' the Clearances.

"Terrible things they were, where people were thrown off the land they had farmed for generations to make way for the rich land-owners' sheep. The crofters in the Braes were denied the right to graze their own sheep on the slopes, though they offered to pay as much as they could. Some agitators grazed their sheep there, defiant like, an' the sheriff an' his men served notices of eviction, but were forced by the people to burn the evictions."

Lucy's hazel eyes were blazing now, and it was obvious how strongly she felt about the Clearances, though she probably had not even been born when they took place. I had heard that the memory of the Highlander is long, and this was proof of that.

"The Chief Constable in Glasgow dispatched

some men to stop the agitators," Lucy continued animatedly, "an' a hundred women an' children fought them wi' sticks an' stones. Morag was one o' them. Ye see, she had left the castle for awhile to tend her ailin' sister an' her children in Braes."

It was difficult to think of people being treated so inhumanely, to think of women and children fighting armed men. But surely, I thought, if Morag had the courage and conviction to do such a thing, she couldn't be the crazy old woman I had thought her.

As if reading my thoughts, Lucy added casually, "The scar does gi' her an odd appearance, but ye must remember that what matters is that she has the sight."

So Lucy believes it, too, I thought wryly. But the truth was that I almost believed it myself.

Later when I went down to the dining room, I found Betheny and Jonathan already there, sitting quietly at the table that seemed much too large for the two of them. I helped myself to some eggs from a covered dish on the sideboard, then poured a cup of tea. I sat down next to Betheny, who had barely touched the plate of food in front of her.

"Have you heard anything about your grandfather?" I asked, trying to sound more hopeful than I felt.

"No," Betheny replied with a long sigh. "He's s-still the s-same."

"I'm sorry, Betheny. But perhaps he'll get better. You can never tell."

She said nothing and I realized how foolish I sounded. Jonathan, too, was silent, and it oc-

112

curred to me that this was an especially momentous time for him. He was seventeen and could expect to inherit Castle Stalker when he turned eighteen, if Sir Duncan died. It was odd to think that he might be a scant few months away from becoming the new laird. I wondered if he was looking forward to the prospect. He was terribly young, really, though he would never admit it. As I looked at him across the table, his pale head bent listlessly and his blue eyes loking nervous and tentative, I thought he was probably very frightened of the responsibility that might soon be thrust upon him.

At the moment he muttered something about riding down to the dock in Portree to wait for the boat, and left.

"Uncle Alex may be on the boat," Betheny explained. "Mrs. MacBean s-sent a wire telling him that grandfather is worse and advising him to return at once."

Her expression darkened as she added sullenly, "He'll certainly bring Antonia with him. Then things s-shall be horrid again."

"What does Antonia do that is so terrible?" I asked bluntly.

"What does s-she do!" Betheny exploded with uncharacteristic vehemence. "She's, she's . . . oh, Chrissa, she's just s-so awful!" and she burst into tears.

"I'm sorry, Betheny," I said quickly, reproaching myself for my utter lack of sensitivity. "I didn't mean to upset you. It's all my fault for being nosy."

No," Betheny insisted, drying her eyes with a handkerchief. "It's not your fault. You don't

113

know what it has been like s-since father died. Sometimes during the past few years I've felt that I would rather die than continue living with her."

"It will be different now," I said firmly. "You're not alone. I'll help you, you know."

She smiled, looking a little less downcast.

Though I tried to keep Betheny entertained that day by reading to her from a copy of *Huckleberry Finn* that I brought from California, the morning and afternoon stretched on interminably. Dr. Ross came and went, saying little but promising to return the next day. I was immensely relieved when night fell and it was time to retire to bed.

In my room I sat in front of the fire, trying to read. After staring at the same page for twenty minutes, I realized that it was hopeless. I was feeling very preoccupied and I knew that it was Morag who was on my mind. Finally, I decided to talk to her again. The castle was dark and silent as I walked through it, filled with an almost tangible air of expectancy—as if something important were about to happen. I had the strong feeling that death was in the castle this night and I felt panic welling up inside me. I began to run down the stairway to the Great Hall, my slippered feet falling noiselessly on the smooth wooden stairs. I ran until I came to the light and security of the kitchen.

I almost collided with Morag who was bent over the long wooden trestle table, putting a cover on a cake. Next to her, a cruisie burned brightly.

She jumped, startled, when I burst in, then said, sighing deeply, "Och, tis *you*. Ye fairly frightened me. I wasna' expectin' anyone at this time o' night."

"Why are you baking a cake in the middle of the night?" I asked bluntly.

" 'Tis a divination cake, miss," she answered in a guilty whisper. "Dinna ye ken aboot sic things?"

I shook my head and she continued easily, "Well, ye leave it at a sacred place. If it disappears durin' the night, the one who is ill will recover. But if it remains untouched 'till the mornin' . . . he will *die*."

"Does this have anything to do with Sir Duncan?"

"Aye. But please dinna say nothin' to the family. They would laugh at sic things, or, worse yet, be angry an' make me stop. But I know better."

This seemed so ridiculous that I couldn't help smiling indulgently at poor old Morag.

"Ach, dinna ye laugh," she admonished, and in the dim light of the single lamp her face, covered by shadows, was strange and distorted.

"There are things ye canna' understand, witches an' sic. When Mr. Ferguson's cow started givin' sour milk after eight years o' the sweetest milk ye ever tasted, who do ye think did it? Witches, o' course. They raise storms an' cause illnesses. Sir Duncan was never sick a day in his life, but was stronger than young men half his age. Now suddenly he's taken ill an' gets worse an' worse. Dr. Ross canna understand it, but I can. 'Tis witches' work, I say."

Then, leaning toward me, Morag whispered hoarsely, "On Beltane they gather, when the charm fires are lit. When that happens, ye'd best stay inside the castle where 'tis safe."

Beltane . . . Betheny had described it as a celebration. And now Morag made it sound like an evil, dangerous night. I shivered, in spite of myself, and for a moment I had a cold feeling of foreboding. But I shook it off, determined not to let Morag's superstitions frighten me. It was quiet for a moment, and I could hear the sound of rain falling hard outside, occasionally interrupted by the roll of thunder.

As Morag picked up the cake in her wrinkled, shaking hands, I stopped her, insisting, "You can't go out on a night like this."

"I must," she replied, stubbornly. "I'm only goin' to the old abandoned kirk doon the hill. Ye may think I'm daft, but I must do this."

"Let me go, then," I offered. "It will only take me a minute to dress, and I'll go to the church for you."

Looking skeptical, Morag asked hesitantly, "Are ye sure?"

"Yes," I answered firmly. "You shouldn't go out on a night as stormy as this."

She still looked skeptical, so I added, "I won't pretend that I believe in this. But I promise you, if it means that much to you, I *will* take the cake to the church."

"All right, then," Morag finally conceded reluctantly. "But ye bundle up in somethin' warm, an' I'll ha' some tea brewin' when ye return."

I hurried back to my room, feeling angry with Morag for forcing me to offer to go out on such a night. But I couldn't let her go. She was old and frail and would be much more suscepti-

116

ble to illness than I would. In my room I dressed quickly in my Levis and shirt, and threw a heavy blanket over my shoulders.

As I walked down the hallway on my way back to the kitchen, I slowed when I passed the portrait of the girl named Brenna. This portrait had begun to hold a strange fascination for me—each time I passed it, I glanced at it, wondering about that beautiful, half-wild face. Tonight, with only the pale light shed by the cruisie, the portrait was in shadows, barely visible. But as I looked at it, I had the eerie sensation that the soft brown eyes were following me, aware of what I was about to do, and mocking me. For a split second I felt utter unreasoning terror before I sucked in my breath and forced myself to calm down, to not panic and run as I had earlier.

Walking slowly, carefully, consciously reassuring myself that I had nothing to fear, I made my way back to the kitchen. But all the while I wondered what it was about that portrait that both fascinated and frightened me. Whereas the portrait in Kit's house of the pale, ethereal blonde girl had merely aroused my curiosity, this portrait, at least a hundred years old, seemed to arouse my deepest instincts.

When I arrived back at the kitchen and found Morag waiting patiently for me, I felt a ridiculous surge of relief.

I picked up the cake and left. Morag stood by the door that opened onto the side of the castle, her shawl pulled tightly around her bent shoulders, watching me as I hurried away into the night.

The rain was coming down heavily, slanted by the wind that blew so hard I could feel its biting cold sting even through the thick wool blanket. My hair whipped wetly about my face, and I hugged the covered cake to me as I ran down the hill, nearly slipping in the mud. I saw the church silhouetted at the bottom of the hill, an empty shell of a building, long since abandoned, with its roof gone and the windows and door merely black gaping holes. When I got to the doorway I hesitated for a moment, reluctant to enter. "This is silly," I told myself. "There's nothing to be afraid of in there."

Carefully I stepped inside, and immediately heard the quick scurrying of mice. I looked quickly around for a place to set the cake, but the moon was hidden by storm clouds and it was too dark to see clearly. Slowly, my eyes grew accustomed to the dark and gradually I began to distinguish shapes. When I saw a pulpit still standing at the rear of the building, I began to walk toward it. Suddenly there was a horrible screech and something sharp was tearing at my legs. I whirled around, almost dropping the cake, my mouth open in a silent scream. Then the thing that had torn at me shot out the door, and for a brief second I saw the vague outline of a cat. Sighing with relief, I hurried to the pulpit, put down the cake, and left.

Later, in my room, lying comfortably in my bed, warm from the tea Morag had given me upon my return, I had no trouble falling asleep. But as I slept, I dreamt. There was a cat, grown huge and menacing, and a strange, ugly woman with a horribly scarred face and

118

blazing green eyes. She was dancing around a tall bonfire, and as she danced she shouted, "Beltane! Beltane!"

Brenna
April, 1746

'Twas in the summer of my fifteenth year that I first met Conal. I was standing in a wee burn that ran past our house, washing myself after the dirty task of cutting the peats for the coming autumn and winter. The hem of my skirt was hitched to the waist in a vain attempt to keep my gown dry, and my fair hair hung loosely past my buttocks.

I heard the sound of a horse galloping down the nearby road and looked up to see a fine red stallion being pulled up sharply by his rider. I had seen Conal MacLaren of the powerful Clan MacLaren before from a great distance, and I recognized him immediately. He was tall—a good two heads taller than I—with brown hair and black eyes. The devil would have such eyes, I thought, and couldn't help smiling at such a disrespectful comparison.

"What a wanton little thing, ye are," Conal spoke with a wry smile, "standin' there half-naked an' no' ashamed. An' laughin', too!"

I must have blushed at his words and his frank stare, for he continued gently, "Who are ye, lass?"

"Brenna Breac, sir," I answered promptly, aware that I was speaking to one of the most important men on Skye.

"Ye're a comely child, Brenna. But take care

119

in the future to keep yer attractions more modestly hidden lest some man be tempted to run off wi' ye."

And with that he spurred on the impatient stallion, laughing as he rode off.

I stood motionless 'till Conal disappeared from sight. To think that I had just spoken to the younger brother of the chief of the Clan MacLaren! And he had found me attractive . . . I could still feel that bold, mocking stare from eyes as black as the Cuillins themselves on a moonless night.

Leaving the burn, I walked over to a deep, dark pool nearby. Leaning over the edge, I looked down at my reflection. This is what Conal had seen . . . full breasts straining against the lacings of my thin bodice, round hips revealed by the wet skirt clinging tightly to them, and long hair curling wetly around a smooth, oval face. Megan had said that I was beautiful, and for the first time I understood what that meant—the power to attract a great and wealthy man like Conal MacLaren.

'Twas more than a year till I next saw Conal. In that long, lonely time, when I saw almost no one save my mother, I thought of little else but him.

And then came the ring dance at the kirn, at the feast celebrating the cutting of the grain. Everyone came, even my mother who usually seemed content with our life of solitude. I was filled with excitement as I watched people dancing to the bagpipe, commencing with three loud shouts of triumph and three times tossing their hooks in the air. Then men grabbed women and swung them around a roaring bonfire. I sat watching, not daring to join them though several lads asked me to dance.

And then suddenly strong arms were around my waist, pulling me to my feet, and I looked up into Conal's black eyes. Laughing, he drew me into the throng of dancers, and whirled me around until I was dizzy with excitement. When I stumbled and nearly fell, he caught me, holding me tightly, and for the first time I knew what it was to feel the strength of a man's arms around me.

Later, when everyone was eating and drinking, Conal led me off to a wee glen, hidden by tall trees. I lay down on soft moss and held out my arms to him, not knowing, really, what would happen, but wanting it desperately, whatever it was. There was a strange stirring in my loins as he unlaced my bodice, and my heart beat frantically with fear and expectation. . . .

Taking my plump breasts in his hands, he kissed them tenderly. Then slowly, gently he began to undress me completely, slipping off my dress and underskirt, until my body was totally exposed to the soft moonlight and the fierce light in his dark eyes. Strangely I felt no shame, but instead a secret exultation.

"A body made by the devil himself for a night like this," Conal whispered roughly, then added tenderly, "Dinna' be afraid, lass. I ken that ye've never been wi' a man an' I willna' hurt ye."

He began to kiss me, first on the mouth, then on my neck, breasts, hips and stomach. I began to moan, at first a low sound deep in my throat, then louder and more urgent as my body began to move, almost of its own will, my hips thrusting upward toward Conal.

When his face came up to meet mine once again, I tore at his shirt until it came open, revealing a broad chest covered with black hair. And then his chest came down on me as his hands pushed open my legs and in a moment he was inside of me, hard and insistent, pushing, pushing . . . and my entire body convulsed in an overpowering feeling of unbearable tension and sweet release . . .

When it was over, the brief moment of intense pain and the long period of unimaginable pleasure, he held me close, whispering tenderly, "My own sweet lass, no other man shall ever touch ye . . ."

And I swore to God and the devil himself that I would never lose the happiness I had finally found.

CHAPTER 7

Torquil's rude thought and stubborn will
Smack of the wild Norwegian still;
LORD OF THE ISLES
Canto Third, XXVII

I was just leaving my bedroom the following morning when I saw Mrs. Laurie, Sir Duncan's pinch-faced nurse, entering his room. I had seen very little of Mrs. Laurie, and never spoken to her, but I disliked her instinctively. There was something hard and unyielding in her consistently grim demeanor, and I never felt quite comfortable in her presence. Still, I knew it was probably very difficult being a nurse, especially with an irascible patient such as Sir Duncan.

Mrs. Laurie saw me coming down the hallway and quickly entered Sir Duncan's room. It seemed funny, actually—she was no more eager to talk to me than I was to talk to her.

As I came down the stairs toward the dining room, I saw Dr. Ross come in, looking tired and disheveled, as if he had slept in his clothes. He asked how I was feeling, then explained that he had been at a crofter's cottage near the castle delivering a baby.

" 'Tis a hard life these poor crofters lead," he said sadly, shaking his head. "Livin' in those cold, drafty cottages, havin' children they canna' feed. When I pulled the poor wee bairn from his mother's womb, I wondered what his lot would be. Whatever, it is likely to be rough. No work for the men hereabouts, no way to provide for their families . . . an' no hope for the future to be any different."

"But why is it that way?" I asked.

"The great landowners like Duncan MacLaren!" he exploded angrily. "Who keep the land for their own pleasure an' refuse to make it possible for the crofters to farm it. Dinna look so shocked, lass. Duncan MacLaren has been my friend for forty years, an' I've told him this over an' over again. But he's like the rest, no' carin' what's happenin' to his own people. Ah, well. At least he lives on the land he owns. That's more than most of these rich landowners can say. They live in London, actin' English, ashamed o' bein' Scottish, an' come to their huntin' lodges for the huntin' each October. An' the rest o' the time the land lies fallow an' the people starve."

Sighing heavily, clearly exhausted, he concluded, "I shouldna' get so angry over what

124

I canna' change, I suppose. An' right now I've Sir Duncan to think of. I thought I might look in on him on my way back to Portree."

"Do you think he'll recover?"

Dr. Ross hesitated for a long moment, before finally answering, "He's verra ill. I dinna' ken why, I may as well admit. He's always been a strong 'un, an' age did little to weaken him. Till lately, that is."

His voice trailed off into a heavy silence. Finally he added, forcing a smile, "Ye can never tell, lass. He may surprise us after all. I'd best go look in on him now."

He walked up the stairway toward the bedrooms as I went on into the dining room. Betheny and Jonathan hadn't come down yet, and I was alone. After pouring a cup of tea, I sat down at the table, thinking about what Dr. Ross had said about the poor crofters. There seemed to be an almost immoral discrepancy between rich and poor in this country. Though I had known poor people back in California, somehow it seemed different. There was always the possibility of a better life there, whereas here, as Dr. Ross said, there was no hope for change. As I was lost in thought, Morag poked her head through the pantry door, whispering urgently, "Chrissa!"

I turned to look at her and she continued tearfully, her voice breaking, "I went doon to the kirk this mornin' an' the cake was still there! The poor laird! He'll die for sure."

Suddenly there were footsteps and Morag ducked back inside the pantry. It was Dr. Ross, with a grim expression on his tired old face. I looked up at him expectantly and he said simply, "I'm sorry, Sir Duncan is dead."

At that moment I found myself thinking, not of Sir Duncan, or even Betheny and Jonathan, but of Morag. Crazy old Morag...

After Dr. Ross left, I went to Betheny's room to break the sad news to her. She was unhappy and clearly worried about the changes that would now take place, but she remained more composed than I had expected. Together we went to Jonathan's room and told him. When he heard that his grandfather was dead, his young face paled and he looked very nervous. But, like Betheny, he remained composed.

It was obvious from the first that there would be no real mourning for Sir Duncan, who had been such a cold, severe man.

It was Jonathan, instinctively assuming leadership, who said that the servants must be told immediately. Though we all knew that the news had probably long since spread through the servants' quarters like wildfire on a prairie, it was still a formality that must be observed. Mrs. MacBean was summoned and asked to assemble all the servants from both the house and the stables in the Great Hall. Though she said nothing, I could tell that she already knew what was going to be said at the gathering.

Twenty minutes later, Betheny, Jonathan, and I were standing at the head of the stairway, looking at the expectant faces of nearly two dozen men and women. Lucy stood in front, looking rather excited and not at all worried. In the rear, near the doorway, stood Willie, stoic as usual. Somehow I was surprised to find that Mrs. Laurie wasn't here. Then I realized that she must have things to do in Sir Duncan's room. I remembered what she had looked like earlier as she had hurriedly entered his room. And I wondered if she had expected to find him dead.

Jonathan began to speak, clearing his throat and trying to sound older than his years.

"I have a very sad announcement to make. My grandfather, Sir Duncan MacLaren, died this morning in his sleep."

There was a low murmur through the small crowd as their suspicions were confirmed.

"My uncle, Alex MacLaren, will return shortly to assume temporary control of the estate until I come of age in February. When he arrives, we will decide exactly when the funeral will take place. Needless to say, Sir Duncan will be buried in the family plot in Portree cemetery. I hope all of you will attend the ceremony. I'm sure my grandfather would want you to be there especially those of you who have served him long and faithfully all these years." Aware of what was uppermost in their minds, Jonathan concluded, "There will almost certainly be no changes in the staff while my uncle is in charge or when I assume responsibility for the estate."

As he spoke, I looked at the faces of the people listening to him so intently. Though there were genuine expressions of sadness on the faces of the older servants, most of them simply seemed relieved that they would retain their jobs. When Jonathan dismissed them, they filed slowly out, talking softly among themselves.

The castle had an appropriately funereal atmosphere that day. For some reason, everyone spoke in whispers and the servants performed their duties silently, with a vague air of expectancy. Things would be different now. With Sir Duncan's death, an era had come to an end. Now Alex MacLaren, a young, dissolute rogue, would run things, and the castle would undoubtedly be a much more lively place. I suspected that many of the servants, especially Lucy, were looking forward to the change.

I stayed inside with Betheny all that day and the next. But finally the atmosphere became so oppressive that I *had* to get away. Late in the afternoon on the day after Sir Duncan's death, I slipped away, leaving Betheny reading in her room and Jonathan going over household accounts with Mrs. MacBean.

After changing into my faded Levis and shirt, I quietly left the castle. I didn't want any company this afternoon, for I had a great deal to think about. With Sir Duncan dead, I didn't know if I should continue to stay at Castle Stalker.

Willie was reluctant to let me ride Charger, insisting stubbornly, "He's nervous today, miss. High-strung. No tellin' what he might take it in his head to do."

But I was equally stubborn and finally Willie relented. As I rode out of the stableyard I saw that he was right about Charger. The big horse was nervous for some reason, as if he could sense the tension that surrounded the castle today. I knew that it would help if I let him run, so I gave him his head and we ran headlong over the heathery moors, my braids whipping behind me.

The sky was completely clear today, and the tall, black Cuillins were sharply visible in the distance. On a day like this I could easily understand why Skye was called the island of the "airy mountain and rushy glen." Criss-crossing the rugged moors were little rivers and small waterfalls. On the sides of the mountains, large waterfalls could be seen flowing down time-worn paths.

When I thought about leaving this strange, isolated island, I grew extremely depressed. Though Skye had at first seemed forbidding, I had quickly come to feel a part of it. All of this—the moors, the mountains, and Castle Stalker itself with its centuries of stubborn pride—all of it touched something deep inside me. I didn't want to leave it.

But I couldn't accept staying on as a poor, very distant relation, accepting charity. And I wasn't at all sure that the dissolute Alex MacLaren would want me to stay. Remembering our highly embarrassing meeting at the inn in Mallaig, I doubted whether I could live under the same roof as such a man.

Then, with a sinking feeling, I thought what life would be like back in America. I could never return to the ranch. I had already definitely decided that that dismal part of my life was over. That meant that I would have to make a living for myself. Since I had only enough money to get to New York, I would have to find a position there as a governess or in a factory. When I thought of such a future, tears stung my eyes. But I held them back. Crying would solve nothing.

After riding for two hours, I turned back,

still confused and depressed. One thing only was clear—I must leave Castle Stalker. Beyond that, my life was a blank. But somehow, I vowed, I would survive. I always had.

I was riding toward the stableyard, keeping the now-quiet Charger to a canter, when suddenly Brownie, a half-grown Border Collie who liked to chase the horses, came rushing out, nipping playfully at Charger's heels. The startled horse bolted, rushing headlong toward the stableyard, nearly tearing the reins from my hands.

In almost the same instant I saw a carriage standing in the stableyard and people stepping out of it. Charger was heading straight toward them, and I knew I must do something immediately. Pulling with all my strength, I managed to swerve Charger aside and bring him to a rearing halt a few feet from the carriage. But as he reared, he tore the reins from my hands, and I slid off his back, cursing the bare pad of an English saddle as I hit the ground with a thud. My fall was softened by a mud puddle left over from the recent storm, but it was an ignominious landing. As the man and woman I had seen stepping from the carriage came hurrying toward me, I blushed deeply, aware that I must look ridiculous.

The man reached me first, and when I looked up at him I was startled to see familiar disheveled brown hair and black eyes. It was Alex MacLaren, glaring down at me as if he would gladly throttle me.

Behind him stood the most beautiful woman I had ever seen. She was tiny, and I thought she must be the woman who had been with

Alex at the inn. But now her head was uncovered and I could see her clearly. Her thick auburn hair was piled high under a plumed hat, and her sea green eyes matched the blue green of her velvet traveling dress. The dress, tight through the waist and hips and billowing at the bottom in a mass of ruffles and lace, showed off a voluptuous figure.

But even in that brief instant that I first looked at her, I sensed something more to her than just a beautiful, undoubtedly vain and self-centered woman. She had the appearance of a sleek, pampered cat; and like a cat, I suspected she had a merciless quality, with claws that wouldn't hesitate to strike when her own desires were at stake. From that first moment, I did not trust her.

"Who the hell are you, and what the devil do ye think yer doing nearly running us down!" Alex thundered in the deep voice I remembered so well.

I didn't know how to respond, then I saw that the woman was laughing at me. That did it. I could accept anger, but I couldn't stand being laughed at.

"Charger was frightened by Brownie," I shot back, carefully ignoring the woman. "I didn't mean to run toward the carriage. Normally I can handle Charger, but ..."

Breaking in roughly, Alex asked curtly, "What do ye mean, normally ye can handle him? Who the devil *are* you?"

Before I could respond, Willie appeared, leading the tired and now docile Charger. He interrupted nervously, "Pardon, sir, but Miss

Chrissa's right. 'Tweren't her fault. *I* let her ride Charger."

Though Willie's tone was carefully deferential, there was a spark in his eyes that betrayed his true feelings—he clearly disliked Alex MacLaren, and was only barely concealing his dislike.

Turning back to me, Alex stared at me intently for a long moment, his black eyes narrowing in concentration. Finally he said slowly, "So you're Carissa Rey."

His tone held a double meaning—he had remembered our meeting at the inn.

"Ye'd best go to your room now and do something with yourself, Miss Rey. I'll speak with ye later."

I was about to respond curtly when the lady standing behind Alex said softly, "Oh, Alex, dear, I think she looks rather charming, all covered with mud like that. Like a little water sprite."

Her tone was maddening, with its underlying mockery and assumption of superiority. I understood immediately why Betheny hated this woman so. I had realized that she must be Antonia, and she was every bit as unlikeable as Betheny had indicated.

I stood up, with some help from Willie, and brushed off some of the mud from my clothes. Watching me, Antonia giggled, saying gaily, "Look, Alex, she's wearing a man's trousers. How quaint."

I glared at her, remembering all of the earthy epithets that the cowboys on the ranch had used. But I held my tongue and stalked off, ignoring both her and Alex, who stared after me with a startled expression.

Back in my room I rang for Lucy, then quickly pulled off my wet, muddy clothes. When Lucy arrived, she took one horrified look at me and gasped, "What happened, miss?"

I started to say something rude, but realized that I had no right to take out my anger on Lucy. So I explained simply that I had fallen into a mud puddle and asked her to prepare a bath for me immediately.

Nodding cheerfully, she headed for the door, then stopped and asked excitedly, "Did ye ken Master Alex and Mrs. MacLaren have returned?"

"Yes," I answered shortly.

"They'll be here for quite awhile now, at least 'till young Master Jonathan comes of age," Lucy continued eagerly. "An' then the gossip will start again."

"What gossip?"

"Oh . . ." Lucy hesitated, but couldn't resist saying, "Master Alex has quite a reputation wi' the ladies. An' there are some as say Mrs. MacLaren finds him quite attractive."

I thought that must be an understatement, if it was indeed Antonia MacLaren's room he was heading for the night we met in Mallaig.

"At least the castle will be gayer now," Lucy continued happily. "I expect Master Alex will gi' balls again, as soon as 'tis proper. An' there'll be Miss Betheny's party on Beltane. What a time that will be! Imagine, celebratin' a bairthday an' Beltane at the same time!"

I had become used to Lucy's incessant talking, always liberally sprinkled with gossip

133

from the servants' hall, especially regarding Alex MacLaren. But just at that moment I didn't care to ever hear anything about him again. I said curtly, "Lucy, weren't you going to get some hot water for my bath?"

"Oh, aye," Lucy answered, laughing, and opened the door to leave.

We were both surprised to see Mrs. MacBean standing there, hand raised, on the verge of knocking on the door.

She said stiffly, "I'm sorry to disturb ye, but Mister MacLaren has asked me to tell ye he wants to see ye in the library immediately."

I felt my heart sink and I answered quietly, "Very well. But he'll have to wait 'till I've had my bath."

"He said *immediately*," Mrs. MacBean retorted sharply.

With Mrs. MacBean I had always acutely felt my status as a poor, distant relation. If anything, her attitude toward me since the first night we met had worsened, and she treated me with a good deal less deference than she showed toward Betheny and Jonathan. Her attitude had always irritated me, and this time I was completely unwilling to meekly accept it.

"He'll just have to wait!" I responded sharply, not bothering to keep the anger from my voice.

Looking shocked and disapproving, Mrs. MacBean left in a huff, muttering under her breath.

I knew what this peremptory summons from Alex meant. There was no question that I would be leaving Castle Stalker. He had asked to speak with me immediately to tell me so.

Taking a long, leisurely bath, I purposefully prolonged the moment when I would have to face him. Then I dressed carefully in my best dress, a pale lavender gown with a black velvet ribbon around the waist, and sat quietly while Lucy brushed my hair. Instead of braiding it, she pulled it back with a black ribbon, a sign of mourning for Sir Duncan.

"I must say, miss, not many people dare to keep Alex MacLaren waitin'," Lucy remarked casually while she brushed my hair.

"I wasn't aware he was held in such respect," I answered acidly.

"He's a MacLaren," Lucy said quickly, "an' there's no one more important hereabouts. People may talk aboot him because he's wilder than most, but still they respect his position."

"I don't think Willie respects him," I replied tersely and was surprised at the strange look in Lucy's eyes.

"Och, well, Willie has his reasons," Lucy answered nervously. "There, yer hair's done now. Ye look really fine, miss, if I may say so."

She was obviously trying to change the subject.

"Ye'd best be goin' now, 'tis late."

My hair hung to my waist and I felt it brushing wetly against my back as I walked down the stairs toward the library.

In the Great Hall, I paused in front of the library door, then, gathering my courage, knocked firmly. Immediately a gruff voice said, "Come in."

As I entered, I saw Alex standing in front of the fireplace, his back to me, one arm leaning on the mantle and one black-booted foot resting on the fender, gazing into the brightly crackling fire. I noticed again how tall he was. He was several inches taller than I, and I was tall for a girl.

I stood in the middle of the room, waiting expectantly, until finally he turned to face me. For a brief moment we looked at each other intently and I could feel the tension in the air between us. There was arrogance in his face, in the aquiline nose and firm chin, and the narrow, piercing black eyes. The ruggedness and harshness of his features seemed to reflect the atmosphere of Skye itself. I sensed that he was a very hard man, one who would never give in if he believed in something. A man who would not be dominated by anyone, as the Cuillins themselves could never truly be conquered by anyone.

His eyes scrutinized me carefully. As I looked into them defiantly, I again had the feeling that I had done so before. A picture flashed through my mind . . . those black eyes gazing down at me with an expression of longing and desire . . . and then the picture was gone, leaving me strangely unsettled and frightened.

Alex was looking me over carefully, clearly surprised at the transformation I had undergone. He began brusquely, "Ye kept me waiting over an hour."

"Would you have preferred me to speak with you when I was still covered with mud, my clothes smelling of horses?" I asked impudently.

His dark, unreadable eyes narrowed in what could have been either anger or a suppressed smile. Then he responded, his voice softening to the gentle, rolling accent of the West Highlander, "No, ye do look much more like a young lady now than a ragamuffin."

And then he continued matter-of-factly, "When I heard of my father's death, I spoke with the family solicitor in Portree. My father remembered you in his will. Ye'll receive a legacy of five thousand pounds when ye reach eighteen, and are to be allowed to live at Castle Stalker as long as you wish. Originally these terms applied to your mother, but with her death, they apply to you instead."

I was stunned! This was not at all what I had expected, what I had prepared myself for. Immediately I felt a tremendous rush of relief—I was no longer a poor relation, but a person who would soon be quite well-off, financially independent. But more important, I didn't have to leave, to worry about eking out a bare existence in New York.

"Until you reach eighteen, I shall serve as your guardian," Alex continued.

"What?" I asked quickly, brought rudely out of my reverie by this incredible statement.

"Someone has to do it," he explained simply. "You are far too young to be on your own. What are you, fourteen, fifteen?"

"I'm seventeen," I answered hotly, "I'll be eighteen in April, and I'm not a child in need of a guardian! I'm perfectly capable of taking care of myself."

"Obviously," he responded drily, "I could see that by the way ye run around in men's trousers and ride horses that could easily kill you."

137

I glared at him; he glared back at me.

In California it was what is known as a "Mexican standoff." There was a long moment of tense silence before he said wryly, "*You* are a very stubborn young lady."

"*You* are a very stubborn man," I countered.

To my surprise he smiled, and his whole face softened to an appealing boyish vulnerability. It was like getting a brief look at a completely different Alex MacLaren. Then he quickly reverted to his usual serious expression.

"We'd best talk of practical matters," He said flatly. "You'll be given an allowance 'till ye receive your legacy. One pound a week should be sufficient. Mrs. MacBean says that ye need decent clothes. There's a dressmaker in Portree who can take care of that. The bills will be sent to me."

"I can make my own clothes," I insisted stubbornly.

"Well, make them then," he shot back angrily. "But get something proper. I don't want to see you in trousers again."

"I always wear Levis and a shirt when riding. They're comfortable. Being a man, you have no idea how cumbersome a skirt can be."

"You'll wear *proper* riding clothes," he said slowly and firmly, and for the first time I came face to face with his iron will.

I stood quietly, not saying anything, but not giving in. He knew I wouldn't give in and it clearly surprised and frustrated him. But he didn't know what to do about it. Finally he dismissed me with a curt, "That is all I have to say—for now."

So, our first interview was to be over, and

138

without a mention of the incident in Mallaig. I could not accept that as easily as he apparently wished I would. Trying not to reveal how terribly embarrassed I felt, I said firmly, "About the incident in Mallaig . . ."

But he stopped me with a curt, "I believe I apologized for my behavior, which was completely unintentional, I assure you. It will not happen again. I don't make it a habit to force my attentions on children."

His tone was maddening—curt, slightly bored, and final. I was furious but had no idea what to say. Rudely, I turned and stalked out of the room, slamming the door behind me.

My relationship with Alex MacLaren had been set from the start—mutual antagonism, flamed by feelings that I suspected neither of us completely understood.

Brenna
April, 1746

I wanted Conal . . . I won him . . . and I threw away everything trying to keep him. He called it treachery, not understanding that it was love.

But in the beginning there were no bad omens to portend our unhappy fate. We met often in the wee glen that quickly became our trysting place. There Conal taught me the many ways of love and I came to know the power of passion. He awakened feelings in me that I had never known existed, and praised me for being a loving, passionate girl.

Sometimes as I lay on the soft moss, feeling the cool breeze softly caressing my naked body, my thoughts would turn to other lovers who might have come here. I wondered if their passion could have been as great as ours. I thought not . . . surely, two people had never loved as we did.

As time passed and Conal said nothing of marriage, I began to think he only wanted me as his light o' love. But I did not mind a great deal. So long as I had his love, I was content.

And then one day in early spring, Conal came late to the glen. I had been waiting all the morning, growing desperate with fear that he would not come, that he would never come again. When I saw him leading his red stallion through the narrow opening that was the only entrance to the glen, I broke down and wept uncontrollably.

"What lass, did ye think I would no' come?" he asked with a teasing smile.

I nodded, choking back the tears, and he burst into laughter. Then, sensing how truly worried I had been, he stopped laughing, took me into his arms and pressed my head against his chest.

"Why, do ye no ken how much I love ye?" he asked softly.

It was the first time he had spoken to me of love, and I thought my heart would burst with happiness. Then he took a small package from his waistcoat pocket and held it out to me.

Conal had given me presents before—a bolt of gold velvet for a gown, an ivory comb for my hair—and I thought this would be the same. But when I tore off the string and opened the cloth, I found a shiny gold ring.

"If ye're to be my wife, ye'll hae to sit for a

140

portrait," Conal said, smiling broadly at my shocked expression. "'Tis expected o' the bride o' a MacLaren. There's a poor, starvin' artist in Portree can do it. An' ye'll ha' to meet Lorn."

Lorn ... Chief of the Clan MacLaren.

CHAPTER 8

And rose the death-prayer's awful tone.
LORD OF THE ISLES
Canto Sixth, XXXV

Sir Duncan's body was "laid out" in the library, according to ancient Scottish tradition. A wooden platter lay on his chest, holding a small pile of earth and another of salt. The earth was symbolic of the corruptible body and the salt represented the immortal spirit. No fire was lit in the room while Sir Duncan's body lay there. The clock was stopped and the mirrors covered.

Betheny and Jonathan came down together that afternoon to pay their last respects to their grandfather. Betheny, who was so frightened of death, was very uneasy at the thought of looking upon her dead grandfather's body. She asked me to come with her, and though I had no desire to look on Sir Duncan's pale, dead face, I went.

Without a fire, the room was cold. And, of course, utterly silent. No one said a word as the three of us filed in. Betheny and Jonathan knelt in front of their grandfather's body and prayed silently for a moment. Both were nervous, anxious to flee the morbid atmosphere of the room, and they hurried through their prayers. I stood back, near the door, as far as possible from Sir Duncan's lifeless body.

Antonia did not make the ritual visit to the library. No one really expected her to do so. Considering what I knew of Alex's relationship with his father, I didn't expect him to come either. But he did come, late the second night, alone. I know because I had been talking with Morag and was on my way from the kitchen to my room when I saw a light in the library and heard a low voice.

Walking silently to the half-open door, I peered inside and saw Alex standing over his father's body, staring at it with an expression of complete and utter hatred. His black eyes were narrowed in anger and his mouth was set in a hard, uncompromising line.

"Perhaps your God will forgive ye, old man," he said bitterly, "but I never shall!"

His whole body was tense with the hatred he had just expressed, his hands clenched so tightly at his sides that the knuckles were white.

It was then I understood what was wrong with Castle Stalker, what had frightened me so the night I had first entered its black interior.

144

There was a dark core of unresolved hatred here, permeating the very walls themselves, and it was centered in Alex MacLaren.

The next day Sir Duncan's body was removed from the library by Willie and some other male servants and taken to the church in Portree for the funeral. All of the family and the servants attended the short, bleak service, except for Sir Duncan's grim-faced nurse who had left hurriedly the morning of his death. At the time I wondered why her departure was so precipitous, but Betheny mentioned that she had another job waiting in London, and I thought no more about it. I had seen little of the woman, and cared for her even less.

Kit was at the service, too, standing off to one side as we all stood around the open grave. I would have spoken to him but he seemed strangely reserved, so I said nothing. It was a grey, ugly day. Black clouds slid silently across a dreary sky. While the young Reverend Mr. MacLean spoke over the grave, it began to rain, a cold drizzle at first, gradually increasing to a steady downpour.

We were divided into two distinct groups—the family on one side of the grave, and the servants on the other. Antonia, looking bored and beautiful, the black of her dress accenting the ivory of her skin, hung on Alex, her arm wrapped tightly around his. Alex looked withdrawn, his expression enigmatic. Betheny was quiet, while Jonathan seemed nervous, undoubtedly very aware of the significance of the occasion. With his grandfather's death, he was only months away from being the laird, controlling Castle Stalker and the vast estate surrounding it.

Once Morag caught my eye as they were lowering the coffin into the grave, and nodded grimly, as if to say, "I told you he would die."

My thin, well-worn cloak was little protection against the rain and cold, and I began to shiver uncontrollably. I was immensely relieved when the service ended with the minister tossing some dirt over the coffin.

At the castle, Morag had prepared a lavish dinner, according to the tradition of a feast following a funeral. But none of us had any appetite and little of the food was eaten.

After dinner we all retired to the drawing room. Everyone had tea except Alex, who drank glass after glass of brandy. It was becoming obvious that he drank a great deal, retreating into the bottle to hide from whatever devils there were plaguing him. The strained silence of the room was getting on my nerves. Finally I asked Betheny to play something on the piano, anything to relieve the unspoken tension.

Betheny immediately went to the gleaming black grand piano that sat on a raised platform in a corner. She was as eager as I to fill the room with pleasant sounds instead of dead silence.

She chose some pieces by Chopin, playing them imperfectly but with great feeling. When she finished a half hour later, she looked up at Alex, her face flushed, her eyes bright, seeking praise for her efforts. He said curtly, his voice a bit slurred from the drink, "Fine, Beth, now you'd best get to bed, 'tis late."

He was so cool toward her—this man whose opinion she had sought out of all the others in the room. I was furious as I looked at her downcast expression, and it was all I could do to hold my tongue. Throughout the past three days, since Alex had returned to Castle Stalker, it had been the same——he was consistently cool toward Betheny, and much of the time he seemed to ignore her very presence altogether. I didn't understand how anyone could be so callous to such an affectionate, likeable young girl.

Both Jonathan and I joined Betheny as she left the room, leaving Alex and Antonia alone. As we walked out of the room, I saw Antonia move nearer to Alex, placing her hand over his, gazing up at him in a disgustingly simpering manner. I was rapidly coming to the conclusion that Antonia was, as Lucy had hinted, interested in making Alex her second husband.

Betheny's room was beyond mine on the third floor, but instead of continuing down the hall, she stopped at my door and asked if she could come in to talk for awhile. I was feeling rather depressed myself and was glad of her company. When we entered my room I was happy to see that a fire had been lit and the lamps were turned up brightly, making the room seem warm and cheerful. Betheny rang for Lucy, and when she appeared, asked for some tea to be brought up. Minutes later we were sitting beside the fire, sipping the tea and feeling cozy and comfortable.

"You know, I feel s-somehow guilty," Betheny began hesitantly.

"Why?"

"Because I don't miss grandfather more," she answered frankly. And then she added in an almost inaudible whisper, "I'm afraid there must be something terribly wrong with me."

"Why do you say that?"

"Because I felt the s-same way about father," she said guiltily. "I wasn't happy that he was dead, but I wasn't horribly unhappy as I s-should have been . . . as Jonathan was. To be perfectly honest, all I was concerned about was myself, about being left an orphan, without a mother or father. Otherwise, it was as if life just went on much the same as usual, except that Antonia was even more unbearable without father around to keep her in line."

"Were you close to your father?" I asked gently.

Betheny was silent for a long moment, then answered hesitantly, "No . . ." She added quickly, "Oh, he was a very good father. Very responsible. But I always had the feeling that it was Jonathan he cared about. He never took much notice of me."

"Well, I don't think there's anything wrong with you, Betheny," I responded sympathetically. "From what I saw of Sir Duncan, and from what people have told me, he was not a man who was generally loved by anyone. It's understandable that you wouldn't miss him terribly. And I can understand your feelings about your father, too. It's hard to love someone whom you feel doesn't care about you."

Tears had come to Betheny's eyes and I handed her a handkerchief. She dried her eyes, looking immensely embarrassed, then we both sat quietly, sipping the hot, comforting tea.

"It's different with Uncle Alex," Betheny spoke again, breaking the silence. "If anything were to happen to him, I s-should be heartbroken. I don't know what I would do without him. You know, when he was traveling about so much, he always s-sent me the most wonderful presents. It was s-so exciting, never knowing when to expect a beautiful doll or lovely new gown. And when I was fourteen, and wanted to go away to Miss Prym's school in London, it was Uncle Alex who managed to get me in s-somehow, though it was terribly exclusive."

Though I said nothing, I couldn't help thinking that he had probably simply wanted to get her out of his way, judging by the way he ignored her most of the time.

And then Betheny continued angrily, "Antonia *can't* marry him!"

"Are you sure she wants to?" I asked without conviction.

"Oh, yes," Betheny answered definitely. "Everyone knows s-she's been after him for years, ever since father died. That was all I could think about during the funeral today, s-seeing her standing so close to him, as if he already belonged to her."

I wondered why on earth Betheny loved her uncle so deeply, since he showed so little affection toward her. She must have assumed that because he sent her presents, that meant he cared about her. I knew differently. My aunt and uncle had always given me all the material things I could possibly want. But there had been no love behind the gifts.

Then I remembered something I had been meaning to ask Betheny. I wanted to know about the mystery surrounding Alex, the two people whose deaths he had caused. But as I looked at her, her young face so sad and worried, I knew I couldn't ask her then.

It was very late. Though it was too dark in my room to see the clock, I knew that it must be well past midnight. I had been sleeping and something . . . some noise . . . had awakened me. I lay in bed, listening for whatever it was that had brought me into this abrupt wakefulness. And then I heard it . . . a heavy step outside my room, heading down the hallway. There was no reason why someone should be prowling the hallway at this time of night—unless he didn't want to be seen. Quickly I left my bed and hurried to the door, opening it slowly, quietly. I peered into the dark hallway, feeling my heart beat faster with fear and intense curiosity. Only a few yards away I saw a shadowy figure standing in front of the door to Antonia's bedroom.

It was Alex. He knocked softly on the door and it was opened immediately. Antonia stood framed in the doorway for a brief moment, bathed in the soft light of the candle she held. She was wearing an emerald-green silk peignoir that outlined her voluptuous curves. Alex bent down to kiss her upturned face, parting the peignoir as he did so to put his arms around her tiny waist. When the peignoir parted, I saw that she was wearing nothing

150

underneath it. For an instant she stood pressed against him, her bare breasts, large and round, pushing against his white shirt. Then she pulled back, he entered her room, and the door closed behind them.

So, I thought, it *is* true. They are lovers.

I was filled with disgust at their illicit behavior. How could she make love to her dead husband's brother, while her step-children slept only yards away? And Alex . . . spending his nights creeping down dark hallways in inns and his own father's house, taking his pleasure without honor or respect. They were a fine pair to be surrogate parents to innocent children like Betheny and Jonathan. The longer I thought of it, the more furious I became. But though my outrage and fury were genuine, there was some other emotion that also filled my heart. It was even stronger and more disturbing, and I refused to face it.

The next morning the dining table was more full than it had been in all the time I had been at the castle. I was finishing my breakfast when Betheny and Jonathan came in, arguing. Moments later, Alex entered, looking tired, followed closely by Antonia who was as lovely as usual in a pale blue morning dress with black velvet bands on the arms and waist, in token respect to Sir Duncan. Her auburn hair shone red-gold, pulled back in a smooth chignon that emphasized her large, round eyes. This morning her eyes appeared more blue than green, reflecting the blue of her dress.

To my utter consternation, Antonia sat next to me at the table. Though I felt uncomfortable sitting so close to her, I couldn't help watching her surreptitiously. Seeing her closely for the first time, I realized that she was older than I had thought. Tiny lines around her eyes and mouth revealed that she was at least thirty, and strands of grey showed in her red hair. She was a beauty, but a fading one.

Surveying my worn brown dress critically, she said in a loud voice, "My dear Carissa, you really should *do* something about your clothes. You're not a pauper, you know, child, and your unfortunate appearance reflects on the family in a very poor way."

Before I had a chance to respond to this unexpected attack, she turned to Alex, sitting across from her, and began chatting animatedly, leaving me feeling angry and yet somehow confused. It was possible, I supposed, that she had meant the remark not as an insult but as friendly advice. A fashion plate like Antonia would naturally be aware of what others were wearing, and would, perhaps, feel free to offer advice. I sat at the table, quietly smoldering, trying to rationalize away my anger.

My attention was distracted from my own problems to Betheny's when her argument with Jonathan grew loud. As usual, he was teasing her unmercifully, but this time the usually meek Betheny had had enough. When he said that she was so clumsy she could barely stay on her grey mare, "a child's mount," she retorted hotly, "That's how much you know! Chrissa's teaching me to ride as well as you. Why, s-soon I'll be riding Charger, s-she says, and that's more than you can do!"

I hadn't promised her she would ever ride

Charger, but I didn't think it wise to correct her at that moment. She was overcoming her shyness, finally standing up to Jonathan's teasing, and that was what mattered.

Alex interrupted the argument with a curt, "What do you mean, ye'll be riding Charger?"

"Chrissa's teaching me to ride like a man," Betheny explained proudly. "We've even fixed up my s-skirt like a pair of trousers, and I can ride ever so much better now."

Antonia gasped, admonishing angrily, "Betheny, how dare you talk about wearing trousers!" Turning to me, she concluded coldly, "Clearly, Carissa has been less than a good influence on you. I've heard California is an uncivilized place. Apparently it's true."

I expected Alex to readily concur with her but to my surprise he merely looked at me intently for a long moment, his expression unreadable as usual, behind those black eyes. Then he said, "Well, perhaps tomorrow we'll go for a ride together and see how ye've improved."

Betheny's happiness at her uncle's encouragement was almost pathetic to see, while across the table Jonathan sat in sullen silence.

Nothing more was said during the meal, but I knew that a subtle challenge had been laid down by Antonia. There was no question in my mind now that she intended to try to dominate me as she dominated Betheny. What she didn't realize was that I was not a shy, insecure child like Betheny who was used to having her life run by others. I was determined that she would soon realize this.

The situation came to a head even sooner than I had expected.

We were having dinner that evening, Betheny, Jonathan, Alex, Antonia, and I. Antonia sat directly across from me, and throughout the meal she made pointed little criticisms of me—everything from the way I dressed to my table manners, which I was uncomfortably aware were still not as polished as hers. I bore her snide remarks in angry silence, becoming more and more furious, until finally she went too far.

She concluded a particularly scathing critique of my gown, which was admittedly rather plain and unfashionable compared to her magnificent turquoise chiffon, with the comment, "But then I understand your mother had little taste either. Or sense, for that matter. Otherwise, she would never have thrown away her reputation by running off with a worthless drifter."

"My mother," I said drily, "had a spotless reputation. Which is more than you can say!"

And then, grabbing the closest thing to me, which happened to be a bowl of soup, I stood and dumped it on her head. I smiled smugly as I watched the thick broth run down her face and neck in tiny rivulets.

"Why, you . . . you . . ." she sputtered, enraged to the point of speechlessness.

Beside me I heard Betheny giggling uncontrollably, then suddenly strong arms were around my waist and I was picked up bodily and carried from the dining room. It was Alex, of course, and though I fought and shouted

154

furiously, he didn't let go of me until we had reached the library.

"How dare you remove me like that!" I shouted. "I wasn't finished with her!"

"You were quite finished," he responded curtly. "A lady would never have behaved as you did."

"A lady would never have insulted my mother as Antonia did!" I answered quickly.

He stared at me silently for a long moment, then said firmly, "Antonia has merely been trying to improve your manners and appearance, to teach you how to be a lady."

"I know enough about being a lady not to open my door to a man in the middle of the night," I responded tersely, my voice hard and stubborn.

The insult hit its mark. Alex looked shocked for a moment before once more retreating behind an inscrutable mask of cool detachment.

"That's all. You may go to your room now."

"I'll go where I please," I retorted hautily, as I strode out of the room, chin held high. After slamming the door behind me, I was stopped dead in my tracks by the unexpected sound of laughter coming from the room I had just left.

The next morning Alex, Betheny and I went riding together for the first time. As we walked out of the castle, I happened to glance up and was startled to see Antonia standing at her bedroom window, looking down at us. To be specific, she was looking at *me*, and her expression was so full of hate and fury that I felt a sharp stab of fear. Her perfect, rosebud mouth was compressed in a grim frown, and her lovely sea green eyes looked daggers at me. Clearly, she was not disposed to forget the incident of the previous evening. I found myself wondering what sort of revenge she was planning.

Though I continued to be vaguely worried about Antonia in the back of my mind, it was too fine a day to be completely spoiled by her fury. Alex took Charger while I was relegated to an aging, but well-bred gelding who had obviously been a fine mount in his day. Betheny was again on her grey mare, and though she was terribly nervous and all-too-aware of her uncle's careful scrutiny, she did well.

Alex chose the direction of the ride, heading inland. The weather was beautiful, a crisp, sunny autumn day. Heather was spread everywhere and in the air was the lilting call of a bird. I still had not quite grown used to the emptiness and loneliness that was Skye, however. There were no people to be seen, and no sign that people had ever been here. Back at the ranch in California there had always been people around, even in the fields—carriages passing by on the nearby roads, ranchhands going about their work. But here on Skye you could go for miles without seeing another living soul.

We rode on, each of us silent for our own reasons. Betheny was concentrating on riding, determined to impress her adored uncle, while my thoughts were on the home I had abandoned with so little regret only a short time ago. Alex silently surveyed the land around him, and I was struck once again by his resemblance to this strange island. Like Skye, he was quiet and hard, with a roughness that would probably never be worn smooth. And, like Skye, there was a mystery about him, a feeling that he could never be fully understood.

Both the man and the island seemed better suited to an earlier time, bolder, less civilized. I could not see either in the new century that would soon be upon us.

My musings were cut short when we came upon a crofter's cottage. It sat alone in a small glen, windowless, roofed with thatch, as usual, with smoke coming desultorily from a hole in the roof. Alex dismounted, and walked up to meet the crofter who came out of the door to meet him.

As they talked, Betheny and I sat on our horses, both of us struck by the dismal scene. It hardly seemed believable that people could still, on the verge of the twentieth century, live in such squalor. I thought how dark and cold and depressing the windowless house must be inside, without even a simple fireplace to provide warmth and cheer.

When I saw four barefoot, grimy children dressed in little more than rags come out to join their father, my heart sank even further. What must these children's lives be like, I wondered unhappily, having none of the brighter things of life, and few even of the necessities, living in utter and complete poverty? Though my own childhood had been emotionally empty, devoid of love after my parents' deaths, I did have the distractions of books and the comfort of a warm, pleasant house. I had never gone hungry. I was sure these children had.

157

After a brief conversation with the father, Alex returned and led Betheny and me away from the cottage. When we were out of sight of the grim little hovel, I turned to him.

"Why do they live like that? So far from anywhere, in such an awful place?"

"They have no choice," he replied harshly, his mouth set in the grim line I was beginning to know so well. "They're among the few who were left after the Clearances when the great landowners, including my own grandfather and father, forced the people off the land. They needed room for their sheep, ye see, and their hunting preserves. Sheep and game were considered far more important than people, who could be shipped off to Canada and America with nothing more than the clothes on their backs."

Whipping Charger into a gallop then, he raced off, and Betheny and I had to hurry to catch up with him. Clearly, he didn't want to talk about it any further. But I was not to be put off so easily. I knew I would never forget the lost, hopeless look in those children's eyes, and I was determined to do something for them.

"Couldn't we help them somehow, send them food or something?" I asked quickly the moment I caught up with him.

"Charity, you mean," he responded coldly, turning those black eyes on me with a look full of contempt. "James Gunn is too proud a man to accept charity, and I won't ask him to."

And with that he turned away, staring stonily ahead.

Back at the castle, Alex and Betheny remained talking with Willie about the horses while I hurried to my room. I was upset, furious with Alex for this stupid notion of pride that kept a family near starvation. When I entered my room I was shocked to see Antonia there, sitting in a chair near one of the tall windows. She rose, walking quickly up to me, and though I was taller than she, somehow I felt inferior to her.

"I've been waiting for you, Carissa," she began coolly. "There is something you had better understand immediately, if you expect to remain at Castle Stalker. *I* am the mistress of this house. I command everyone here, and that includes Alex MacLaren, your guardian. I can have you removed if I choose. So, in the future, tread softly around me. Or you shall be *very* sorry, indeed."

She left, without waiting for a reply. I don't think she expected any. I stood there for a long moment, taking in her threat, for it was clearly that. I had no doubt that she meant every word she said. If she decided to do so, she would get rid of me somehow.

The next morning Betheny and I were out walking, heading toward the beach where we intended to search for seashells. But we had barely walked out the front door when Kit came riding up. We stopped when we saw him, and he guided his horse over to us.

"Good morning, Beth, Chrissa," he said, smiling broadly.

"Good morning, Kit," Betheny responded. "What brings you here?"

"Why, I came to see Alex, of course, and to pay my respects to you two lovely lassies."

Betheny gave me a sly, knowing look, and I felt myself blush. Then Kit turned to me and asked, "Are you quite recovered from your fall, Chrissa?"

"Yes, quite," I answered, trying to ignore Betheny.

"Then perhaps we might go for a ride sometime. That is, if you think you could stay in the saddle this time," he finished with a wink.

"I have no trouble with the old mare I'm riding nowadays," I replied noncommitally, then added quickly, "We'd best get down to the beach, Betheny. Good day, Kit."

And I hurriedly led Betheny away.

As we rounded the corner of the castle, out of Kit's sight, Betheny's eyes grew wide with excitement. She glanced back surreptitiously over her shoulder.

"S-see, Chrissa, I told you he's rather gone on you."

"That's ridiculous," I responded curtly. "He's a good deal older than I am, and besides, I'm hardly old enough to have a suitor."

"He's a bit younger than Uncle Alex," Betheny replied quickly. "Only thirty or thereabouts. And seventeen isn't so young. He's got quite a reputation with the ladies, you know. Just like Uncle Alex. They s-say that between the two of them they've broken every heart on Skye."

"Perhaps that's what Mr. Farren was warning me about," I said absently, carefully picking my way down the steep path to the beach.

"Who's Mr. Farren?"

"Just a man I met on the coach during the journey. He warned me that terrible things happen to pretty girls on Skye. I suppose he must have meant that they get their hearts broken by Kit MacKenzie."

I was laughing as I spoke, but when I turned toward Betheny I saw that her face had gone pale and she was utterly silent.

"Did I say something wrong?" I asked quickly.

Betheny vigorously shook her head no, but it was obvious that my joke about Kit had upset her for some reason. I knew that if I pressed her, she would relent and tell me what was wrong. But I felt that would be unfair. She was still recovering from the upheaval surrounding her grandfather's death, and now had to deal with the subtly vicious Antonia. This was no time to add to her problems.

Still, as we walked along the rocky beach, looking for shells, my mind was on this latest mystery. There was so much that I didn't understand at Castle Stalker. I still felt that Alex was somehow at the center of it, but I didn't know quite how. And now it seemed that Kit, also, was involved.

It began to rain just before lunchtime. By then Betheny and I had gathered quite a few shells, which we hurriedly carried back to the castle wrapped in a cloth. As we walked up to the front steps of the castle, I noticed that Kit's horse was still tethered there. I felt both nervous and excited at the thought of seeing him again.

As we entered the Great Hall Betheny left to

161

go to her room to deposit the shells. Telling myself that it would be interesting to try to identify the shells we had found, I headed toward the library to find a book on seashells. The truth was that I suspected that Alex and Kit would be in the library.

The library door was ajar and as I walked up to it I heard voices. Kit and Alex *were* there, talking boisterously. I heard Kit say, laughing, "A child to you, perhaps, Alex, but not for long. I think you'll be in for quite a surprise someday soon."

Alex responded sarcastically, "Little Chrissa's still in braids."

"I can assure you, Alex, old friend, that beneath those drab clothes and childish braids is the body of a woman . . . quite a mature one."

I felt my face go red in acute embarrassment and I waited breathlessly, with a sinking feeling in the pit of my stomach. Surely now Alex would tell Kit that he, too, knew what my body was like and would comment on its attractions.

But to my surprise, he changed the subject abruptly, saying curtly, "Tell me, Kit, how is your new grieve doing? I hear he's a sharp man and good with your tenants."

As Kit responded to Alex's questions, I backed away silently. Despite the fact that I was admittedly headstrong and independent, until that moment I had considered myself a child in a sense, not really grown up. I hadn't thought of myself as a woman, whose sheer physical attractions were discussed bluntly by men, with all the possibilities that suggested.

Somehow the thought bothered me tremendously.

At that moment Alex and Kit came out of the library together, laughing. When they saw me, they stopped, surprised. They stood framed in the doorway, the pale, fair-haired Kit, slightly taller than the dark, black-eyed Alex. For a moment no one spoke, nothing moved, and it was like a moment frozen in time . . . the air in the shadowy hall grew heavy as I thought, I have seen them here before, at Castle Stalker . . . they were both smiling at me, Conal and Lorn . . . one evil, one good . . . and the good one died because . . . because . . .

"Chrissa, what are you staring at?"

It was Kit's voice, light and full of laughter, pulling me back to the present, to the sound of the rain outside and the crackle of the fire in the library.

"Chrissa?" he asked again, growing concerned. Then he walked quickly over to me, looking down at me curiously.

"Are you all right?"

I nodded, then looked over at Alex, still standing perfectly still in the doorway, saying nothing but staring at me intently.

"You look as if you'd seen a ghost," Kit continued lightly. "Which is to be expected in an old place like this, I suppose."

"I don't . . . feel well," I said slowly. "Excuse me."

I walked slowly, carefully up the stairway, feeling dizzy and unsure of myself, as if I couldn't quite feel my feet touch the floor. At the top of the stairs I turned and looked down at them. They were staring up at me, Kit's ex-

163

pression questioning, Alex's hard and guarded. He had felt it, too, I knew, whatever it was that had just happened, and in that strange, timeless moment he had been filled with hatred for me.

As I hurried to my room, I could still feel his hatred, communicated through those cold black eyes, touching my very soul.

Brenna
April, 1746

'Twas at a great feast at Castle Stalker that I first set eyes on Lorn MacLaren. And from the very beginning I sensed there was terrible evil in the man, for he held a fatal fascination that only the blackest of men possess.

Conal took me to the castle the night of the feast. I felt very gay in the gown I had made from the gold velvet Conal had given me. But when we came to the castle, I became frightened and my gaiety disappeared. I knew that many grown men would not pass the castle alone in the night, and that local girls would rarely stay long as servants. Some said that the castle was haunted by the ghosts of past MacLarens, while others whispered secretly of wicked deeds performed by Lorn himself.

Whatever the truth was, the castle was indeed an eerie sight at night, standing like a grey ghost from which there is no escape.

It was late in September and word had come that Bonnie Prince Charlie had taken possession of Edinburgh, sleeping that very night in the Palace of Holyrood itself. The feast at Castle Stalker was a celebration of the Prince's great victory. Conal led me into the huge banquet room where men and women feasted at a long wooden trestle table covered with food. Hounds quarrelled over the bones that were flung aside, as a piper played a pibroch. At the head of the table sat the chief—Lorn MacLaren.

He was much like Conal—tall and dark-haired, with coal black eyes. But he was much older than Conal, with a hard expression in place of Conal's teasing smile. Even his laughter was harsh and somehow frightening.

But he was unmistakably the laird—every man there deferred to him and many were quite fearful when he gazed upon them intently. I felt great trepidation as Conal led me through the crowded room toward Lorn . . .

"So this is the lass ye claim ye'll marry, little brother," Lorn said, eyeing me carefully as Conal introduced us proudly. "Yer a bonnie thing—I dinna blame Conal for being so smitten."

Blushing, unsure what to say to such a great man, I bowed my head and stared nervously at the stone floor. Suddenly Lorn's hand shot out, cupping my chin roughly and raising my head so that my gaze met his.

"Dinna look away, lass. I may no' be as handsome as my brother, but I am the chief."

"Oh, no, sir, I didna' mean . . ." I stammered stupidly. Lorn cut me short with a burst of laughter, then grabbed me in his powerful arms and, pulling me toward him, kissed me full and hard on the mouth. Then he pushed me away, saying, "There, I've taken my kiss from the bride early," and laughed again.

I stood there, feeling a wave of something—

could it be passion?—subside in my trembling body. He was terrifying, and yet my body had responded to his kiss.

Later, Conal said that I should not mind Lorn, that he meant no harm. But though I said nothing, I couldn't forget the way Lorn had kissed me, nor the way his dark eyes had followed me all the evening in his strange, mad way...

CHAPTER 9

Embarrass'd eye and blushing cheek
Pleasure and shame, and fear bespeak!
LORD OF THE ISLES
Canto Sixth, VIII

I was lying in bed the next morning, in that hazy state between sleep and consciousness, when Lucy knocked on my door then hurried in without waiting for me to answer. Bristling with excitement, she began eagerly, "Miss Chrissa, ye've got to get up an' come see!"

"Come see what?" I asked tiredly, sitting up slowly and rubbing the sleep from my eyes.

" 'Tis a present for ye, from Mr. MacKenzie! He sent this note," she finished, thrusting an envelope into my hand.

As I opened the envelope, Lucy watched me

167

impatiently, filled with curiosity as to what the note said. It read simply:

> I hope you will accept this gift as a
> token of our growing friendship.
> Kit MacKenzie

I couldn't bear to see Lucy standing there, consumed with curiosity, so I read the brief note to her.

"Och, miss, what a fine gentleman he is," Lucy said, sighing dramatically. "An' the best catch on all o' Skye, except for Mr. Alex o' course."

"But where is the gift?" I asked quickly, interrupting Lucy's absurd romantic imaginings.

"Ye must come outside," she answered mysteriously, " 'Tis waitin' for ye there."

I dressed quickly, then sat impatiently while Lucy brushed my hair hurriedly, pulling it back with a ribbon. We left immediately, Lucy leading me down the stairs, through the Great Hall, and out to the stables. There, in the middle of the stableyard, stood the most beautiful horse I had ever seen. She was a black Arabian mare, with a fine, small head and a compact, perfectly formed body. Willie was holding the reins and stroking her velvety muzzle. I saw immediately that she was very high-strung, for when Lucy and I walked up, she shied away, prancing nervously.

"Calm down, lass," Willie spoke to her softly. "Ye ken who I am. I've handled ye often enough."

Then he turned to me and said proudly, "Her

name is Taj. Mr. MacKenzie brought her over only minutes ago."

Kit couldn't have given me a nicer present, but it was terribly extravagant and I had grave misgivings as to whether or not I should accept it. Still, I told myself, the least I could do was return the horse to him, which would give me a chance to ride her at least once. Hurrying back to my room, I changed into my riding clothes, then returned to the stable. By then, news of Kit's gift had spread through the castle, and Betheny and Jonathan were in the stableyard, admiring Taj.

"Oh, Chrissa, isn't she beautiful!" Betheny exclaimed when she saw me. "You should be very pleased. Taj was Marianne's horse."

Before I could ask who Marianne was, Jonathan interrupted sullenly. "You probably can't ride her. Arabians are high-strung, too much for a girl to handle."

His jealousy was obvious, and I couldn't help smiling at him, which only made him angrier. Instead of replying to him, I simply mounted Taj, grabbed the reins from Willie, and raced off, giving the spirited mare her head. As I raced out of the stableyard, I caught a glimpse of a stunned Jonathan and a gleeful Betheny.

Taj was as fast as Charger and she covered the moors effortlessly. Instinctively she headed toward MacKenzie House, toward home, and I let her. When we grew near to the house, I slowed her to a trot, entering the stableyard just as Kit left the paddock, walking toward the house. Smiling broadly, he walked quickly over to me. While I sat on Taj, stroking her neck, he held the reins to make sure she would stand still.

"Do you like my gift, then?" he asked happily.

"Oh, yes, but I really can't accept it," I answered doubtfully. "She must be worth a good deal of money. I don't think it would be at all proper."

"Proper is an empty, ridiculous word that does not apply to someone as original and delightful as you," Kit responded firmly, his blue eyes twinkling merrily. "If you don't take her, I'll just have to sell her to someone who probably will not appreciate her as much as you clearly do. And besides, with Alex back at the castle, you'll never get a chance to ride Charger, you know. You'll be stuck with that old mare you were telling me about. You'll need a good horse if we're to go riding together."

His expression as he finished was amused and mocking. I was being charmed and I knew it, but I was completely at a loss as to how to handle it. I had never known anyone quite like Kit before.

"I'll take good care of her," I finally managed to say after an awkward silence.

"I know you will," Kit responded softly. And then he added, "She's a fine animal. You know, the Mohammedans believed that Allah created the Arabian out of a handful of the south wind. Because they run like the wind, I suppose."

"Indeed, I've never ridden a horse so fast and smooth. She's as easy to sit as a child's rocking chair."

Kit smiled, then asked softly, "Are you feeling better today? You didn't look at all well yesterday."

"Oh . . . yes, I'm feeling fine, thank you," I responded hesitantly. I had made a determined effort to put the strange incident of yesterday out of my mind, and it bothered me greatly to be reminded of it.

Kit offered to ride with me a ways back toward Castle Stalker to see how I handled Taj, and I accepted readily. We rode across the moor and down through a rocky glen that lay in a dark hollow of the grim mountains. Rocks lay piled up in the hollow and showed their heads above the peaty moorland where the heather grew.

"This is Glen Sligachan," Kit explained, stopping his horse. I stopped beside him, waiting. In a moment he continued softly, "I sometimes think Valhalla might be like this . . . you know, all Skye names are a mixture of Norse and Gaelic. Skye was Viking land in remote times. Norsemen colonized it. Many of us have the pale hair and blue eyes of our marauding ancestors," he said wryly. "The Vikings named the hills, the lochs, and the peaks. My old nanny used to say that the ghost of Thor surely walks the Sgurr-nan-Gillean when the lightning cracks from peak to peak and the thunder rolls and rocks from Portree to Dearg."

Turning to me, he smiled and finished with a shrug. "Well, it was an impressive story when I was a lad, anyway."

"It's an impressive story now," I answered,

171

smiling. "The people of Skye certainly seem to be a superstitious lot."

"You're thinking of old Morag, aren't you?" Kit asked easily.

"Yes. She seems to believe in quite a lot of strange things. She's even been warning me to beware of some imagined danger." I tried to laugh as I said the words, but somehow my laugh sounded hollow.

"I wouldn't let her worry you. She's very old, you know, and inclined to be a bit batty." Then he continued more soberly, "However, there *is* something I would like to warn you about if I may."

I looked at him curiously, and he continued uneasily, "This is rather difficult since Alex is my oldest friend. But you're so young and inexperienced, I thought . . . well, hang it all, what I'm trying to say is to be rather guarded where Alex is concerned."

"You mean because he is a philanderer?" I asked frankly, touched by Kit's concern.

"Well, that is as good a reason as any, isn't it?" Kit answered enigmatically. Then, "Enough said. I'll leave you now. You're sure you know the way back to the castle?"

"Yes," I said quickly, feeling strangely ill at ease suddenly. When Kit spoke of the Vikings his expression had changed, growing intense and strange. And when he warned me of Alex, he seemed preoccupied, as if he were holding back what was really in his mind. Did he really mean to warn me about Alex's seduction of women? Or was there something more, something that he couldn't bring himself to say? I had grown so used to Kit's light, joking manner that I could not help feeling disturbed by this unexpected depth to his personality.

As he turned to ride off, I said quickly, "Thank you again, Kit, for Taj."

" 'Twas nothing," was his brief, smiling response before he turned his horse and galloped off.

As I turned Taj toward home, I felt thoughtful and almost grim. I wondered about Kit, and the curious, contradictory emotions he aroused in me. I had begun to suspect that I had no real idea what Kit was actually like, deep inside. I wondered if I would ever know.

Back at the stable, Willie happily helped me down from Taj. "Have a good ride, miss?" he asked politely.

"Oh, yes, Willie, marvelous."

"Ye always will on this horse, miss. Taj never gave Miss Marianne a moment's fright. I always thought she knew the value of the rider she was carryin' . . ."

His voice trailed off and, shaking his head sadly, he led Taj off toward the stalls.

That name again . . . Marianne. Whoever she was, Willie had clearly been fond of her . . .

"Well, what happened?" Betheny asked excitedly when I walked into the dining room a moment later.

"Nothing, really," I said casually, pouring a cup of tea.

"Oh, Chrissa, you know what I mean! Are you going to keep Taj?"

"Yes, I suppose so," I answered coolly, trying hard to make as little of the situation as possible. "Apparently Kit has no need of her."

"Oh, I think it's marvelous!" Betheny exclaimed dramatically. "You and Kit..."

"There is *nothing* between Kit MacKenzie and me," I interrupted briskly.

"Oh, of course not, if you s-say s-so," Betheny agreed too quickly, obviously feeling otherwise.

The truth was, though I wouldn't admit it to anyone, even Betheny, I was beginning to realize that there was something very special about Kit. My relationship with him was not nearly as unimportant as I tried to pretend.

"Do you think I might ride Taj s-sometime?" Betheny asked, changing the subject.

"Of course you may," I assured her quickly, pleased that she would want to learn to ride a really spirited horse.

Then I remembered her comment about Taj belonging to Marianne. And I remembered the way Willie's eyes had softened when he mentioned Taj's former owner. I asked, "Betheny, who is this Marianne that Taj belonged to?"

Immediately Betheny grew somber and quiet, and her excitement disappeared. She looked down at the cup of tea in front of her for a long moment, then said hesitantly, "Marianne . . . was Kit's sister. She died last year."

I waited, feeling somehow that there was something more she wanted to say, but she was silent. And then suddenly she said nervously, "I must be going. Uncle Alex is taking me into Portree today to do s-some sh-shopping."

She added, almost as an afterthought, "Would you like to come, too?"

"No," I said politely, "You go ahead. Perhaps I'll ride Taj in later and meet you."

"We'll probably have tea at that little tea shop when we're finished. Look for us there."

"I will."

Betheny smiled and left, leaving me sitting alone at the huge table. Marianne . . . there was something about her that made Betheny intensely nervous. And then I realized that it must have been Marianne's portrait that I had seen at MacKenzie House the first day I met Kit. Trying to remember what the girl in the portrait looked like, what immediately came to mind was not so much her pale, ethereal beauty, but an overwhelming sense of sadness. Or was it madness?

An hour later I decided to ride into Portree. There were some things I needed from the village and it would give me a chance to take Taj for a really long ride. But I knew that I could not appear in the village in my Levis and shirt, and for a few minutes I didn't know what to do. Then it occurred to me that Lucy might know of an extra riding habit stored away that I could use. I rang for her and she came up to my room immediately.

When I explained my predicament, she said easily, "Aye, there must be sich a thing somewheres. Let me see . . ."

Then she continued excitedly, "The old clothes are stored in a room below the drawin' room. There might be a ridin' habit of yer mither's doon there."

Together we went to the drawing room, and

Lucy went directly to a door in the northeast corner. It opened onto a roughly built narrow service stair in the thickness of the north wall of the keep, which lead down to a vaulted basement. This was the ancient kitchen, Lucy explained, and still retained its huge arched fireplace. To the right a narrow, steep and cramped little flight of steps led down to another chamber. It was dimly lit by two narrow loopholes and in a corner was the remains of a privy.

"This was the dungeon," Lucy said in a hushed voice, clearly rather awed by the bleak room.

I looked around at the room, now full of trunks and boxes, all covered with dust, and thought how horribly oppressive it would have been to have been confined here.

As if reading my thoughts, Lucy said in a low voice, her hazel eyes narrowed, "This wasna the worst o' it." And, pointing to a heavy stone flag with an iron ring set in it, she continued, "Under that trap door is another room, a horrible place. Years ago when I was verra young an' had just come into service at the castle, one o' the lads who worked here lifted the flag an' showed me the room below. I can still remember clearly what it looked like when he stuck a candle down for me to see. 'Twas dark an' terrible smellin'. He said that a mistress o' the castle once put her own two daughters there after they had sought to escape from the castle wi' their lovers."

Lucy's voice had lowered to a whisper, and in the cold, poorly lit room, I found myself growing frightened.

"Let's hurry," I said quickly. "It's cold down here."

"Aye," Lucy agreed, shivering from both cold and fear.

She opened a box and began rummaging through the contents.

Pushing open the heavy, dust-covered lid of an old trunk, I looked down at a pile of old-fashioned clothes made of rich silks and velvets. They had surely once been quite beautiful, but were now faded and torn. There was one dress, made of deep golden velvet with a low-cut bodice and black silk ribbons that laced up the front. The sleeves were long and tight, the skirt full and billowing. From the style, I guessed that the dress must be about a hundred and fifty years old, at least.

I ran my fingers tentatively over the heavy, soft velvet . . . in the pale light shed by candles it would glisten like moonlight. And in a dance the full skirt would sway back and forth like the waves going in and out on a beach . . . Conal, unlacing the ribbons, saying that I was so beautiful the devil must have created me to beguile men . . .

"Miss!" Lucy's voice was sharp and insistent, with a shrill note of fear.

I looked up at her slowly.

"Miss, I've called ye three times an' ye wouldna' answer. Are ye no' feelin' well?"

The golden velvet gown fell from my fingers back into the musty trunk.

"I'm all right, Lucy," I managed to answer, in a voice that seemed somehow removed from my body. "What do you have there?"

" 'Tis a ridin' habit, miss, an' no more than

177

fifteen or twenty years old. I'd say it belonged to yer mither."

"Let's take it up to my room then," I said quickly.

Lucy nodded and led the way back up the narrow stairway. As we reached the drawing room, she turned back to me and asked uneasily, "Are you sure yer all right? Ye looked . . . so strange for a moment back there. An' ye're still so pale."

"I'm fine!" I snapped, then immediately felt guilty when I saw the hurt look on Lucy's face. "Come on, let's go try this old thing on," I continued more gently.

In my room I changed into the lovely dark blue habit and was relieved to see that it was an almost perfect fit. Complete with a white silk blouse and silver pin shaped like a whip, it was still remarkably stylish. Though I was sure Antonia would have looked down her nose at it, it was more than good enough for me.

Lucy quickly helped me sew the skirt as I had done Betheny's so that I could ride astride, all the while voicing grave misgivings as to the propriety of such attire for a "fine lady" like myself.

"Antonia's the only 'fine lady' around here, and frankly, judging from her example, I'm much happier to be the simple girl I am," I responded smiling broadly.

Lucy laughed wholeheartedly, wiping tears of mirth from her eyes, relieved to see me back to my old self. My strange behavior in the dungeon was now completely forgotten.

Finally the alteration was completed, and though it was past one o'clock I still was determined to ride into Portree. The few minutes I had spent in that dark little room had made me feel almost claustrophobic, as if I were imprisoned there myself, and I desperately wanted to get outside, to the fresh air and endless moors.

An hour later I was nearing Portree. Though Taj at first had wanted to run, eventually she had grown tired and been content to walk the final two miles. As I headed down the main road leading into the village, I saw the old stone church and beside it the graveyard where Sir Duncan had been buried. And then I saw something that I had not noticed on the rainy day of the funeral. Off to one side, outside the low stone wall surrounding the cemetery, was an elaborate headstone carved from gleaming pale green Skye marble standing alone in a patch of white heather.

Guiding Taj over to the headstone, I dismounted and walked close enough to read the inscription. It said simply: "Marianne Edith MacKenzie, 1870–1898."

Here was the final resting place of Marianne MacKenzie, that beautiful, strangely compelling girl in the portrait. But why was her grave apart from the others in the cemetery? It was, in fact, completely outside the churchyard itself. Though Betheny had been clearly reluctant to talk about Marianne, I was determined to ask her about this.

I rode on into Portree, looking back once at the lonely, isolated grave.

After completing the small amount of shopping that I had to do, I went to the tea shop. Inside, Betheny and Alex were sitting at a

179

table covered with empty plates and cups. Alex was facing the door and saw me the moment I entered. For a split second he looked completely surprised and off guard, but he recovered quickly, saying something in a low voice to Betheny, who turned and smiled at me.

"Chrissa, you decided to come after all," she said happily when I reached their table.

As Alex rose and held a chair for me, I said, "Yes, I rode Taj in."

"Ah, yes, I heard of Kit's rather extravagant gift," Alex said lightly, but with an undertone of disapproval.

Then he added, "That habit is much more suitable than yer usual riding attire."

"Yes!" Betheny agreed enthusiastically. "Wherever did you get it?"

"It belonged to my mother, I think. Lucy found it in an old trunk."

The waitress came then and Alex ordered some tea and cakes for me. He and Betheny had already eaten and had, in fact, been on the verge of leaving when I arrived. But Betheny insisted on staying with me while I ate. It was an awkward meal. I ate with little relish, listening absently to Betheny's excited chatter about the shopping she had done, while Alex remained silent. All the while I wondered why he disapproved so of my accepting a gift from Kit.

When I had finished eating, Alex left immediately to get the carriage.

"Naturally you'll ride back with us," Betheny said hopefully. And before I could protest, she added, "You can tie Taj to the rear of the carriage."

I gave in reluctantly for I had been looking forward to the ride back over the moors. But I knew Betheny's feelings would be hurt if I declined. And besides, I had something important to ask her.

"Betheny," I began quickly, wanting to ask the question before Alex returned. "On my way into Portree I passed the church and I noticed a grave outside the cemetery."

Betheny's expression changed immediately. Her mouth tightened and her hands moved nervously in her lap. She knew what I was going to ask.

"Why was Marianne MacKenzie buried outside the churchyard?"

After a long, drawn-out silence Betheny answered in a barely audible whisper, "Suicides are always buried outside the kirkyard."

I sat back, stunned. I had not expected that. So there *was* great sadness behind that beautiful face, I thought grimly. Was that why Kit had never mentioned Marianne? Her memory was too painful...

But it didn't make sense. Marianne was only twenty-eight, and very beautiful and rich. And she had Kit, who must have adored her.

"But why would she do such a thing?" I asked.

"I can't talk about it here," Betheny said brokenly, on the verge of tears. "Please, wait till we get back to the castle."

Betheny was more shaken than I had ever seen her and I felt horribly guilty for upsetting her. But I was determined to know why Marianne MacKenzie had killed herself.

Alex returned then and we went out to the

carriage. It was an almost completely silent journey back to Castle Stalker, and all the while I thought of Marianne.

When we arrived at the castle I went to my room, waited a few minutes to give Betheny time to collect herself, then went to her room. She was sitting on the window seat, waiting for me, looking so forlorn that I decided I couldn't force her to talk about something that was upsetting her this much.

"If you'd rather not talk about it . . ." I began, but Betheny interrupted me.

"You're bound to hear it from s-someone," she said softly. And then she began gravely, "Most people know about it, and it's ruined Uncle Alex's reputation on Skye. No one thinks I know because I'm s-so young. Late one night s-shortly after Marianne died I overheard an argument between grandfather and Uncle Alex. That is how I know."

Sighing heavily, she continued, "Kit and Marianne were identical twins and they were uncommonly close. She was his only relative in all the world after their parents died. He loved her very much and thought s-she was better than anyone. They used to come here together quite often. It was touching, really, to s-see how protective Kit was of her.

"For awhile Uncle Alex escorted Marianne about, and naturally most people thought they would marry. But then they s-stopped s-seeing each other and a few days later Marianne . . . killed herself. She walked into the s-sea and later they found her body washed up on the s-shore of Loch Stalker. She had left behind a note. In it, she revealed that s-she was . . . with

182

child . . . and s-she killed herself because the child's father refused to marry her."

Finally I understood what the man had meant who had accused Alex of causing the deaths of two innocent people. He had been referring to poor, abandoned Marianne and her unborn child.

My expression must have been revealing for Betheny continued quickly, defensively, "You're thinking as many people do that Uncle Alex was the father of the child. But that isn't true! That night when he and grandfather argued, Uncle Alex insisted that he was innocent. He and Marianne were merely good friends and he knew that s-she was in love with s-someone else. *She* s-stopped seeing him, *he* didn't abandon her!"

"Did Kit know all of this?"

"Yes, Uncle Alex told him all about it as s-soon as he heard about Marianne's death. Kit was upset, of course . . . Dr. Ross s-said he had never s-seen anyone so grief stricken. But Kit knew Uncle Alex well enough to believe he was innocent. And he has remained his true friend, though many people on Skye vilify Uncle Alex behind his back. It's only ignorant religious zealots who condemn Uncle Alex!"

I said nothing more. It would have been needless cruelty to tell Betheny that I didn't share her passionate belief in her uncle's innocence.

Later that day I found out that Willie didn't either. I had gone down to the stable with some sugar for Taj, so enchanted with her and amazed at my good fortune in actually owning such a magnificent animal that I took every opportunity to see her. Willie was brushing her himself when I walked in, which surprised me for it was a job one of the stableboys would normally have performed.

He grinned when he saw the sugar in my hand, and said, "Spoilin' her already, miss? Well, I canna' blame ye. She's a rare animal, as perfect as any I've ever seen. Miss MacKenzie spoiled her somethin' dreadful, too."

I responded slowly, trying not to appear too curious, "I can imagine how much Miss MacKenzie must have loved her."

"Aye, she did that. Mr. MacKenzie gave the filly to her when she was just weaned. Miss MacKenzie insisted on trainin' her hersel', though I'm proud to say she asked for my advice at times. She said once that I ken more aboot horses than any man alive, an' she would listen to no one else when it came to trainin' the filly she loved so much. She came over often, wi' questions, an' I even went to MacKenzie House at times when Sir Duncan could spare me."

"You must have thought a great deal of her to go to so much trouble," I said quietly.

" 'Twas no trouble," Willie answered softly, and his dark brown eyes held a sad, faraway look. "She could never be any trouble at all. Except to the one who drove her to her death."

He looked up at me sharply, aware that he had gone too far. "Excuse me, miss, I hae other work to do."

And he left.

That night as I lay in bed I thought about passion, a sensation I had never experienced. Passion had led to Marianne MacKenzie's tragic death and the death of her innocent, unborn child. And passion was somehow connected with the name Conal that I remembered so vividly from those strange few minutes in the dungeon . . . In that brief, unreal time I had felt my face flush and my legs quiver as inexplicable erotic visions filled my mind . . . rough hands slowly unbuttoning a soft velvet gown, slipping it over my shoulders . . . eyes hungrily gazing at my waiting breasts . . . fingers circling my nipples . . . a mouth covering mine then dropping to my breasts and stomach . . . my breath coming fast, my chest heaving . . . a frightening, oddly pleasurable sensation in my loins . . .

Was this passion? Was this the deeply buried instinct I had felt stirring as I looked closely at the portrait of Brenna?

Brenna
April, 1746

In the spring, only one month from the wedding day that Conal and I had chosen, Lorn came to the hut where my mother and I lived our simple lonely lives. My mother was visiting her sister in Portree and I was alone the night that Lorn came riding up on his fine white horse.

I had seen him often since that first night at Castle Stalker, but always Conal had been with me. I was glad of his presence for I was frightened of Lorn . . . his hard, narrow eyes followed me constantly, betraying his desire for me.

I was standing outside the hut when Lorn rode up and pulled viciously on the reins bring-

ing his horse to a rearing halt. I was stunned. I had not expected the great Lorn MacLaren to come to a humble stone hut. But he had come . . . at night . . . when I was alone.

I stood frozen near the doorway, fighting a strong desire to run. Lorn walked up to me, towering over me, smiling drunkenly.

"Well, Brenna, will ye no' ask me into yer house?" he asked.

There was nothing I could do. I nodded and walked slowly, reluctantly, inside.

The peat fire provided the only light and it was dim inside the small room. I sat down near the fire, waiting.

Lorn walked around nervously, then finally stopped next to me. Slowly he ran one dirty hand through my hair.

"Ye're an uncommon lovely lass," he said softly. "I thought so when Conal first brought ye to me."

I stood abruptly, intending to walk away from his cold touch. But before I had taken a step, he grabbed me and held me tightly.

"Ye can have me, lass," he whispered roughly, his mouth only inches from my face, "an' I'm the Chief of all the MacLarens! Ye dinna want that boy, Conal."

"I love Conal!" I screamed desperately. "I want nothing to do with you."

"Don't ye now. Are ye so sure o' that?" he asked wickedly. Then, with one hand still holding me in a painful grip, his other hand ripped my thin gown down the front. With another swift movement he pulled the gown completely away, and I stood next to his foul-smelling body, completely naked.

He had expected me to quake with fear, I was sure, and though I was frightened I was also strangely excited. I stood proudly in front of him, not bowing my head in shame or trying to hide my full breasts or ruddy triangle.

"Ye can take me if ye will, but ye'll know all the while that it's Conal I'm thinking of and wanting," I said fiercely.

He slapped me . . . so hard that I fell down on the cold stone floor, scraping my hands.

"Stupid lass," he said easily, only the tightness of his mouth and the strange light in his dark eyes betraying his fury. "I could take ye here an' now in this miserable little hovel."

Then he knelt down, his legs straddling my body. And when I tried to move, his arms shot out pinning my hands to the floor. I felt the coarseness of his breeches against my hips and the hard leather of his jacket brushing against my breasts.

"I could tak' ye here an' now," he repeated slowly. "An' I think ye would no' mind it so very much. I ken what sort o' lass ye are, Brenna Breac. But I dinna' want ye this way. Ye'll come to me . . . ye'll come to me, begging."

And with that he rose and stalked out, leaving me lying on the floor, trembling with the fear that his mad prophecy might actually come true . . .

CHAPTER 10

For rarely human eye has known
A scene so stern as that dread lake
LORD OF THE ISLES
Canto Third, XIV

In early October when he had been at Castle Stalker for scarcely a month, Alex left for a prolonged stay in Edinburgh, taking Antonia with him. Though Antonia had made no secret of the fact that she was bored and longed for the attractions of the city, no one believed that was why Alex left. It had become obvious to everyone that he was extremely uncomfortable in his role as caretaker of the estate for the few short remaining months till Jonathan would come of age.

Jonathan and Alex were still friendly, and I

knew that basically Jonathan worshipped his dashing uncle almost as much as Betheny did. But they completely disagreed as to how the estate should be run. Alex wanted to restore the estate to its former position as a self-sustaining entity by pouring money into modern farming methods and equipment. But Jonathan wanted to live as his grandfather had—in luxury, spending money on his needs and on the castle itself, while ignoring the surrounding farmland and the desperate plight of the crofters who eked out a living on it.

I was walking along the hallway on the first floor of the castle early one morning when I heard raised voices coming from the small office opposite the library. It was Alex and Jonathan, arguing bitterly.

"You don't understand what a waste it all is!" Alex roared. "The crofters are starving, the land lies fallow. The laird should do something about this, he should be a leader among his people and provide for them."

Jonathan responded stubbornly, in a rare show of defiance toward his uncle, "They are not my people. They don't belong to me, their lives are their own responsibility. For God's sake, Uncle Alex, you want things to be as they were hundreds of years ago, but it won't work. It's nearly the twentieth century, you know, and it's time these people learned to fend for themselves. I am *not* responsible for their welfare. And *I* am the one who will be the laird soon, not you. Things will be done *my* way."

"Ye're right, Jon," Alex said tersely. "All of this will soon be yours to do with as ye please."

And with that he came stalking out of the

office, brushing roughly past me without speaking. The next day he and Antonia left for their prolonged stay in Edinburgh. Kit joined Alex almost immediately and for a fortnight things were very quiet around Castle Stalker, with no visitors and little to do. Betheny and I rode quite a bit, while Jonathan busied himself with learning how to run the estate.

And then, without any warning, Kit suddenly turned up one day as Betheny and I were preparing to leave on our regular morning ride. He came riding up to the castle, dressed immaculately as usual, in a deep blue riding coat that brought out the sharp piercing blue of his eyes. To my surprise I felt my stomach tighten nervously and I realized that I was ridiculously happy to see him. I compensated for this bothersome realization by consciously assuming a cool, diffident demeanor, in sharp contrast to his broad smile and affectionate greeting.

"Good morning to you, my two favorite lassies on all of Skye," he began merrily.

"Really, Kit?" Betheny asked, laughing.

"Very well, then, my two favorite lassies in all of Scotland!" he answered, grinning impishly.

"I'm surprised you would have left the excitement of Edinburgh to return so soon to poor, dull Skye," I observed drily.

"Skye has delights that Edinburgh does not," he answered quickly, and I felt myself blush furiously under his mocking gaze.

"It looks to me as if you two are going for a ride. May I join you?"

"Of course, Kit," Betheny responded happily. I knew she was glad of his company, finding him as charming and entertaining as I did.

We left the castle grounds at an easy canter and rode along the cliffs overlooking the sea. I was happier than I had been in a long while. Purple bluebells and yellow and white buttercups were in bloom, and in the clear sky above us a golden eagle circled lazily, his wings stretched to their full six-foot span. Towering above everything were the mountains—tall and dark, sharply etched against the pale blue sky.

On this rare bright clear day, Skye looked like a place Morag had told me about—Tir nan Og, the legendary Celtic Shangri-La, the land of the ever-young.

As we slowly walked the horses, Kit between Betheny and me, he began telling us a scandalous story of a séance he, Alex and Antonia had attended in Edinburgh.

"We were all seated round this large, oval table in a rather shabby room," he began. "The medium, Mrs. Lowrie, went into a trance and called out that the spirits were descending upon us. Then all the lights went out and one of the ladies screamed. I believe it was Antonia. At any rate, Mrs. Lowrie assured us we were safe and told us that it was very important that we remain seated. After a minute, we saw a white, ethereal object floating near the table. It spoke in a strange, high voice, identifying itself as the late wife of one of the gentleman present.

"Well," Kit paused, grinning, "naturally the gentleman was quite overcome with emotion and fainted straight away. I think the fact that he was with an extremely attractive young lady whom the late wife had always been jealous of, had something to do with it. And what do you think happened next?"

"What?" Betheny asked breathlessly.

"Well . . . the lights went on and we saw the medium, Mrs. Lowrie, caught in flagrante delicto, as they say, having left some of her garments in a closet while she walked barefoot as a spirit. The lady wore a startled expression on her face, to put it mildly. Alex had switched on the electric lights, you see, catching her in the act, so to speak."

"Uncle Alex?" Betheny exclaimed.

"Aye, Betheny, your uncle is not a believer," Kit said wryly. "He thought there was some trick to it, you see. Mrs. Lowrie tried rather unsuccessfully to convince us that some mischievous spirits had made her disrobe, but, needless to say, no one accepted that explanation."

I laughed heartily at that, and at other stories Kit told. He was marvelously entertaining, full of stories that poked fun at himself as often as others.

We were headed back toward the castle, only about half a mile from there, when Betheny said mischievously, "Kit, when are you going to stop having adventures and settle down with a wife?"

Looking directly at me, Kit replied, with a half-serious, half-joking expression, "When Chrissa's old enough for me, of course."

Though I laughed and teased Kit that he was setting himself up for a breach of promise suit, I was actually rather embarrassed and ill at ease. What made it worse was my conviction that he was well aware of my discomfort and was amused by it.

When we rode into the stableyard, I saw Jonathan standing with Willie. As Betheny rode up to Willie and dismounted, Jonathan said in a surprised tone, "Beth, you're not a bad rider."

Since Betheny had started standing up to her brother, he had begun to show a grudging respect for her, and complimenting her on her riding ability was the ultimate accolade.

Betheny was extremely pleased at this compliment and responded, smiling, "It's all due to Chrissa. She's a good teacher."

"Aye," Jonathan replied, looking at me as I dismounted. Then he added slowly, "You're a great deal different than the girls here on Skye, or even in London, Chrissa."

"Is that a compliment?" I asked, laughing.

"Yes," he answered seriously, "You're . . . quite something."

Then he quickly mounted the horse Willie was holding for him and rode off rather recklessly, as usual trying to show off.

"I shall have to watch that young man," Kit said to me slyly, "or he'll capture your affections before I can."

"Kit, everything you say is in jest. Nothing you say can be taken seriously," I responded, trying to sound flippant.

But it soon became clear that Kit was right about Jonathan. It seemed that wherever I went I ran into Jonathan. I would be in the library reading when he would appear, ostensibly to get a book. But when I asked which book, he would look nervous and stammer that he wasn't sure. No matter how late I came down to breakfast he was always there, toying with his food. And whenever Betheny and I went riding, he invariably asked if he could come along.

I gradually had to accept the fact that he fancied himself in love with me. Though Kit's teasing flirtation with me made me feel nervous and ill at ease, I wasn't very bothered by Jonathan's clumsy devotion. I saw it simply as a schoolboy crush that would disappear in time, though I knew that to him it was perfectly serious so I did not make fun of him. Instead, I tried to pretend that I didn't see the obvious.

Sometimes it was rather difficult to remain blasé. His face betrayed his every emotion and his actions were patently clear. He went to great lengths to surreptitiously discover my birthday, then casually mentioned that he was older than I—by two months.

And then one day when Betheny and I were out riding alone, Jonathan suddenly appeared. He came charging past Betheny recklessly, his horse coming so close to hers that her little mare reared, nearly throwing Betheny off. She barely managed to control the frightened horse and was terribly shaken. Jonathan rode on, laughing, thinking, no doubt, that he had impressed me with his wild, fearless horsemanship.

We were close to the castle and it took no more than two or three minutes to arrive at the stables. Jonathan and Willie were standing together as I guided my horse over to them. While Willie went to help a still-shaken Betheny dismount, I jumped off Taj and strode angrily up to Jonathan.

He started to greet me but I interrupted him with an icy glare. He stopped and I said furiously, "That was a rude, dangerous stunt you pulled! Only an immature child with no consideration for others would do such a stupid thing!"

As I turned and walked away, Jonathan, livid, shouted after me, "How dare you! You forget who I am!"

Turning and facing him, I responded sarcastically, "I didn't forget who you are. You're a stupid, self-centered child and it's about time you started acting your age."

Then I turned and walked on toward the castle. As I did so I heard Betheny say merrily, "Well, Jon, you've been properly chastised."

Half an hour later I was sitting in my room, reading, when there came a knock on my door. I said, "Come in," expecting Betheny, and was surprised to see Jonathan.

He stood in the doorway, looking very embarrassed and awkward, his arms dangling clumsily at his side. Finally, with great difficulty, he said haltingly, "I . . . I want to apologize for my behavior today. I didn't mean to frighten Beth. I . . . hope you'll forgive me and not think too badly of me."

I knew it was probably the first time in his life he had, of his own accord, apologized for anything, and I felt very proud of him.

"I don't think badly of you, Jonathan," I answered, smiling. "In fact, I admire you more than ever now."

Grinning broadly, he mumbled, "Thank you," and ambled off.

After that, Jonathan seemed to change, to grow more mature. I could see that he was trying very hard to refrain from teasing Betheny, although occasionally the effort became too much. But now when he teased her, she answered back with growing confidence, and their arguments often ended with both of them giggling at something the other had said.

It was touching to see how close they had become. And that made what was to happen all the more tragic.

Betheny came down with a cold and was confined to her bed for several days. She wasn't terribly ill, but with winter setting in, Dr. Ross thought it wise for her to take care of herself. I was sitting by her bedside, reading to her from her favorite novel, *David Copperfield*, when Jonathan came up to ask me to go riding with him. I declined and he left, obviously disappointed.

It was the last time that I saw him alive.

When he didn't return that evening a search party was sent out, headed by Willie. I waited in the drawing room, pacing back and forth, growing more and more anxious as the hours crawled by slowly. I had a horrible feeling of dread that grew stronger as time passed.

And then, just before midnight, the search party returned. When I saw them coming I ran out to meet them. Willie looked utterly exhausted and terribly worried. Seeing the questioning look on my face, he shook his head negatively. They had found no trace of Jonathan.

" 'Tis too dark to see anythin', lass," Willie said tiredly. "We'll go out again in the mornin'."

Then he and the others went into the kitchen where Morag had prepared some hot soup for them.

Very early the next morning when the sun was just coming up over the Cuillins, I met Willie in the stableyard. He looked surprised to see me in my riding clothes, but before he could say anything, I began firmly, "I'm going to look, too."

"Ye dinna ken the island that well, miss," Willie responded, but I interrupted him. "I'll not wait around here again. I'm going to *do* something."

"Verra well," Willie gave in with a sigh. "But ye'll stay wi' me an' no' go off on yer own."

I agreed and we set out immediately.

It was a cold, dark, windy day. The wind came howling down through the mountains to whip the heavy branches of the sturdiest trees. Along the cliffs overlooking the sea, the less hardy trees were permanently bent inland. Above us, the thick dark storm clouds kept moving and changing shape, throwing brief patches of sunlight on different parts of the mountains.

Willie led me toward the mountains, and as we reached their rocky lower slopes I could hear the crunch of the horses' hooves on the rough, stony path.

"There is a place near here where Master Jonathan often went," Willie shouted to me above the roar of the wind. " 'Tis called Loch

198

Coruisk, a corrie o' water a mile or two into the mountains."

Loch Coruisk . . . why did I shiver when I heard that name? I had never heard of the place before, surely there was nothing in it to frighten me so . . .

We rode on, our heads lowered against the sting of the wind, following a track that crossed the valley and wound up a ridge. Cairns, pyramids of stone, marked the path into the mountains. As I entered their dark, dismal depths for the first time I felt a surge of claustrophobia, as if I were being swallowed up by them. It was all I could do to force myself to go on.

And then we came to Loch Coruisk.

It was a small lake scooped out of solid rock by ice hundreds of thousands of years before. I looked at the dead, dull lake, and then up through the murky clouds at the towering rocky pinnacles surrounding it. There was no living thing anywhere—no sound nor movement, nothing but a dead, stony, seemingly God-forsaken world. As I looked at the lake itself it almost seemed to have a life of its own, a stony life and consciousness with its fixed look and stern sphinx-like repose. The silence was overwhelming in this dark, brooding place, and my very thoughts seemed to ring loudly in my ears. As an inexplicable sensation of intense cold spread through my body, I thought, this is where I would come to die . . . throwing myself into the black, cold water because I no longer wanted to live . . .

"Miss! Miss!" A man's voice rose insistently above the wind and I turned to look at him.

For a moment I didn't recognize this plain-featured stranger. I was dazed, consumed by a bitter cold.

"Miss, I see somethin' by that large rock," he said urgently, and suddenly I remembered that it was Willie speaking to me.

Following his gaze I saw a dark, crumpled form lying by the rock. Willie spurred on his horse and I followed, no longer dazed, but still almost unbearably cold.

The crumpled form was Jonathan. Willie dismounted and knelt beside him for a moment, then looked up at me, slowly shaking his head. When I looked down at the body I saw the jacket covered with dried blood from a single bullet wound in the chest.

We arrived back at the castle in the early afternoon. I watched helplessly as Willie laid Jonathan's stiff body on the sofa in the library. Mrs. MacBean, looking drawn and grim, sent a servant to fetch Dr. Ross and the local magistrate in Portree. I remained with the body, wondering how on earth to tell Betheny. I didn't want her to see Jonathan's body, his face looking so young and pale, and I knew I must go to her soon.

Then suddenly Betheny was standing in the doorway of the library, asking, "What's wrong? Did you find Jon?"

Walking over to her quickly, I put my arm around her thin shoulders, trying to turn her away.

"Let's go back to your room," I said softly, trying to keep my voice from breaking.

She looked at me intently for a moment, a

frightened awareness dawning in her large black eyes, then broke away and hurried toward the sofa. Willie stood there silently, his expression helpless. When Betheny saw Jonathan's body she stopped abruptly. Her face went ashen and her lips moved but no sound came.

She fainted. Willie caught her and somehow managed to carry her up to her room.

I stayed with Betheny until Dr. Ross came and mercifully gave her a sleeping draught. As the doctor and I left her room, I looked back at her, lying so still and pale on her bed, and wondered if she would be able to survive all of this.

As if reading my thoughts, Dr. Ross said gently as we walked down the hallway, "She's young an' stronger than ye might think. 'Tis a terrible blow, but Betheny will survive. Though she's frail-lookin', she's still a MacLaren, an' they're made o' strong stuff."

"Have you examined the . . . the body?" I asked hesitantly.

"Aye," he answered soberly. "'Twas a hunter's bullet, I think. These things happen this time o' year. At least there was no pain. The lad died instantly."

Mrs. MacBean met us at the foot of the stairway in the Great Hall to ask the doctor if he would care for some tea. He declined politely, saying that he had to be getting on to see a crofter who had broken a leg.

"The magistrate will ha' to tak' Jonathan's body back wi' him to Portree," Dr. Ross told Mrs. MacBean, looking rather awkward. And he added, "There'll ha' to be an inquest. 'Tis a matter o' form in a violent death, though the cause o' this seems clear enough. Poor, poor lad . . ."

Mrs. MacBean nodded silently, then said, "I've sent wires to Master Alex and Mrs. MacLaren. They should be here tomorrow night. Master Alex will make the arrangements for the funeral."

"Och, another funeral so soon," Dr. Ross said sadly, shaking his head. "This poor family has had more than its share of misfortune lately. 'Tis almost as if a curse were on the MacLarens."

"*Was* it misfortune?" I asked boldly. "Could Jonathan have been murdered?"

Looking shocked, the doctor replied quickly, "O' course not, lass. There's no one would ha' wanted to kill Jonathan MacLaren. He was a mere lad an' had no enemies. No, 'twas an accident. I've seen it happen too many times before, when hunters dinna ken what they are aboot."

"But why would hunters be in a place like . . . like that?" I asked desperately.

Taking off his glasses and slowly cleaning them with a handkerchief, Dr. Ross answered slowly, deliberately, "Lass, ye're gettin' excited an' dinna realize what yer sayin'. Take my advice—ha' a nice cup o' tea an' rest. This has been a terrible ordeal for ye."

As Mrs. MacBean showed Dr. Ross to the door, I turned and ran up the stairs. Alone, in the privacy of my room, I cried myself to sleep.

When I awoke it was night and my room was dark. Quickly lighting a lamp, I splashed water on my face from the bowl on the washstand. When someone knocked on my door I was so nervous that I jumped, startled. I was immensely relieved when I saw that it was Lucy. Her face, normally so bright and cheerful, was drawn and her hazel eyes were red-rimmed from crying. Jonathan's death had upset everyone greatly, I realized, unlike Sir Duncan's demise.

"Mister MacKenzie is here, miss," Lucy said softly.

I nodded, not quite trusting myself to speak, and after quickly changing into a clean dress, I followed Lucy down to the drawing room where Kit was waiting. When I walked in, he hurried over to me, taking my hands in his.

"My poor little Chrissa," he said gently, looking down at me kindly. "I heard about Jon and wondered if there might be something I could do to help you."

"No, but it was terribly nice of you to come. We're still waiting for Alex and Antonia to return from Edinburgh."

"Poor Alex," Kit said with a long sigh. "What a shock it will be for him. First his brother, then his father, now his nephew. It almost seems like fate, doesn't it?"

I looked at him and was shocked to see that his pale blue eyes held a strange, wild expression, as if his mind held disturbing thoughts that he was trying to conceal. Did he really think Alex would be shocked at the news, I wondered suddenly?

"Alex still has Antonia," I said tersely.

Kit looked at me sharply and saw that I was staring at him. "You really think he cares for her?" he asked drily.

"Of course. They're always together. And

she's very beautiful. Everyone seems to think they'll marry soon."

"I'll tell you something, Chrissa. The only reason Antonia is here is because Robert didn't leave her enough money to move to London. That's where she really wants to be. She hates Skye and Castle Stalker. Alex is well aware of her feelings and doesn't care. They are lovers, yes, I won't insult your intelligence by denying that," Kit continued bluntly. "But neither of them really cares a fig for the other. Antonia merely wants what she can get from Alex and he is incapable of truly caring for any woman."

"What you say about him may be true," I responded frankly. "But I still wouldn't be surprised if she persuades him to marry her."

Kit was quiet for a moment, looking thoughtful, then muttered under his breath, "If I thought you were right . . ."

But he didn't finish the sentence. At that moment there was the sound of a carriage pulling up in front of the castle and a moment later Alex entered the room.

I was surprised and confused to see him here so unexpectedly. There was no way he could have gotten here so quickly from Edinburgh. And then I thought of what I must tell him, and I felt my stomach tighten into knots.

Alex smiled easily at Kit and began, "Ye should have stayed in Edinburgh a bit longer. The night after ye left, Antonia and I . . ."

His voice trailed off as he saw Kit's sober expression, and he continued slowly, "At any rate, I decided I'd gotten enough of Edinburgh and had best return before the local constabulary asked me to leave. Antonia stayed to do some shopping."

Then he continued tightly, "What is it? Ye both look so bloody solemn."

"Something has happened, Alex," Kit said simply.

"What's happened? Is it Betheny, is she all right?" he asked quickly.

For a brief moment I wondered why he should suddenly show such concern for Betheny whom he had always treated so coolly. But there was no time to dwell on this.

"It's Jonathan," I said shakily. "There was an . . . accident. He's dead."

Alex stared at me in disbelief, then repeated incredulously, "Jon is dead?"

I nodded, my throat constricted and my eyes filling with tears. Walking over to the window, I looked out onto the moonlit ocean in the distance, trying to hide my face.

"What happened?" Alex asked tightly.

"Dr. Ross said it was a hunting accident," I answered without turning around, my voice shaking.

"Where is the body?"

"The constable took it into Portree."

Without saying another word he turned and walked out of the room. I heard him calling loudly for Willie to saddle a horse.

Kit and I stood silently in the drawing room. Finally he said gently, "I'd best go now. And you should go to bed, Chrissa. Sleep is the only thing that will help now."

I nodded dully and he came and kissed my cheek tenderly before leaving.

After toying with a supper that I didn't

want and couldn't eat, I went up to bed. But finally, long past midnight, I accepted the fact that I would be unable to sleep. The specter of Jonathan's pale young face kept haunting me until I could bear it no longer. I decided to go down to the kitchen for a cup of tea, hoping that Morag would still be awake and I could talk with her. Since the experience at Loch Coruisk early that morning I had wanted desperatly to talk to her, hoping she could explain the frightening feelings that had taken hold of me.

I slipped on the thin cotton robe that did little to keep out the bitter late-night cold of the castle and lit a cruisie. As I walked down the hallway, my hair swinging loosely against my back, I felt a sense of tragedy in the air. The castle that night was a horribly oppressive place.

As I passed the library door, I was surprised to see a pale light shining inside. Walking close enough to peer inside, I saw Alex sitting in a chair by the nearly dead fire, his black-booted legs sprawled in front of him, an empty bottle of brandy on the table next to him. He was staring glassy-eyed at the dying embers of the fire, his brown hair falling over his forehead and into his black eyes. He was a pitiful sight and my heart went out to him.

I walked over to him softly and knelt beside his chair. He looked down at me, the expression on his rough, unshaved face cold and hard.

I said gently, "You should go to bed . . . it's terribly late."

He responded bitterly, his words slurred

206

from too much drink. "I've lived all my life as I chose, not as others thought I should. I've taken what I've wanted, an' the devil be damned! An' now I have what I wanted most—Castle Stalker. 'Tis no good thinking of anyone else, Chrissa Rey, for they always go away . . . or die. This place . . . this solid, timeless place is all that matters an' 'tis mine now."

He laughed, but it was a harsh, bitter sound, without joy. "I've been celebrating, ye see, drinking toasts to my good fortune."

He raised the glass in his hand and quickly swallowed the last of the brandy, clumsily wiping away a drop that fell on his chin. Then he looked down at me, staring intently as if seeing me for the first time. Suddenly he reached down and ran a hand through my hair and down my back. I could feel his rough hand through the thin cotton of my robe and my body shivered at his touch. Frightened by the wild look in his black eyes, I started to rise. But he grabbed the back of my neck so hard that it hurt, forcing me to remain kneeling, looking up at him helplessly. He leaned down till his face was only inches from mine and I felt my breath coming hard and fast.

"Damn yer eyes! I've seen ye looking at me as if . . . as if ye could see somethin' that no one else can!"

And then as he looked closely at me, his expression changed and he looked bewildered. He said slowly, "I've seen *you* before." Running a finger down my cheek, he finished, "I've touched you before . . ."

His finger continued down my throat, and I struggled, trying to pull away.

"Master Alex!"

It was Morag, standing in the doorway in her nightgown, her shawl pulled tightly around her bent shoulders. She was holding a cruisie and looking very hard at Alex. He looked up at her, then let me go and dropped back into the chair, closing his eyes and sighing deeply. I rose and walked quickly to Morag.

"Come, lass," she said softly, "I'll tak' ye to yer room."

In my room, Morag began quickly, "Master Alex didna' mean ye any harm. He had been drinking because o' Master Jonathan's death."

"Morag . . . there is something . . . something going on, something I don't understand." My voice broke and I burst into tears. My whole body was shaking and I felt as if I must be on the verge of madness.

Morag sat me down on the edge of the bed, then sat next to me, holding me and stroking my hair. "Pull yersel' together, lass, an' tell me what it is that's upsettin' ye so."

"I keep . . . remembering things," I explained haltingly. "Only it's not really remembering because it's things that happened a long time ago. I see things as they once were and I feel that I was a part of them. Once I saw Kit and Alex in the hallway, only they weren't Kit and Alex, they were Conal and Lorn. But I don't know who Conal and Lorn were!" I finished wildly.

"Hush, now, child," Morag said gently. She looked past me for a long moment, preoccupied with something. Then she continued slowly,

208

"When I was a wee bairn I was taken to a ceilidh. 'Twas a gatherin' held round a peat fire, an' songs were sung an' stories told. Young an' old alike would sit round the fire, listenin' to their elders' stories o' the past an' Scotland's great an' glorious history. I remember 'twas held in a crofter's cottage an' a storm was ragin' outside. But inside we were warm an' cozy. Some women twisted heather rope an' others sat at spinnin' wheels while they listened to the tales o' the past an' stories about the fairies, ghosts, an' the evil water-horse that lures people into the loch where it lives an' then eats them.

"One verra old man told the tale o' the battle o' Culloden an' when he spoke everyone stopped what they were doin' an' listened, for Culloden had been the biggest battle o' them all. An' this old man's father had fought in it. He described the battlefield first—a level stretch o' heath land, wi' the mornin' mist still ghost-like in the few trees as the two armies faced each other . . . the English on one side an' the Scottish under Tearlach himself, Bonnie Prince Charlie, on the other. He was tryin' to reclaim the throne for his poor faither ye see, an' everythin' rested on that one battle.

"It began. The brave clansmen flung themselves on the bayonets o' the Sassenachs an' soon the moor was covered wi' bodies in blood-soaked tartans. Gillies MacBean of Kinchyle stood wi' his back to a dyke, wounded, but he slew thirteen before he died. The clans were badly outnumbered an' 'twas suicide. The drums sounded an advance an' the English moved forward. The battle was over . . . lost. An' the dyin' men wondered what had become o' the MacLarens o' Skye. They had stood on a hill overlookin' the battle, three hundred strong, an' could ha' made the difference for they were known to be fierce warriors. But they didna' fight—no, they didna' fight.

"The clan chief was Lorn MacLaren an' wi' him was his brother, Conal. Lorn kept his men back but Conal went onto the battlefield an' died bravely. 'Twas said there was treachery involved—a lass named Brenna, famous for her beauty, who they both loved. Because o' her, the Clan MacLaren didna' fight an' Culloden was lost."

"Brenna . . . the same girl in the portrait upstairs?" I asked softly.

"I wouldna' know, lass, tonight is the first time I hae been further from the kitchen than the dinin' room "

And then she added soberly, "That is what ye're rememberin' . . . ye were there, in another life. Ye knew Conal an' Lorn MacLaren."

As I looked at her, disbelieving, she concluded simply, "This is no' the only life we are given. We live many times."

She sighed deeply, exhausted from her long speech and the terrible events of the day.

"I must go now," she said in a tired voice.

"Morag, just one more thing," I said quickly, stopping her as she rose.

"Aye, what is it?" she asked kindly.

"Your vision of my death . . . surely you were mistaken. You must have meant Jonathan "

"No," Morag said heavily, " 'Twas yer spirit I saw, Chrissa, no' Master Jonathan's. I canna

210

always see what will happen, but wi' you ... I feel a strong bond wi' *you*, Chrissa. Somehow, we are connected, an' I feel strongly what will happen to ye. Ye must take care, child, or death will visit this house again ... an' it will come for *you*."

Brenna
April, 1746

April came ... warm and clear, a perfect time for lovers to be together. But now when Conal and I were alone in the wee glen, which was seldom, it was different. All his talk was of Prince Charlie, ensconced in Holyrood, sending the clans out to battle. On one of the few occasions when Conal and I saw each other, he talked of the great victory at Prestonpans and how Cope's army ran like rabbits. Conal was excited, as I had never seen him before, full of praise for the Bonnie Prince.

And then came the day when Conal told me he would have to leave, that our wedding must wait. Prince Charlie was marching on London, he said, with 500 cavalry, 5,500 foot, and 13 pieces of cannon.

I could not believe it. During all these months when everyone talked of the Prince in Edinburgh, I had never thought that Conal would somehow be involved.

"But has Lorn pledged the clan to fight, then?" I asked, stunned.

"Lorn willna' say for sure," Conal said tersely. "But he will fight when it comes to it ...

the Clan MacLaren must fight, and soon. Cumberland's army is on its way, they say."

I burst into tears then. I told Conal he must not go for he would surely die, everyone said it was a lost cause, and I could not bear to lose him. He was taken aback by my words and sat silently while I screamed and cajoled, trying anything I could think of to change his mind.

But it was useless.

Finally he stood abruptly and said curtly, "My clan will fight and I with them. That is how it must be. If ye love me truly, Brenna, ye'll understand an' stay by me. Ye must trust that I am right. I dinna want to go into battle knowing ye're no wi' me."

But I could not say the words he wanted to hear, and he left, looking very sad.

I cried for many long hours, cursing God and Prince Charles Edward Stuart himself. And then slowly, gradually, an idea came to me. There was a way to stop Conal . . . to save him from what would surely be a bloody, senseless slaughter . . . if I dared . . .

CHAPTER 11

His soul a rock, his heart a waste?
LORD OF THE ISLES
Canto Third, XVII

Castle Stalker was once again placed in mourning, and this time there was a pervasive sense of genuine loss. Everyone wore black and our collective mood matched our dress. It seemed especially tragic that Jonathan should die a senseless death while he was still a boy.

A week after the funeral the family solicitor in Portree came to the castle to read the new will. All of us were called into the library for the somber occasion to listen to Mr. Syms, a short, thin man with a long face and receding hairline.

"The terms are quite simple," he began with-

213

out emotion. "Now that Jonathan MacLaren is dead, the estate is to be divided equally between Alex MacLaren and Betheny MacLaren, aside from some bequests which you are already aware of. Mr. MacLaren will have Castle Stalker and the immediate grounds. Miss MacLaren will have the rest of the land, including the farms and cottages."

"I assume that means that my meager allowance will remain the same," Antonia observed drily.

"The amount of yer allowance was determined by yer late husband, Mrs. MacLaren, and he would presumably know best in such a matter," Mr Syms replied tersely.

Antonia flushed, angry and frustrated.

Mr. Syms turned to Betheny and said coolly, "Until you reach your majority at eighteen, your uncle will act as your guardian and have full responsibility for the running of the estate. When you turn eighteen, half the estate will be legally yours to do with as you please, to pass on to your children when they come."

I glanced at Alex, wondering if he had been aware that he would not inherit all of Castle Stalker. Did it bother him that Betheny would soon control half the estate? But he stood quietly, his face a mask, revealing nothing of his inner thoughts. If he was shocked or disappointed by the terms of the will, he did not show it.

During those first few weeks following the funeral I could hear Betheny crying in her room at night. I went to her each time, comforting her as best I could. Sometimes I

214

talked about my life in California, trying to divert her attention from Jonathan's death. At other times I read to her until her eyes closed and her breathing grew deep and regular, and I knew that she was finally asleep.

Gradually as time wore on, Betheny began to pull herself together again. Dr. Ross was right—she *was* stronger than I realized. She had to be strong to survive the series of tragedies that seemed to plague her life; first her mother's death during childbirth, then the loss of her father and grandfather, and finally Jonathan's tragic death. Through the ordeal of Jonathan's death, Betheny changed, matured, and I no longer looked on her as a wounded animal in need of protection. She was rapidly growing into womanhood, still a shy and stammering girl in some ways, but with a subtle strength that even Antonia sensed and respected. Though Antonia still dominated her, she had begun standing up for herself, and was less likely to burst into tears when Antonia gave vent to tart criticisms.

For her part, Antonia began acting more and more like the mistress of the castle. Her feelings were transparent. She was convinced, I knew, that soon she would marry Alex, and Castle Stalker would be hers. The castle itself meant nothing to her, but the MacLaren fortune . . . that was entirely different. She wanted it desperately, and I doubted that she would let anything, or anyone, stand in her way.

As the people changed, so did the atmosphere of the castle, becoming more busy and noisy, with a constant stream of crofters tramping in and out. Alex was instituting sweeping changes in the running of the estate, especially with the farms. Farming equipment was brought in and disbursed among the crofters, and at the same time Alex spent much of his time teaching them modern farming methods. Castle Stalker was being brought slowly into step with the times, though I knew Alex's motives were actually old-fashioned. He wanted to be the respected owner of a self-sufficient estate whose workers appreciated what he provided for them . . . he wanted to be the all-powerful laird.

To my surprise, Betheny showed a keen interest in the work her uncle was doing. She spent many hours in the library with him, questioning him about the changes that were being made and offering her own suggestions for further improvements. Though Alex didn't seem to mind Betheny's involvement in the running of the estate, I felt that he must secretly resent it. He was the sort of man who would want to be in complete charge of whatever he was involved in.

I said little but constantly watched Alex. I had not forgotten the way he behaved and the things he said the night we found Jonathan dead. Dr. Ross had insisted that Jonathan could not have been murdered for no one had any reason to kill him. But that wasn't true. Alex had a historically powerful reason— Castle Stalker.

I found myself dwelling on the question of Alex's possible guilt. Could he have killed Jonathan? I knew that it was all too possible. He had, after all, been on Skye, not in Edinburgh,

216

when Jonathan died. And they had argued fiercely when they had last been together. But was Alex cold enough, inhuman enough, to take a life? I thought immediately of Marianne MacKenzie. If he *had* seduced her and then refused to accept responsibility for the result, it was his fault that she felt driven to commit suicide. And that, in my mind, was tantamount to murder.

Still, Jonathan was Alex's nephew, and it had always seemed that Alex was genuinely fond of the boy. Then I remembered Betheny's words—"More than one man has committed murder for Castle Stalker. Brothers have killed brothers, uncles have killed nephews . . ."

And there was something else that had been bothering me for some time—Sir Duncan's strange, inexplicable illness and demise. Even Dr. Ross had admitted he was baffled by Sir Duncan's sudden illness. I had always been bothered by the nurse's precipitous leavetaking. Did she know something—or was she actually a party to murder?

And there was the other . . . the tragedy from the past. Somehow it was all connected. The evil that had existed then, existed now. I was sure of it . . . could feel its very presence here in the castle itself, especially when I gazed at the half-finished portrait of Brenna. Had Alex been the treacherous Lorn, watching his countrymen and his own brother die, all so that he might possess the woman he desired?

And then as I was caught up in these confused and frightening thoughts, I realized that if Alex *was* a murderer, killing everyone who stood in his way to controlling Castle

217

Stalker, then Betheny was not safe. She was the final obstacle to his deadly plan.

Suddenly I felt utterly terrified.

After that I watched Betheny closely, rarely leaving her alone. I think she believed that I was merely concerned for her because of her depression over Jonathan's death. But the truth was that I feared for her very life. And the person I feared was the one person she trusted completely.

Coming down to breakfast late one morning in November, I found Betheny hurriedly finishing a cup of tea. She looked nervous and excited, and I noticed that she was wearing her riding habit.

"I'm sorry I can't stay and talk with you while you eat," she said quickly, "but Uncle Alex is taking me for a ride. He said he wants to see how I've improved. It will be just he and I. He made it clear to Antonia that she isn't welcome."

She was smiling happily, so pleased at the prospect of having her adored uncle all to herself that she didn't notice my grave expression.

"That's wonderful," I said with forced humor. "Where are you going?"

"I don't know. Uncle Alex will probably decide where we'll go. You know how he always likes to be in charge."

"Yes."

She rose and left then, and I sat at the table, thinking hard. I was filled with a terrible sense of foreboding, but didn't know what to do about it. Finally I decided that I could at least follow them, and I ran to my room, quickly changing into my riding habit.

218

Down at the stables, Willie told me that Alex and Bethany had left only minutes before, pointing in the direction they had ridden. I was so anxious to be off that I helped Willie saddle Taj, then hurried off in the same direction Bethany and Alex had gone.

It was a bleak, cold day but fortunately it wasn't snowing. However, it had snowed the night before and the countryside was covered with a thin layer of white powder. Everywhere I looked, there was empty white moorland enveloped in an almost unearthly silence. I saw no sign of Bethany and Alex: in fact, the land looked totally devoid of human life.

I headed toward the path by the sea first. After I had ridden on it long enough to determine they hadn't gone that way, I turned back and took a path that Bethany and I often took. But there was no sign of them there either. I rode on for three hours, feeling desperation rise within me as the time passed. My mind was filled with horrible visions of Bethany lying dead on the frozen ground, her face as pale and lifeless as Jonathan's had been.

I found no sign of them anywhere, and finally had to turn back toward the castle. By now both Taj and I were exhausted and cold, and when it began to snow lightly it only increased my depression. The light snowfall had stopped by the time I rode into the stableyard. As I dismounted, feeling forlorn and overcome with worry, I looked up to see Bethany and Alex inside the stable, talking to Willie. I felt a tremendous surge of relief as tears came to my eyes. The stableboy who was helping me with Taj looked at me strangely, then asked if anything was wrong. I shook my head no, unable to speak, afraid that at any moment I would burst into embarrassing sobs.

Betheny saw me and waved merrily. I waved back, waiting patiently as she hurried over to me.

"Chrissa," she said excitedly, "we rode all the way into Portree and had tea at the hotel! It was such fun and Uncle Alex said I've really become quite an accomplished rider."

Smiling, I responded softly, "It sounds like fun. I wish I'd been there with you."

Then I looked beyond her and found Alex watching me, a cool enigmatic expression on his face.

December arrived. Black December they called it, because of the terrible losses on the battlefields of the Transvaal, the heaviest losses of the Boer War.

On a bitterly cold night in mid-December when snow fell lightly on the Cuillins, Kit came to dinner, the first time he had been at the castle since Jonathan's death. After dinner, the five of us—Kit, Alex, Betheny, Antonia and I—retired to the drawing room. While Kit and Alex drank brandy and talked, I listened avidly to their conversation, at the same time helping Betheny with a shawl she was knitting. Antonia sat next to Alex, leafing through a fashion magazine and looking unutterably bored.

"This war is insane!" Alex roared angrily. "The Scottish regiments suffer the most casualties and what are they dying for? For the damn English! Those rieving Sassenachs take over our country, enslave our people, then

220

force them to die for their own selfish interests overseas."

"You talk as if we have a choice, Alex," Kit said placidly. "You're not a realist. You like to see yourself as an ancient clan chief, kowtowing to no one, with the power of life and death over everyone. You remind me of the story of the MacNeill who used to send his trumpeter to his castle tower every evening after dinner to proclaim: 'Ye kings, princes, and potentates of all the world, be it known unto you that MacNeill of Barra has dined—the rest of the world may dine now.'"

Smiling wryly, Alex responded, "That may be true, but it is also true that in the Highlands we are all gentlemen. And the poorest man of a clan is as good as his chief. Our forefathers were living here, following the laws of the clan, when the Romans were occupying England."

"If you insist on speaking the truth, then you must also admit that the English have dominated Scotland for almost a hundred and fifty years and that isn't going to change. We might as well accept it."

"It's that kind of attitude that has kept us in bondage to England!" Alex responded harshly. "We were free once and we can be free again. There is no reason why we should be considered part of England. We are different than they—we have our own heritage, art, history, even our own language."

"All of that died at Culloden," Kit said sharply.

My head, which had been bent over a ball of yarn, came up sharply and I stared intently at

Kit and Alex. Culloden . . . a blood-soaked field and a doomed prince . . . Lorn and Conal arguing bitterly . . . "We must fight!" . . . . "No!" . . . and Conal looking at me accusingly, then back at Lorn, shouting, "Sell yerself for this harlot, then, but I will fight!" . . . Lorn holding me back as Conal rode off, but later . . . at the well of the dead . . .

I must have screamed for suddenly everyone was staring at me, dumbstruck.

"Chrissa," Betheny began hesitantly.

I interrupted her rudely, "Excuse me, I don't feel well."

And I ran from the room, leaving them all staring after me. It was to Morag that I went, bursting into her small room without knocking. She was asleep in a chair by a brightly crackling fire, her grey head resting heavily on her shoulder, her scar livid in the bright light. And suddenly I realized that I didn't even know how to say what I was feeling. The strange images that had suddenly filled my head a moment earlier had faded and I no longer felt the sense of urgency that had propelled me to Morag. I started to turn, to leave quietly, but my shoe squeaked, awakening her.

Morag looked up at me sleepily, through heavy-lidded eyes, obviously confused, and said thickly, "Why did ye come back, Sally? Is it the bairn?"

Taken aback by her words, I hesitated for a long moment, then responded softly, "Morag, it's me—Chrissa."

Raising her head slowly, she looked at me as if I were a stranger. Then she shook her head and responded in a whisper, "Oh, yes, Miss Chrissa, o' course. I dinna ken what I was thinkin'. Sit doon an' I'll make some nice tea."

I sat quietly while she put the kettle over the fire to boil and measured out a generous teaspoonful of *Earl Grey*. Looking closely at her while her face was turned toward the fire, I realized for the first time that she was really very old. Her face was deeply wrinkled and her hair was thin and white. She's getting senile, I thought, confusing me with someone named Sally who had a baby.

"Now then, child," she continued kindly, settling back in her worn chair. "What is it that has frightened ye so?"

"It . . . it happened again," I began hesitantly. "I was seeing things as they once were."

"If ye're no' used to it, it can be a fearful thing," Morag said easily, "whether 'tis the future or the past ye're seein.' What vision came to ye?"

"It was the battle . . . Culloden . . . where it all happened. Kit and Alex were arguing, you see, and suddenly I was seeing Lorn and Conal arguing."

"I see," Morag spoke slowly, not looking at me.

"What is it?" I asked frantically.

Slowly she raised her eyes to meet mine and her expression was grim. " 'Tis all happenin' again, ye see," she began softly. "This is the danger I foresaw for ye so many months ago. What happened all those years ago is happenin' again. The evil that was wi' Lorn an' Conal

MacLaren an' the lass named Brenna . . . 'tis here again."

She continued gruffly, "Ye must take care, Chrissa Rey. Ye must be stronger than Brenna was. This time, ye must overcome the evil."

Suddenly she threw up her hands, continuing in great frustration, "Och, that my powers o' the sight should fail me now! I canna' see . . . I canna' see what will happen, only that there is great danger for ye, lass, from evil that comes down through the centuries. But I *do* ken that evil thrives on Beltane . . . ye must be watchful then!"

Beltane . . . she kept coming back to that superstition-shrouded night. Suddenly I felt bitterly cold and unbearably tired, as if I had carried a heavy burden for a long, long time. If only I could find some place warm and sleep . . . forever . . .

Later, as I walked down the third-floor hallway toward my bedroom, I stopped in front of the portrait of Brenna. I looked closely at her, at the golden hair and tawny eyes . . . what had she been like? Had she meant to betray her country, or had she been an innocent pawn?

Christmas Eve came a week later, a subdued celebration. An atmosphere of sadness and loss remained from Jonathan's death. Everyone still looked at me strangely, remembering my odd behavior on the night that Kit had come to dinner. But surprisingly, the evening went rather well. Kit came by, his arms laden with

224

presents, and his cheerful demeanor lightened the tension in the air.

Antonia and I greeted him together as he walked into the drawing room, and helped him place his presents under the tree with the others already there.

"Looks like a fine Christmas Eve," he remarked happily, looking out the window at the gently falling snow.

"Let's just hope that tonight Carissa can control herself and not have one of her strange little fits," Antonia said bitchily, her sea green eyes looking at me archly.

Before I could respond, she hurried off to speak to Alex standing alone in a corner near the piano. Since I had dumped soup on her she had always been careful to flee to safety after insulting me.

"I don't know why that woman hates me so," I muttered angrily.

"Don't you?" Kit asked easily. "It's obvious enough. Before you came, she ruled things here, domestically speaking, of course. She was the only attractive woman for miles. Now there's you. And you're not only pretty, you're *young*. Poor Antonia is well past her first youth and staring unhappily into middle age."

"I've never felt competitive toward Antonia."

"You don't have to. She automatically feels competitive toward every other woman around her."

Just then some children from the nearby hamlet of Uig drove by in a cart pulled by a large sway-backed horse and stopped in front of the castle, singing Christmas carols in

225

Gaelic. I looked out the window at them, bundled in heavy coats and scarves, warm air rising from their open mouths as they sang. When they finished, Alex went out to thank them and invite them into the kitchen for a traditional cup of hot punch.

A few minutes later Alex returned to the drawing room where we were all waiting impatiently.

"Well, don't you think we ought to open the presents, Alex?" Kit began smiling. "I, for one, want to see what I've gotten!"

We all laughed, then gathered around the tree. The presents were piled under it, wrapped in bright paper and satin ribbons. Alex began to hand them out, reading the cards to see for whom they were intended.

Betheny was still enough of a child to feel tremendously excited about presents, tearing the paper off each one eagerly as Alex handed it to her. She squealed with delight when she discovered a pretty, expensive gold broach shaped like a horseshoe from him, and immediately walked over to him by the tree, thanking him profusely. I watched them standing together, the tall, brown-haired man, with coal-black eyes and the brown-haired girl with equally black eyes . . . she looked so different from her father, the pale, blue-eyed Robert MacLaren. Really, she looked much more like Alex . . . I stopped, thunderstruck. Suddenly I knew . . . I knew as surely as if someone had told me.

Alex was Betheny's father, not Robert. Confused, speechless, I watched them, the shy young girl gazing up adoringly at the smiling man who seemed so pleased that she liked his gift.

And then I noticed that Kit was looking at me strangely, and I knew that I had been staring at Alex and Betheny too obviously. Smiling with forced gaiety at Kit, I began opening my packages, trying to look calm.

Kit's present to me was a silver necklace with a single, tear-shaped diamond suspended from it. The diamond reflected the flames of the fire, flashes of blue and gold coming from the very center of it. Though the necklace was quite simple, I knew it must be expensive.

My discomfort at receiving such a costly gift must have shown, for Kit said quickly, "Don't you like it, Chrissa?"

"Oh, of course I do!" I responded honestly. "But, it's so expensive . . . Kit, you're too extravagant. You shouldn't have done it. Taj was quite enough."

"And why shouldn't I have done it?" he asked sardonically.

"But . . . it's so beautiful."

"Not half as beautiful as you are," he said simply, for once completely serious, his pale blue eyes staring into mine.

I felt myself blushing, with no idea how to respond to his compliment. Next to me Antonia, who was elegantly attired, as usual, in a lavender silk gown, gave me a look of pure jealousy. And though I had at first considered returning the necklace to Kit, I decided to keep it.

Somehow I was surprised to discover that Alex had given me a present. Though I had given him one, also, it was merely a scarf that

I knitted myself, made more out of a sense of obligation than generosity. But his present to me was very significant—a complete riding habit, including leather boots, all in a soft shade of grey to match my eyes. I noticed with a barely suppressed sense of victory that the skirt was slit up the middle, and I knew that Alex must have ordered it specially to be made that way. When I looked up from opening the package, I saw that he was watching me carefully. I managed an awkward "Thank you," that seemed to amuse him.

" 'Twas nothing," he responded wryly, then turned and began talking to Antonia.

The last present I opened was from Antonia. I don't know what I had expected, but it wasn't this. It was a ball gown made of satin. The color was a sickening fuchsia, the design was atrocious and out-of-date with a high neckline, huge leg o' mutton sleeves, and endless ruffles cascading down the bodice. I looked at Antonia silently while she smiled back at me as if nothing was wrong. But I knew that she had done this on purpose.

"I knew that you'd be needing a gown for the Beltane ball," she said with mock sweetness. "Now you have one, Carissa, *dear*."

I was furious, but I forced myself to remain calm. It would give her too much satisfaction, I knew, if I let her see that she had succeeded in angering me.

Gathering together my presents, I wished everyone good night and Merry Christmas and started to retire.

"You're not retiring so early?" Kit asked with obvious disappointment.

"Actually it's getting to be rather late and I'm feeling very tired," I lied.

"Perhaps you're right. I should be getting home myself," he responded, covering a yawn with his hand.

While Alex saw Kit to the door, I went up to my room and deposited my presents on the table near the bed. Then I sat down by the brightly crackling fire and thought about Betheny and Alex. I had no proof that he was her father . . . but somehow I *felt* it to be true. It would explain his behavior toward her—usually so cool and distant, but on occasion, as tonight, clearly affectionate. He would not want anyone to guess that he was her father, and would try to keep it a secret, probably even from her. Suddenly there was a knock at the door and when I opened it I found Betheny standing there dejectedly, holding a box with a dress in it.

"May I come in for a moment?" she asked sadly, and I nodded.

"Look at this!" she continued angrily, holding up a dress almost as ugly as the one Antonia had given me.

"It's from Antonia, isn't it?" I asked knowingly.

"Yes," Betheny answered in surprise. "How did you know?"

"Because she gave me this," I responded, holding up the fuchsia satin gown.

"Oh, how could s-she!" Betheny burst out furiously. "She's, s-she's . . ."

"She's a great many things, all of them bad," I interrupted quickly. "But it won't do any good to talk about it."

229

"You know I was actually beginning to think the ball might not be s-so bad. I was looking forward to wearing the beautiful broach Uncle Alex gave me. But if I have to wear this . . . this thing, it will be even worse than I feared!"

"Oh, Betheny, we'll fix it somehow," I reassured her. "I'm not a bad seamstress, you know. Here, let's have a look at your gown."

She handed it to me, holding it by the tips of her fingers as if it were a dead rodent that she couldn't bear to touch. I couldn't blame her. The gown was made of silk, cut much too full for Betheny's slender, girlish figure, with a high neckline and rows of lace, much like my gown. But as I examined it, I began to see ways it could be improved. The color was good, a pretty soft blue. Without the rows of lace, and with a lower, more stylish neckline . . .

"Betheny, you're going to have a beautiful dress after all," I said confidently.

"Do you really think s-so?" she asked, unconvinced.

"Definitely. Tomorrow morning after breakfast we'll have a fitting and I'll start working on it. I think it will turn out rather nice actually."

"Oh, I hope so," Betheny sighed deeply. "Thank you, Chrissa. I don't know what I s-should do without you."

"It's nothing, really. A little cutting here and there is all it needs. But you'd best go to bed now. It's very late."

Smiling happily, she left. When I was sure she was inside her room, I, too, left. Although it was late I knew there was a good chance

Morag would still be awake. The servants were having their own Christmas party downstairs and I suspected that it would last longer than the family's sedate celebration. Hurrying down to the kitchen, I found most of the servants standing around the long trestle table, sipping hot punch, talking and laughing. I saw Morag sitting in a corner talking with Willie, and I quickly went over to her, ignoring the surprised stares of the others.

"I've got to talk with you, Morag," I said gravely.

She looked at me quietly then nodded her head. I had the uncanny feeling that she knew why I had come. We went into her room and after closing the door, she poured me a cup of tea from the teapot that always seemed to be waiting on the table. After sipping a little of the hot liquid, I said slowly, "Alex is Betheny's father, isn't he?"

Morag looked down at the worn carpet, saying nothing for a long moment. Finally she nodded, then said quietly, "It has always been a wonder to me that no one ever saw. She looks so much like him."

"What happened?"

Morag sat down heavily in the large overstuffed chair in the corner near the fireplace. Then she began in a tired voice, "It all happened so long ago. Master Alex was verra young, only seventeen. Sally was a maid here then, sixteen an' a bonnie lass. They fell in love an' when they discovered Sally was wi' child they determined to marry. But Sir Duncan would hae none o' that. He sent Master Alex to Edinburgh, an' it took two strong sairvants to drag him to the coach. Then Sir Duncan sent Sally away to hae the bairn. He gave her money an' told her never to return to the castle. By the time Master Alex managed to return, Sally had gone an' no one knew where she was."

Sighing heavily, Morag continued softly, "It fairly broke his heart, it did. Master Alex truly loved Sally. He changed after that. He had never gotten along wi' Sir Duncan for he knew that Sir Duncan preferred Master Robert. But after that, he hated his father even more. He started runnin' wild an' gettin' into all sorts of mischief, all to hurt his father, ye see. An' when he was old enough, he left, travellin' all over the world, even goin' as far away as India."

"But how did Betheny come to be here?" I interrupted impatiently.

"Sally returned," Morag answered in a tired voice. "Her bairn had come an' she could stay away no longer. She was ill, ye see, an' knew she would die. How she made it here, so sick an' on a night such as that one . . . well, she came to gi' the bairn to Master Alex, but he was long since gone. An' the rest o' the family an' sairvants were doon at the kirk. But Louisa, Master Robert's wife, was here. She had stayed behind, no' feelin' well, ye see, for her own bairn was due in a month."

Morag paused, then continued, "I think ye must ken what happened. Louisa's bairn came that night, ahead o' its time an' stillborn. Poor Louisa died before the night was out. I took her bairn an' buried him in the garden. 'Twas a wee boy, ye see. An' then I hid the ailin' Sally in the storeroom that once was the dungeon, an' told everyone her bairn, a little girl, was Louisa's. Sally agreed to all this for she knew that it was her bairn's only chance o' a decent life. She died soon an' late one night I buried her next to Louisa's little boy."

Though even sixteen years ago Morag would have been an old woman, I could see her burying a woman and a baby. She would have the strength and courage.

"Does Alex know this?" I asked slowly.

"Aye. He was the only one I told. He had a right to know. At first, he wanted to claim the bairn, but he knew it would go hard on wee Betheny if it were known she were illegitimate. It ha' been a hard thing for him all these years, knowin' she is his own, yet no' able to claim her."

We were both quiet for a long moment. The fire had gone out while we talked and it was cold in the small room. Morag pulled her shawl more tightly around her bent shoulders. My hands were so cold they had goosebumps, so I got up and began rebuilding the fire. Almost immediately there was warmth once more in the room, as a shower of sparks flew up the chimney and the small fire grew. I stood in front of the slowly growing fire, with my hands stretched out in front of it. It seemed that I was always cold nowadays . . .

Alex . . . he had been cruelly treated and had good reasons for becoming as hard and selfish as he was. But were those reasons good enough to excuse murder? After hearing Morag's sad story I was more than ever convinced that Alex probably had something to

233

do with his father's death. I could still remember the look of utter, unbending hatred on his face as he stared at his father's dead body in the library.

"Does anyone else know that Betheny is Alex's daughter?" I asked Morag suddenly.

"I didna' tell anyone," Morag insisted firmly. "But I think . . . Mr. MacKenzie has known Master Alex for so long . . . I think he might ken the truth."

I remembered the way Kit had looked at me, so intently, as I stared at Alex and Betheny earlier in the evening. I thought, he *does* know. And he knew that I, too, had guessed the truth.

Brenna
April, 1746

On a warm evening when the air was sweet with the scent of bog myrtle and the only sound was the wild call of the cuckoo, I prepared myself for the terrible thing I had determined to do. After washing in the cold burn, I donned the golden velvet gown that showed to perfection my firm breasts and full hips.

By the time I reached Stalker Bay, night had fallen. There was no moon and the castle was a vague spectral outline in the distance. I hesitated, terrified of the black, ominous place that I must enter alone. I felt my stomach tighten and my throat grow dry with the knowledge of what I was about to do. But finally I forced myself to move on, toward the castle. For this was my only hope of saving Conal . . .

Minutes later I was shown into a small, windowless room where Lorn sat in front of a peat fire. When he saw me, he rose, walking drunkenly toward me.

"So, lass, ye've come . . . as I knew ye would."

I nodded, unable to speak. Lorn came closer, until he was towering above me and I could smell his foul breath. There was an evil glint in his black eyes . . . eyes that were the color of Conal's, but infinitely harder and slightly mad. I believe it is true that eyes are the window to the soul, and in Lorn's eyes I saw a soul as devoid of good as the devil himself.

"Take off that gown," he ordered.

I obeyed, slowly unlacing the bodice and slipping off the sleeves, then letting the dress fall to the floor around my feet. I stood there naked, for I had worn nothing under the gown, not even slippers to cover my feet. In that moment as Lorn looked at me, I knew the power my body held over men. And I knew that he would grant me what I asked in exchange for my favors that night.

As his rough hands cupped my breasts, I said coolly, "There is one thing . . . ye must no' let Conal fight for the Prince."

Lorn looked at me in surprise, then that strange, mad smile returned.

"The Clan MacLaren will no' fight for Prince Charlie," he said carefully.

And then he took me . . . in ways that to this day I cannot bear to remember, quickly destroying the flicker of passion I had felt for him.

CHAPTER 12

*A long, long course of darkness, doubts,
and fears!*

LORD OF THE ISLES
Canto Sixth, I

On a rare sunny morning in January Betheny came bursting into my room as I was preparing for dinner. Her face was aglow and she was grinning widely. I knew that something wonderful must have happened to make her so transparently happy, and whatever it was, I was grateful for it. It had been so long since she had been truly happy.

"Chrissa, you'll never guess, you'll just never guess!" she burst out excitedly.

"Well, if I'll never guess then you'd best tell me," I responded wryly.

237

"Uncle Alex is giving me my very own colt to raise and train and be mine forever!"

"You mean the colt from the sorrel mare that's in foal right now?" I asked. It wasn't a brilliant guess—the young mare was the only one in foal on the estate.

"Yes, isn't it wonderful? Imagine, it will be all mine, right from the very beginning of its existence. And I shall take very good care of it."

"I imagine the mare will help a bit, too," I said, smiling broadly. It was so good to see Betheny excited and happy, looking forward to something instead of moping in the castle.

"And you know what else," she continued proudly, "I'm going to be there when the little fellow is born. Uncle Alex said I could. In fact, he said it would be quite educational. I shall be part of the mystical experience of birth."

"I don't want to disappoint you, but the experience of birth is more messy than mystical."

"Have you seen a colt born before, then?"

"Yes, back on the ranch in California. But actually your uncle is right. It will be an educational experience for you and will make you feel very close to your colt."

"Oh, I can hardly wait. I'm going to spend every waking moment in the barn. Willie says you can't tell for sure when it will happen and I don't want to miss it."

Betheny was true to her word. In the days that followed, she spent most of her time in the barn, impatiently watching the sorrel mare who seemed in no hurry at all to give birth and satisfy Betheny's curiosity.

One afternoon Kit came over to tea, and as

we were talking, he suddenly said, "You know, I just realized I've been here over an hour and I haven't seen a trace of Betheny."

"She's probably down at the stables again," Antonia responded dully.

"Ever since I told her she could have the sorrel mare's colt, she's spent all her time there, waiting for it to be born," Alex explained with a wry smile.

"Ah, I can imagine her excitement," Kit said, grinning. "I remember the first time I was given my own colt. I actually slept in the barn for several nights before the little bugger finally arrived."

"Betheny's almost done that," I said. "She's fallen asleep down there the past two nights and I've had to go down and wake her and insist that she come back to her room."

"Well, it will all be over soon," Alex continued. "Willie told me this morning that he thinks the colt will come any day now."

It will all be over soon . . . later I remembered those words and wondered exactly what Alex meant when he said them.

It was late that night. I had gone to bed early with a headache and a dull book that nearly put me to sleep. Then I realized with a start that I hadn't heard Betheny go into her room. She must still be down at the stable. Though I wanted more than anything to simply let myself fall off into sleep, I forced myself to get up and get dressed. I knew that if I didn't get Betheny she would probably spend the night in the barn, and in this freezing winter weather, that could be dangerous. Later, I would wonder with a shudder what would have happened if I *had* let myself fall asleep and not gone down to the stables . . .

I was still several yards from the stables, clutching my cloak tightly around my shivering body in a vain attempt to keep out the cold, when I noticed a strange light in the stable window. And then I heard it—the frightened neighing of horses. Instinctively I sensed what was happening and I began running even before the flames burst through the stable roof and the heat burst the glass in the window.

As I reached the stable doors I was shocked to see they were bolted. Who would have barred them with Betheny inside? I wondered desperately as I drew back the bolts and flung open the doors. Several horses that had somehow managed to break out of their stalls ran past me and I had to flatten myself against the door to avoid them. The place was thick with smoke and rapidly growing flames that raced through the old wooden structure. Coughing painfully, my eyes watering, I searched urgently for Betheny. There was no sign of her, no response to my calls, and I knew that if she had been asleep when the fire started she might have been overcome by smoke without even awaking. As I made my way through the center of the barn, opening stall doors and letting loose the remaining terrified horses, I heard voices outside. The stablehands must have finally become aware of the fire, but the stable was beginning to fall apart around me now, and I knew it might be too late . . .

And then I saw Betheny. She was lying unconscious in the empty stall next to the sorrel mare who was pacing and whinnying, consumed with fear. My eyes were full of tears now from the smoke and my throat so constricted that I couldn't speak as I knelt next to Betheny to feel her pulse. She was alive, thank God, but how was I to get her out of here? I was so weak now from inhaling smoke that I couldn't possibly carry her.

Then she groaned and opened her eyes slightly.

"Betheny," I whispered, the word torturing my burning throat. "Come . . . get up . . ." and I pulled at her desperately.

Slowly she rose, leaning on me heavily, but as I turned and started to lead her toward the door, she stopped.

"My horse . . . my horse . . . Chrissa, we can't leave her to die like this."

I was close to fainting and desperate to leave while there was still a clear path to the door, but I knew that Betheny would never leave the mare. Quickly I turned and unbolted the stall door. But the mare was completely terror stricken now and refused to leave her familiar stall to walk out into the flames and falling timbers. Tearing a strip from my petticoat I wrapped it over her eyes so that she could not see what was around her. Then I pulled hard on her headstall, praying fervently.

It worked. The mare hesitated for a split second, then followed me slowly, her swollen body swaying back and forth. Betheny put an arm around her neck, leaning on her as we stumbled out of the rapidly burning stable. We were nearly at the door when Willie, who was standing just outside, saw us and came running toward us.

"My God, I didna' ken there was anyone in there," he shouted, horrified. Then, as I fainted, he picked me up bodily and carried me outside, while another stablehand grabbed Betheny and pulled the mare outside.

As I lay on the frozen ground, gulping the cool, soothing air, I watched the servants trying futilely to fight the fire. And I wondered why Alex was nowhere around . . .

The disaster could have been much worse. Though Betheny and I were both ill for several days from smoke inhalation, there were no actual fatalities from the fire. All of the horses survived, a few with burns that required prolonged care. The sorrel mare gave birth that same night to a healthy, pretty little white filly. The first day that Betheny and I felt well, we went down to the makeshift building that the servants had quickly constructed to house the horses. And when Betheny saw the filly—her filly—standing long-legged and wide-eyed next to the mare, she burst into a wide grin. I was glad then that I had risked the time to save the mare.

Alex spent much of his time down at the stableyard, overseeing the clearing up of the charred timbers and planning the construction of the new stable that would permanently take the place of the destroyed one. He offered no excuse for his lateness in coming down to the stable the night of the fire. I knew that it was possible he had been in Antonia's room. Her room was at the far end of the castle from the stables, and if he had been there, he would not have seen the fire or heard the noise of the horses and the servants.

But a persistent, frightening voice inside my mind said that it was also possible he hadn't come down sooner because he himself had set the fire—to kill Betheny. Thus, the last obstacle to his complete control of Castle Stalker would have been removed. It was a sickening thought, but a man who would kill his father and his young nephew would probably not hesitate to kill his daughter.

Still, I had no proof of this, and I tried hard to persuade myself that such a thing could not possibly be true.

Confined to the castle while I recovered from the lingering effects of the fire, I grew more and more restless. I wandered through the castle, finding rooms that I had never known existed, until I had combed every inch of the place. But I did not return to the dungeon.

Finally there came a day when I felt perfectly well. I was determined to get out of the castle, at least for a little while. Betheny tried to dissuade me from going, insisting that the weather was changeable this time of year and though it was now clear, could quickly turn bad again. But I was adamant and I left her looking terribly worried.

At the temporary stable, Willie, too, tried to persuade me not to go, but it was useless. I assured him that I would return at the first sign of a storm and minutes later I was galloping Taj out of the stableyard. Taj was as restless as I, since she hadn't been ridden in the days following the fire, and wanted to run. I let her have her head for a couple of miles, then slowed her to a canter. We headed in a new direction, south from the castle, on a path I had never tried before. But I wasn't worried about getting lost. I knew that as long as I kept the sea in sight I could follow it back to the castle.

It was bitterly cold in spite of the pale sunshine, and when the wind began to blow I started to shiver. I had just decided to turn back when it began to snow. At first it was just light snowflakes that melted when they touched the ground, but it quickly turned into thick snow swirling around me. One minute there was nothing but the howl of the wind over a grey landscape, and the next everything was white. Taj was so frightened that at first she stood still, refusing to move. Finally I prodded her into a jerky gallop, but she kept tossing her head nervously and I had to concentrate hard to control her.

The snow began coming down harder and thicker until suddenly I discovered that I could no longer see the ocean. In one terrifying moment I realized that I was lost in a swirling sea of snow, with no idea how to reach the castle.

I refused to let myself panic. I knew that if I did, it would communicate to Taj, who might then go racing off into the storm and stumble blindly over a cliff into the sea that was out there somewhere. Forcing Taj to stand still, I tried to get my bearings. I thought I could see enough of the sun to have some idea which direction to proceed in, though deep inside I suspected this was only wishful thinking. Still, I had to do *something*, so I prodded Taj carefully in what I hoped was the right direction.

I rode that way for an hour, unable to see more than a few feet in front of me, straining to listen for the sound of the sea, using all my energy to keep Taj under control. Finally, when I felt exhausted, my hands aching from holding the reins tightly, I saw a dark object looming ahead of me. As I came closer I saw that it was an old abandoned crofter's cottage with a small barn attached. It was obviously uninhabited, but that didn't matter. It was a refuge from the storm, and I cried in relief as I urged Taj toward it.

The barn was in disrepair but enough of it was still standing to provide an adequate cover for Taj. After tying her carefully to a post, I unsaddled her, then hurried into the cottage. As soon as I walked through the doorway into the blackness of the cottage I heard the scurrying of mice. Or rats, I thought uneasily. Unable to see what was ahead of me, I was afraid to step further inside. For a long moment I stood poised just inside the door, with the storm raging at my back and the blackness in front of me.

As my eyes gradually grew accustomed to the darkness, I began to see better. The room was empty, devoid of furniture. In the corner was a fireplace with some old peats piled next to it. I walked carefully toward the fireplace, hearing the boards creak under my feet, and began piling peats into the fireplace. Even though I was wearing gloves, my hands were nearly frozen and I handled the peats clumsily, dropping them at first until my hands grew warmer. As I bent to pick up the final peat, I saw a pair of gleaming yellow eyes staring up at me. I screamed, dropping the peat, and heard something, probably a rat, scurry away.

I stood there shaking for a moment, then bent down and tossed the last peat into the fireplace. Snow was coming into the room through the open door, so I shut it tightly. There was one small window that allowed in some pale light, enough to help me make my way back to the fireplace. It was then that I realized I had no matches. A desperate search around the small room revealed nothing, not even a flint. I was cold and wet and exhausted, surrounded by darkness and the constant sound of rats' claws scraping against the floor. Utterly miserable, I began to cry, my shoulders shaking uncontrollably.

Suddenly the door flew open so hard that it banged against the wall and snow came swirling in once more. In the doorway was framed the dark figure of a man. He stood there for a moment, peering into the darkness, while I stared back silently, not moving, barely breathing.

"Carissa?"

It was Alex's voice and it sent chills through my body.

Then a rat ran over my foot and I screamed in spite of myself.

"Chrissa!" he said again, loudly, then hurried toward me. In a moment he was beside me, looking down into my face.

"Are you all right? Why didn't you answer me?" he asked gruffly.

"I . . . I was frightened," I answered stupidly.

246

Looking at me as if I had suddenly gone mad, he shook his head. Then he noticed that snow was coming through the open doorway and he quickly walked back to the heavy oak door and closed it.

"Why didn't ye start a fire?" he asked curtly.

"I didn't have any matches. And I couldn't find a flint."

"Well, I've got matches," he said, then immediately started to light a fire. As he bent down over the fireplace, working with the tiny flame that at first refused to grow, he explained, "When the storm came and ye didn't return, we formed a search party. I saw your horse in the barn and knew ye'd be in here. You were lucky to find this old place. Ye'd never have lasted out there."

I heard the storm howling outside and saw the snow swirling heavier than before outside the window. And I knew that Alex was right. I *would* have died out there. But the thought occurred to me that I might just as easily die here. I was alone with a man who might be a murderer, and no one knew where we were.

By now the fire was glowing softly, filling the room with the sweet reek of peat. Satisfied that the fire would last, Alex stood, turning toward me. His black eyes surveyed my bedraggled appearance carefully, then he said matter-of-factly, "Your clothes are soaking wet. Ye'd best take them off and lay them near the fire, such as it is, to dry."

"But..."

"Don't worry, I've got a blanket outside on

Charger. I thought it might be needed. So, ye see, ye needn't worry about your modesty."

And with those last curt words, full of sarcasm, he left, returning in a moment with a large, heavy wool blanket.

"Now, get out of those wet things before ye catch your death of cold," he ordered, handing me the blanket.

I hesitated until he realized what was bothering me. Laughing, he turned his back to me while I undressed.

"You are surprisingly proper at times for such an unconventional lass," he said wryly.

Ignoring him, I quickly slipped out of my jacket. It was so cold and wet from the snow that it was nearly stiff. The silk blouse underneath was wet also, clinging damply to my shoulders, outlining my breasts. I hung my jacket and blouse on pegs next to the fireplace, then quickly slipped out of my skirt, which had gotten completely drenched. My chemise followed, leaving me standing naked in front of the small fire, gratefully feeling its warmth spread over me.

Wrapping the huge blanket around me, I sat close to the fire. The wool felt coarse and stiff next to my bare skin.

"You can turn around now," I said curtly over my shoulder.

Alex turned and walked over to the fire. Taking off his wet overcoat, covered with snow, he shook it out and laid it next to my clothes.

Then he knelt next to the fire, holding out his hands toward it to warm them.

"This fire won't last long, unfortunately.

And then it'll be nearly as cold in here as it is out there. But we're not far from the castle, thank God. If this storm clears up by morning you'll be able to see the sea not far in the distance. The castle is only a few miles up the coast."

"Oh. I hadn't realized I was so close."

"It doesn't matter. Even if it were only a mile away we'd never make it in this storm. We'll just have to hope it's over by morning."

Then, looking at me quizzically, he asked, "Why did ye scream when I came in?"

I was silent for a long moment, then answered simply, "A rat ran over my foot."

To my surprise he laughed, and when he did his entire demeanor changed. The rough lines of his face softened and he looked almost boyish.

"Afraid of mice, eh? I would have sworn there was nothing *you* were afraid of, judging by how recklessly ye behave most of the time."

I suspected that he was teasing me, but I wasn't sure. I had the horrible feeling that he was a cat and I was a mouse he was toying with before destroying.

I responded guardedly, "I don't believe I'm reckless."

"You are reckless, headstrong, stubborn, and contrary," he insisted, clearly smiling now. "You don't behave as a young lady should. You speak your mind, are independent to an unfeminine degree, and refuse to accept the fact that women were meant to be governed by men. Ye'll never find a husband and I'll continue to be your exasperated guardian until we are both in our dotage."

249

I didn't know how to respond. A smiling, teasing Alex was a surprise and a mystery.

Then he added, more seriously, "You have pride, too much for a girl, perhaps—but 'tis better than having none."

I bridled at that remark but before I could retort, he said awkwardly, "There's something . . . something I've been meaning to talk to you about."

I waited, sensing somehow that I was in for a lecture.

I was right.

" 'Tis about Kit. I have noticed that you spend a great deal of time together. I can understand why you would enjoy his company. He is charming, great fun at times. But ye must know he is not very responsible in his relationships with women."

He stopped, embarrassed and obviously relieved that his lecture was over. He had done his duty.

I replied tartly, "Strange, that's exactly what he says about *you*."

For a brief moment there was no response, then Alex burst out laughing, a surprisingly gentle, attractive sound.

"I can see 'tis no use talking to you. Ye'll go your own way always. Very well, ye'd best try to sleep now. The storm will be with us till morning, I think."

He folded his overcoat into a pillow on the floor, then motioned to me to lie down there. As I lay with my eyes closed, too nervous to fall asleep, I heard Alex sit down on the floor across the small room.

I was very aware of his presence, his sheer

physical nearness in the tiny hut. The sound of
his breathing, deep and regular, filled the
room, and somehow I knew that his dark eyes
were watching me—I could feel their piercing
look through the heavy blanket and my own
closed lids.

What kind of man is this, I wondered, with
whom I am sharing a lonely shelter on a bitter
night. Was he a cold murderer? Willie thought
so, I suspected. But then, Willie thought many
things, had deep feelings that few people would
credit. For the first time I realized that Willie
was something of a mystery—not simply the
obedient servant. He had dared to nurture a
deep and abiding love for the beautiful
Marianne MacKenzie, a lady far above him in
station. And now he hated Alex MacLaren, his
laird, for driving her to her death.

Yet Morag, who knew Alex best, insisted he
was innocent, a victim of unhappy circum-
stances. Still, Morag was a very old woman
who tended to think of Alex as the mistreated
boy he once was. She would not be likely to see
him as he *really* was.

But none of this speculation answered the
question—who killed Jonathan? For I was
convinced that it was murder, not an accident.
And Betheny's close brush with death, too, was
planned, I thought. Of all the people on Skye,
only one, Alex, had any reason to kill Jonathan
and attempt to kill Betheny. The reason was
Castle Stalker.

Castle Stalker—everything came back to it
eventually. It was the catalyst in all our lives,
silent and immobile, yet influencing our
thoughts and actions, wielding an awesome in-

251

fluence. Had it been so for the others—Brenna,
Conal and Lorn—had Castle Stalker somehow
played a role in their tragedy?

Thoughts, dark and swirling, filled my exhausted mind—love and betrayal, pain and ec-
stasy. Confused images—a portrait of a lovely,
pale, mad girl, another portrait of a wild, wanton creature with whom I felt a strange
communion...

Brenna-Chrissa, Chrissa-Brenna . . . I fell
asleep with the two names intertwining in my
mind...

It is dark and bitter cold. I lie next to a
small peat fire that has burned down to a bed
of hot coals, glowing golden-red in the
darkness. I cannot remember where I am, why
I am wrapped in a thick blanket. And I am
cold . . . so cold that my body shivers uncontrollably.

"Conal!" I shout into the darkness.

In a moment he is beside me.

"What did you say?" Then, touching the
hand I hold out to him, "God, you're cold as
ice. You'll freeze at this rate."

Quickly he pulls the blanket aside and lays
down beside me, covering us both with the
thick wool, taking my shivering, ice-cold body
in his arms. Gratefully I feel his strong arms
encircle me, his shirt smooth against my skin.
As I press my body against his, my breasts feel
the soft, curling hair on his chest where his
shirt is open. And my hips push against his
hips, feeling the hard, throbbing pressure between his legs. My mouth reaches up to meet
his. Suddenly he pulls back, his body stiffens

. . . then as I slip my leg between his, my arms pulling him toward me, he relaxes, melting as a thick tallow candle does, slowly, completely. A groan escapes his lips before I kiss them . . .

His hands are all over me, caressing the secret places they know so well. But there is a strange sensation here, as his fingers run lightly over my belly, finally reaching the hairy triangle. It is as if my body, asleep for a long, long time, is being gently awakened. My back arches at his touch, my breathing grows fast. While his fingers probe between my legs, gently prying them apart, his lips brush my cheek, my neck, the hollow between my breasts. And then his tongue is circling my nipples, first one, then the other, making them grow erect.

Pushing me back against the hard floor, his body hovers over me, his chest pressing against my breasts, his knees pushing open my legs . . .

He is inside me, and suddenly there is pain, horrible, blinding pain as he forces me to accept him, to be filled with him.

Why is there pain? It should not be so!

As quickly as it has come, the pain is over, and my body shudders with relief. Then comes the gentle, rocking motion and my body begins to move with his, perfectly, as always. The movement grows faster, more urgent, my nails dig into his back as I try to pull him even closer to me, to become part of him. His lips are on mine, his tongue probing my mouth, while his hands pull my hips up to meet his.

And then comes the fire, a spark at first, quickly growing, igniting my loins, making my body as taut as a bowstring stretched to the breaking point. Somehow it continues, my body rigid, as wave after wave of cool fire spreads through my quivering body . . .

It is over. I lie in his arms, my mind giving over to sleep, and just before unconsciousness I know I have come home . . .

When I awoke, it was morning and the storm had passed.

And I was alone.

I looked quickly around the room but there was no sign of Alex. My clothes remained by the fire, dry now, but his were gone. Only the blanket that I was wrapped in was tangible proof that he had been here. I sat up, surprised at an unexpected soreness in my body. It must have been the hard floor, I thought. As I quickly dressed I had the vague feeling that there was something I should remember, something about last night . . .

I was folding the blanket when I noticed a dull red stain—blood, barely dry. And then I remembered in a rush of shameful knowledge—Alex and I, together, touching each other intimately. Oh, God, no! I shouted to the empty room. How could it have happened? Surely it must have been rape . . . and, yet, my mind recoiled from that. I tried desperately to remember all of it, but the only images that came to mind were of lust and passion—not just his, but *mine*.

I couldn't bear to face such thoughts. Running out to the barn, I discovered that Taj was saddled and ready to go. Alex must have saddled her before leaving.

In the distance I could see the sea, deep blue beyond the snowy cliffs. Mounting Taj, I headed north, where I knew Castle Stalker would be, trying not to think, not to remember . . .

A half hour later I rode into the stableyard, in time to meet Willie and some other servants mounting horses, preparing to continue their search for me. Willie's plain face stretched into a broad smile and I was touched to see tears come to his eyes.

"Miss Chrissa! Ye're safe!"

He helped me down from Taj, continuing exuberantly, "Thank God, miss, we thought for sure ye were done for when Mr. MacLaren returned earlier an' said he hadn't seen a sign o' ye."

"Alex is here?" I burst out.

"Aye, miss," Willie responded slowly, looking at me strangely. Then, "Ye'd best get inside, now, Miss Betheny has been worried sick. An' I fancy Morag has some nice hot soup waitin' for ye."

I went inside, immediately encountering Betheny in the hallway. Bursting into tears, she hugged me, too overcome to speak. Then she hurried me to my room, clucking like a mother hen, in a direct reversal of our usual roles. After helping me change into a nightgown and putting me to bed, she insisted that I swallow a few sips of soup brought by a smiling Lucy, then left me to sleep.

But I couldn't sleep. My mind was a jumble of fears and unanswered questions. When Betheny looked in on me two hours later, I burst out immediately, "Is your uncle here?"

"Uncle Alex?" she asked, confused. "No, he waited until he heard you were all right, then he and Antonia left. For Edinburgh, I think. He said he would be gone for a very long time."

Brenna
April, 1746

Lorn betrayed me to Conal. I shall never forget the look of fury on Conal's face when he came riding up early in the morning following my night with Lorn. I was standing in the burn behind our hut, trying to scrub away the terrible, dirty feeling that I was left with after lying with Lorn.

Conal pulled his red stallion to a rearing halt, then jumped off and strode angrily over to where I stood, motionless and expectant, filled with a sickening dread.

"Brenna!" His voice, usually so soft and full of love, came harsh and loud. And when he came closer I could see that his black eyes were narrowed in anger.

"Lorn is boasting to all o' Skye that he's had ye!"

I looked at him helplessly, knowing that it would do no good to lie. My silence was answer enough for him. The cold fury in his eyes changed to a great and compelling sadness. One hand reached out toward me and for a moment I thought he would strike me, but he only touched my cheek softly.

And then he turned, walking swiftly back to his horse.

I ran after him, crying and trying to explain, but he would not listen.

" 'Twas for you, Conal!" I shouted urgently. "Oh, love, 'twas all to save ye, for I dinna want ye to fight an' die."

His face was cold, his eyes unmoved, as he mounted his horse. He said simply, "I asked ye to stand by me, Brenna, but ye went to Lorn instead."

And he rode off, leaving me standing in the roadway, alone.

CHAPTER 13

And from his pale blue eyes were cast
Strange rays of wild and wandering light
LORD OF THE ISLES
Canto Second, XXX

The remainder of that bleak winter passed
quickly and uneventfully. Antonia and Alex remained in Edinburgh. Though Betheny re-
ceived regular letters from her uncle, I heard
nothing from him. Apparently what had
passed between us in the crofter's cottage the
night of the storm was simply to be forgotten.

I was ill for awhile, but the illness passed,
leaving me feeling rather tired and yet at the
same time restless. This lingering feeling of
tiredness led me to develop a habit of taking
naps in the afternoons, something I hadn't

done since I was a small child. At first I merely thought it was due to the unaccustomed harshness of the cold Skye winter. Gradually I began to realize that the true source of my tiredness and restlessness was something altogether different ...

Betheny and I led a quiet, fairly happy life during that period. When the weather was nice, we often went riding, occasionally accompanied by Kit, who began to spend a great deal of time at the castle. Hardly a week passed that we didn't see him at least two or three times, for dinner or tea or to go riding.

I still enjoyed being with Kit but somehow there had been a subtle change in our relationship. I found myself looking on him only as a friend, not as a romantic possibility.

During the faolteach, or storm days, I either read in the library or worked on Betheny's ball gown. I spent many evenings in Morag's small, comfortable room, listening to her reminisce about my mother. I had no more visions and Morag did not mention them, or her warning about Beltane, again. But I thought she seemed watchful, as if she was waiting for something to happen.

My birthday came on April 14th. With so much else on my mind, I had actually forgotten it, until I went down to breakfast and was greeted with a gay, "Happy birthday, Chrissa," from Betheny, who was grinning broadly. On the table in front of my chair was a huge package that stood at least two feet tall and four feet long. I couldn't imagine what could be in such a large box.

"It's from Uncle Alex and me," Betheny explained proudly. "I wrote to him, explaining what I wanted, and he found it in Edinburgh and sent it. He even insisted on paying for it, though I had been saving my allowance to do so."

As I stood there, looking surprised and happy, Betheny said impatiently, "Well, aren't you going to open it?"

Laughing, I began untying the ribbon and tearing off the thin tissue paper. When I finally opened the top of the box, I saw why it had to be so large. Inside was yards and yards of golden velvet, thick and soft and smooth. When I touched it, I remembered the golden velvet dress in the storeroom and for a moment I froze.

But Betheny noticed nothing. She continued easily, "I hope you like the color. I thought you could make a ballgown out of it to replace that hideous thing Antonia gave you. I know there is only a fortnight till Beltane, do you think you'll have enough time?"

"What?" I asked, distracted. Then, pulling myself together, "Yes, I think so. Your dress is nearly finished now, and if I make something simple with this..."

My voice trailed off as I thought about a plain dress adorned only with black silk ribbons lacing up the bodice...

Smiling happily, Betheny confided, "You know in his letter to me Uncle Alex was rather disapproving of the color and fabric. He tends to think of you as a child, you know, and he suggested something 'younger,' such as my gown. But I wrote back, saying that you are a woman now, eighteen years old, and he would

261

just have to accept the fact. You *do* like the material, don't you?"

"Yes, I love it," I answered with a forced smile.

"I thought it would be perfect for you, a nice contrast to your dark hair and complexion," Betheny continued easily. "Somehow I couldn't see you in pale pink or blue."

"It was nice of your uncle to take the time to find the material," I said slowly.

"Oh, I don't think he minded. Despite his gruffness and the fact that you two argued a good deal when he was here, I think he's rather fond of you. He always asks about you in his letters to me, you know, wondering if you're feeling well or need anything."

She finished sadly, "I don't know why he's staying away so long."

I didn't either—unless it was actually possible that he still retained enough of a sense of morality to be ashamed of what had happened between us. It was more likely, however, that he didn't want to face me because then he would have to accept some responsibility for me.

Betheny talked about the ball gown throughout breakfast, and afterwards brought a copy of one of Antonia's old fashion magazines, "Le Salon de la Mode," to my room. There we planned the style of the gown. I made a pattern out of newspapers, copying a dress from the magazine. It had a scandalously low neckline, tight waist, and full, billowing skirt. It was simple, without ornamentation, and, except for the ribbons, much like the golden velvet dress in the storeroom.

I worked on the pattern until late in the afternoon. Then just before teatime, Lucy came into my room and informed me, with a sly, knowing look, that Kit had come to visit me. As I hurried down the portrait-lined hallway, consciously avoiding the half-finished portrait of Brenna, I wondered what Kit might want. Though he was a frequent guest at Castle Stalker, he had never specifically asked for me before.

He was sitting in the drawing room, talking to Betheny. When I entered, he stood, saying politely, "Good afternoon, Chrissa. You look particularly lovely today. Is that a new dress?"

It *was* new, one of several new dresses Betheny had persuaded me to buy after a long period of determined resistance on my part. It was bright green with tiny yellow and white flowers, a far cry from the few drab dresses I had brought from California.

We made small talk about my dress and the weather, until Betheny said hopefully, "You *will* stay to tea, won't you, Kit? I shall pretend I'm all grown up and the lady of the castle and s-shall be the hostess."

Laughing, Kit responded, "Well, if you put it like that, how can I refuse? Besides, by a strange coincidence, my social calendar happens to be completely free today."

Betheny rang for Lucy and asked that tea be brought in immediately. A few minutes later, Lucy deposited the tea tray on a small table in front of Betheny, who carefully poured us each a cup. Then she passed around a plate of cucumber sandwiches, offering them to us with a formality that was totally unlike her. She was playing her part to the hilt and clearly enjoying it immensely. It made me feel awfully good to see her once more enjoying herself after her long battle to overcome her depression following Jonathan's death.

Kit, too, was enjoying the situation. Once he caught my eye and winked while Betheny was concentrating on slicing the cake. But though the conversation was as friendly and enjoyable as ever among the three of us, I had the impression that Kit had something else on his mind. And I remembered that he had asked for *me* when he came.

Finally Kit said a little too casually, "Betheny, if you don't mind, I think I'll take this young lady for a stroll in your garden before I take my leave. 'Tis an unusually warm and lovely evening."

Betheny glanced at me, her feelings obvious. "Something is up," she seemed to say. Aloud, she replied, "Don't let her stay out too long and catch cold, though. It's her birthday today, you know, and it would be a terrible time to become ill."

"I know that it is a very special day," Kit answered slyly, then took my arm and led me downstairs and out to the garden.

We stood in front of the stone balustrade surrounding the garden, overlooking the sea below. The sun was still shining, as it did nearly until midnight in the spring, bathing the mountains in a strange dusky grey light. The sky itself was a deep, deep blue, almost devoid of clouds. The moors were covered with brown, shriveled heather that wouldn't come to life again until later in the spring.

Somehow there was a barren look to the landscape. A sense of death, rather than renewed life, as you might expect in spring. As I looked out at the Cuillins, I once again had the horrible feeling of cold—bitter, unrelenting cold, and I shivered suddenly.

"Are you cold? Can I get a wrap for you?" Kit asked solicitously. "I thought it was rather warm this evening . . ."

"I'm all right," I insisted. "It's just . . . a rather strange evening."

"We call it fey," Kit responded easily. "It means other-worldly . . . special in an almost supernatural way."

He had described it perfectly. I had a sense of foreboding about this evening, as if almost anything could happen. I knew that Morag would say that fairies were about, making mischief and bewitching people. Fairies, she had explained to me, make little sound, no more than a gust of wind, the swish of silk, or the whistle of a sword cutting through the air. Small they are, she said, no more than four feet tall, living in grassy knolls. She called them thieves, but added righteously, "They only tak' what men deserve to lose."

Am I about to lose something, I wondered thoughtfully.

"You look very different from the girl I found lying on the moors in a man's trousers and a shirt too large for you," Kit began softly, interrupting my morbid thoughts. "You're a woman now, and a very beautiful one."

I was surprised to feel myself blush and was about to respond with an embarrassed "Thank you," when Kit reached into his coat pocket and withdrew a small package wrapped in silver paper.

"This is your birthday present. I bought it some time ago but I waited until today to give it to you. I thought this would be an appropriate time."

Handing it to me, he said soberly, " 'Tis yours if you want it."

Looking up at him, somehow I knew what was in the small silver package. Nevertheless, when I slowly unwrapped it, I was amazed at the size of the emerald and the number of small, round diamonds surrounding it.

"I love you, Chrissa Rey," Kit said huskily. "I've wanted you since the first time I saw you all those long months ago."

He took me in his arms and kissed me . . . not gently but with great passion. Passion . . . again that horrible, unrestrained feeling that frightened me so.

I broke away and stood staring at him, on the verge of tears.

"I'm sorry," he apologized quickly. "I didn't mean . . ."

I felt a mass of conflicting emotions. Kit had always been so kind to me, and there was no denying that he was attractive—fearfully so. I genuinely liked him. There was no reason why I should not be thrilled. Two months ago I *would* have been thrilled . . . before that stormy night in the cottage with Alex.

My silence revealed my feelings. Kit continued urgently, "I'm very serious about this, Chrissa. I want you to be my wife. I know you think I'm a bit wild and carefree, but I assure you that I would be a model husband. No more carousing, no more philandering. I would be faithful and dependable, and so grateful that you are mine."

Still I couldn't speak, and Kit finished in a whisper, "I'm so alone and I need you so much."

It was not what I had expected him to say. I had never seen him look so vulnerable, and I knew then that I had to say something.

"Kit . . . I am deeply touched by your proposal . . . I had no idea that you felt this way. You know I am fond of you, but . . . I can't marry you."

When I finished this woefully inadequate speech, there was a long, awkward silence. Finally Kit responded slowly, a hardness replacing his touching vulnerability, "I think I understand. It's Alex, isn't it? Since you were lost in the storm and he left here the very next day, things have been different. First Marianne, now you."

His expression was frighteningly intense, his mouth set in a thin, hard line. His pale, ice-blue eyes were shining brightly with a strange excitement.

"Kit . . ."

But it was too late. He was already walking quickly back toward the castle.

I felt thoroughly miserable and confused, aware that I had handled the entire matter badly. I had hurt Kit deeply and I hated myself for it. But how could I explain to him that our relationship was doomed?

Finally, after several minutes, I went back into the castle. Betheny was waiting impatiently in the drawing room, and as I walked in, she asked excitedly, "What did Kit want?"

Walking over to the roaring fire in the marble fireplace, I held out my shivering hands, warming them, and responded with a long sigh, "He asked me to marry him."

"Oh, Chrissa, how exciting! Did you accept?"

"No," I answered slowly. "I couldn't."

"Poor Kit," Betheny responded kindly. "He must have been s-so hurt. No wonder he left in such a hurry, without even saying good-by."

I looked at Betheny then said softly, "He thought it was because of Alex. He said, 'First Marianne, now you.' And then he ran off."

Betheny looked away from me, her face suddenly gone pale.

I spent nearly all of the next two weeks sewing. Betheny's gown was finished the day after my birthday and turned out even nicer than I had hoped. When she tried it on, I was amazed at the change in her appearance. She looked very much like a young lady in the gown, instead of an awkward little girl. She was so pleased with her gown that she even began to look forward to the ball, though she was still worried about being a wallflower.

The fact that Alex would be returning for the ball added to her excitement. And even the knowledge that Antonia would be with him couldn't dim her happiness. It had been two long months since she had seen him, and she missed him sorely.

The moment Betheny's gown was finished, I began working feverishly on my own. I was not especially looking forward to the ball, but I was desperate to bury myself in some kind of activity that would fill my mind and take my thoughts off Kit's disturbing reaction to my refusal of his proposal. As I worked on my gown, I made a conscious effort not to think about the golden velvet gown in the storeroom . . .

I didn't see Kit at all during that brief period. However, I knew that he had been invited to the Beltane celebration and I thought he would probably come, if only not to hurt Betheny's feelings. When I thought of seeing him again, I felt nervous and tense. This nervousness was surpassed only by my dread of seeing Alex again.

Such nervousness was unlike me, but then lately I hadn't been behaving like myself at all. And I knew at least part of the reason why.

On the morning of May first, I awoke to the sounds of frantic preparations. The gardeners brought in hundreds of flowers from the hothouse and dozens of potted plants from the garden to decorate the ballroom. Bottles of champagne were brought up from the wine cellar, dusted off, and stood on the huge sideboard in the dining room, waiting to be put in buckets of ice that evening.

Morag had prepared an overwhelming amount of food, enough to feed a small army. That afternoon I went down to the kitchen to look in on her and found her the center of a bustle of activity. She proudly showed me the food she had cooked, rattling off a list of enchanting names, everything from cullen skink, to haggis and neeps, musselburgh pie, roast grouse Rob Roy, and a delicious looking pudding quaintly called Tipsy Laird Trifle.

Though the kitchen was a culinary heaven, filled with delicious sights and smells, Morag wouldn't let anyone, even me, touch anything. " 'Tis for this evenin'," she said sternly when I started to dip a finger into a bowl of trifle. Finally she ordered me upstairs to my room for a nap, saying, "The ball will last till the wee hours o' the mornin' an' ye'll need yer strength."

As she led me out of the kitchen, she stopped and said in a low voice, "But mind 'tis Beltane . . . dinna leave the castle. There will be evil outside on this night."

Up in my room, I couldn't sleep as Morag had ordered. I was still working on my gown. It had taken me longer than I had expected to complete, and an hour before the ball was due to start, I was still hemming it. As I worked, I thought about Morag's stern warning. She had been trembling with fear when she asked me to stay inside the castle—where, she insisted, I would be safe.

Late in the afternoon, Betheny came bursting into my room with the news that Alex and Antonia had returned. As I sat by the window, sewing, she perched on the edge of my bed, happily describing their return.

"Antonia looked thoroughly bored, of course," Betheny began with a sly smile, "I'm sure she did *not* want to come back. She hates Skye, you know, it's far too provincial for her taste. Oh, Chrissa, the whole thing is almost worth it just to s-see her looking so miserable."

She giggled, and I smiled in return. I could

well imagine Antonia's displeasure at having to return to dull, socially unexciting Skye after two months in Edinburgh.

"But Uncle Alex looked happy to be back. He hugged me tightly and s-said that he had missed me terribly. You know, Chrissa, I think he's changed lately. He never used to be so affectionate. Anyway, it's wonderful having him back. I asked him if he would s-stay and he wouldn't say exactly, but I think he wants to."

"Did he . . . ask about me?" I asked slowly, trying hard to sound casual.

"Yes, right away, in fact," Betheny answered easily. "He seemed very concerned when I told him you had been ill for awhile. But I explained that it was just a passing influenza or something."

If he was truly concerned, I thought bitterly, why had he abandoned me?

Betheny was too happy at her uncle's return to sense that something was bothering me, and she continued excitedly, "You should s-see Antonia's ballgown. I saw her maid, Yvette, ironing it, absolutely yards and yards of peach-colored chiffon. Exactly what you would expect. She won't be outdone by anyone, as usual. Though you know, I think your gown is much nicer. It's rather plain, but somehow much more tasteful and elegant than Antonia's."

"Thank you for the compliment, but I think it's a foregone conclusion that Antonia will be the belle of the ball," I said drily.

"Well, we'll just s-see about that," Betheny countered pertly as she left to go to her own room to begin dressing.

When she had gone, I stopped sewing for a moment and looked out at the slowly darkening sky and the dark mountains in the distance. So Alex was back at last. In a few short hours we would see each other for the first time since that stormy night of passion.

Brenna
April, 1746

I cannot think of Conal without remembering Culloden and everything that happened during that fearsome battle. Of all of it, what I remember most is the hail. It fell so thick and hard that the warriors were obscured and looked like ghosts grimly reenacting an ancient battle . . .

I had not seen Conal since our confrontation after my night with Lorn. Then I heard that he had gone off to join the Prince's forces at Culloden. Immediately I ran to Castle Stalker, stumbling over the stones on the rocky moor, splashing through the streams, desperate to talk to Lorn. He had promised! How could he have let Conal go?

But when I arrived at the castle Lorn refused to talk to me. The place was filled with men, every member of the clan who was able to fight, and Lorn was organizing them to march off to Culloden. Finally I managed to force myself through the shouting, excited mob and reached Lorn.

"You swore he would not fight," I began angrily through bitter tears.

"The clan must make an appearance," Lorn responded curtly. "The other chiefs expect it.

But I told you, the Clan MacLaren will no' fight. Come with me an' you'll see."

Picking me up bodily he sat me on a horse near his, and we set off at a gallop. All that night we rode, arriving at the crest of a hill overlooking Culloden Moor just as the sun was beginning to rise in the sky. Culloden was a bleak heath, broken only by a wee burn, hardly more than a sogginess of the grass, that flowed into a small spring. The morning mists were still ghost-like in the few trees and during the night some great colony of spiders had covered the furze-bushes with silver gauze.

I looked down at the two armies, lined up opposite each other—on one side, Prince Charlie himself, with 500 hungry clansmen wearied by a night march; forty yards away, the Duke of Cumberland and 9,000 regular troops. The Duke sat his white horse rigidly, looking toward the slight rise of ground directly opposite where the tall, red-haired Prince sat his horse.

For two hours not a shot was fired as the armies formed for battle. I looked around desperately for Conal but could not find him. Then at a little after 1:00 the Highlanders fired their cannon. From the enemy came a bombardment of grapeshot which cut lines through the clans. The second shot was aimed at the Prince himself and fell among the horsemen surrounding him, spattering his face with mud.

Then the skirl of the war pibrochs began and the battle started in earnest. With a wild shout, the Mackintoshes broke from the right center of the line, dashing through the hail, toward the enemy guns . . . and the slaughter

273

began. McGillivray of Drumglass was pointed out to me, leading a charge, waving his claymore, taking his men through grapeshot and musket fire. Through smoke and hail the Highland front line moved forward to suicide, wave after wave of clansmen flinging themselves on the English bayonets and dying ...

I knew that somewhere among them was Conal, and my heart ached as I looked around for him. Then I saw a familiar red stallion leave the fighting throng and race up the hill toward us. I burst into tears and thanked God when I saw Conal. His face looked exhausted, his clothes were covered with blood, but he was alive.

Pulling his horse to a halt in front of Lorn, he begged him to lead the men into battle. But Lorn refused, saying the battle was clearly lost.

I ran to Conal then, hanging onto his stirrup, beseeching him to stay with us where it was safe. But he scorned me and rode back to fight, not once looking back ...

Then I looked at Lorn's cold, impassive face, and I knew that he had truly betrayed me ... he had known all along that Conal would insist on fighting, even alone. When he had said that the Clan MacLaren would not fight, he had not meant Conal wouldn't.

When it was over, I walked across the battlefield, past the bloody, maimed bodies of dead and dying men and horses. The silence was broken only by the occasional agonized scream of a wounded horse or the low moan of a dying man. The stench of death was overpowering and I had to hold my kerchief to my nose to keep from fainting.

I finally found Conal . . . lying face down at the well of the dead, one hand lying limply in the blood-red pool.

He was dead.

CHAPTER 14

The damsel dons her best attire,
The shepherd lights his beltane fire,
LORD OF THE ISLES
Canto First, VIII

The night of May 1st was clear and warm, perfect weather for the Beltane celebration. As I looked out of my window onto the rear of the castle, I saw Willie and some of the other male servants piling huge stacks of wood on the lawn. Later, these would be giant bonfires, to ward off the evil that was supposed to be loose on this night.

Finally at 7:30, a half-hour before guests were due to begin arriving, I finished my dress. Just then, as I sat back and sighed, letting the dress fall to the floor, Betheny came into my room. I hardly recognized her. Lucy had pulled her brown hair back in a dozen ringlets that fell down past her neck, and a bright blue satin ribbon was entwined in her curls. As she walked in, her blue satin gown made a swishing sound along the floor.

"Betheny, you look very pretty!" I exclaimed, smiling.

She grinned in a touching combination of embarrassment and immense pleasure, and said hesitantly, "Do you really think so?"

"Of course! You certainly don't have to worry about being a wallflower now. In fact, I take back what I said about Antonia being the belle of the ball. I dare say you'll outshine her."

Blushing, she responded softly, "I'm so glad you'll be there. If I do turn out to be a wallflower, at least I won't have to go through it alone."

"Oh, Beth, it will be great fun, you'll see. And wait 'till your uncle sees you in that gown. He'll think you're quite the grown-up young lady."

"Uncle Alex *has* seen me," she answered excitedly. "He told me that I am the prettiest girl he's ever seen. I know it isn't true, but it was so nice of him to say so."

"I think it probably is true. You look very lovely."

"He seemed surprised," Betheny continued quietly. "As if he suddenly realized that I'm not a child any longer. And he said that he is *very* proud of me. Do you know, Chrissa, that's the first time he's ever said that to me."

I could well imagine what Alex MacLaren's feelings were at such a time—seeing his daughter nearly grown and not able to acknowledge her as his own. I felt intense pity for the man. Whatever he was, whatever he had done in his wild life, he had certainly paid for his sins.

Betheny was looking at me oddly, wondering why I had suddenly grown so quiet and serious, I knew. To distract her, I said brightly, "He *should* be proud of you. You've grown up a great deal since I first met you."

"Well, if he thinks I've grown up, wait till he sees *you*," Betheny responded gaily. "He tends to think of you as being my age, you know, and he's certainly going to be in for a surprise when he sees you in that gown."

We both laughed happily, and then Lucy came in, insisting that tonight I couldn't wear my hair in my usual style, braids, but must have something special. She had just been getting some last-minute instructions from Yvette, Antonia's maid, on a fancy new hairstyle. I sat at my dressing table, continuing to talk to Betheny while Lucy worked on my hair. Lucy constantly interrupted the conversation to say peevishly, "Hold still, miss, or I canna' do this right."

When she finished several minutes later, my hair was arranged in what Lucy proudly called a "French knot," an elaborate bun at the nape of my neck, with tendrils of hair curling around my forehead and cheeks.

"Oh, miss, 'tis verra late, we must get ye into yer gown quickly."

As I stood and picked up the gown where it was still lying on the floor in a golden heap,

Lucy took a corset out of the top drawer in my dresser.

"Now, miss," she began firmly as I looked askance at the uncomfortable contraption, "I ken ye usually dinna bother to wear this, but tonight ye must. People would be scandalized to see yer body unconstrained."

"Oh, very well," I gave in reluctantly. "I suppose I can bear the stupid thing for a few hours."

When Lucy finally got it laced up as tightly as she insisted was necessary, I was immensely uncomfortable. But before I could take off the ridiculous contraption, she dropped my gown over my head and began buttoning the row of tiny buttons in the back.

When Lucy finished and I turned around to face her and Betheny their expressions were surprised and admiring.

"Ach, miss, ye're a beauty for sure," Lucy said proudly, and I knew that she felt a good deal of the credit went to her hair-dressing efforts.

"Chrissa . . . you look so different!" Betheny burst out awkwardly.

Turning to look at myself in the full-length mirror on my wardrobe closet door, I saw the reflection of a stranger—a sophisticated young woman in a beautiful gown of billowing golden velvet, the material shining softly in the lamplight. My body, a good deal of which was revealed in the tight, lowcut bodice, was that of a woman, not a girl.

As I looked at my reflection in the mirror, it seemed to waver and move, as if it was a dark pool . . . thus had I seen myself in the pool before I lay with Lorn . . . offering him my full hips and milk-white breasts in exchange for my lover's life . . . Conal, all for Conal . . .

"Chrissa, are you all right? You look ill."

I didn't respond. I was feeling what it was like to be a passionate, wanton female, possessed of surpassing beauty, capable of committing any sin for her love. . .

"Would ye like some brandy, miss? Ye do look a bit pale," Lucy added, and I knew she was remembering that I had been like this in the dungeon that day.

"I'm just . . . tired," I said slowly, my voice strangely husky and drawling.

Looking at the clock on the mantel I saw that it was 8:30, and I said quickly, "We'd best get down to the ballroom."

"Yes . . . you're right," Betheny answered hesitantly, still looking at me strangely.

As we walked side by side down the staircase, we could hear the sounds of music, laughter and talking coming up from the ballroom below. Apparently, a good many of the guests had already arrived.

When we reached the bottom of the stairway where it flared into a wide curve facing the huge double doors that opened onto the ballroom, we came face to face with Kit. My stomach tightened and the exhilaration I had been feeling, slipped. But he smiled broadly, without even a trace of tension, and spoke gallantly, "Two more lovely lasses I have never seen. I don't know which to dance with first!"

His dilemma was resolved when a young man, an acquaintance of Betheny's from a neighboring estate, came up and asked her for the dance. I was relieved to see that the evening was starting out so successfully for her.

When they had gone, Kit bowed and said, "Shall we?"

I nodded and he led me into the ballroom where we joined several other couples in a waltz. I had never danced before, but Kit was an expert and he taught me quickly. In a moment we were whirling smoothly around the room. As we danced, Kit holding me lightly, he looked down at me and said coolly, "I always knew that you were a beauty, Chrissa, but you've surprised even me tonight."

"It's just the gown," I said huskily, looking up at Kit seductively.

"No . . . it's more than a beautiful gown and a new hairstyle. You're different . . . more womanly."

He was right—I *was* different. I felt bold and carefree, eager for new sensations. I looked at Kit, and every other man in the room, differently, wondering if they found me attractive, if they wanted me . . .

And then I saw Alex.

He was standing next to Antonia near the orchestra, wearing the full, traditional dress of the Highlander. The kilt was the red and black MacLaren tartan. Over the scarlet doublet was a gold sash, and over that the plaid, also in the MacLaren tartan, secured by a gold shoulder pin. With his black eyes and thick, unruly brown hair, he looked magnificent and terrifying—a wild Highland warrior-chief from a time when honor was more important than life itself. I stared at him, mesmerized, overwhelmed by the feeling that I was looking the past in the face. He stared back, with a look of surprise and something else . . . hatred?

It only lasted for a second, though it seemed an eternity, then Kit whirled me around in a different direction, and soon I was at the other end of the room.

I couldn't get the picture of Alex and Antonia out of my mind. She was easily the most beautiful woman at the ball in a gorgeous gown of peach-colored chiffon over emerald green silk. And she had been holding Alex's arm tightly, as if to say to the world, "He is mine."

And Alex—he had looked exactly like . . .

"Antonia is very nearly the belle of the ball," Kit said lightly, interrupting my dark thoughts. "As was to be expected. But you've upstaged her, with your hair as black as night and your simple gown. Not even Antonia can hold a candle to you tonight, Chrissa. You're very beautiful and . . . seductive. There isn't a man here tonight who hasn't stared at you with undisguised desire. And there isn't a woman who doesn't wish she had your special quality. It's more than just lovely grey eyes that a man could get lost in, and a figure that epitomizes womanhood. Whatever it is that set apart the great sirens of history, Helen of Troy and Cleopatra and the others, *you* have it. That dark, mysterious thing with all the power of instinct, that gives a woman power over a man, despite his greater strength."

I was lightheaded with Kit's extravagant compliments. And yet when the dance ended just then, I wasn't disappointed. I was somehow tired of Kit, and when he asked me for the

283

next dance I lied, saying I preferred to rest for a bit.

Laughing, gay, once more his charming, lighthearted self, Kit responded easily, "You'll get used to the pace. I'll be back for another dance later. Don't forget."

I sat in a quiet corner, watching the ladies and gentlemen in their beautiful clothes. I had never met most of these people before and I knew that they were wondering who I was. One elderly lady who looked quite formidable in a heavy diamond necklace, stared at me openly, then turned to her companion, a rather short, anemic looking man, saying in a loud voice that carried to the corner where I was sitting, "Who *is* that young woman?"

The old man glanced at me, then said something in a soft voice.

"Humph!" the woman responded arrogantly. "I wouldn't say *pretty*. If you ask me she has *that* sort of look—you know what I mean. One of *those* women."

Just then a stranger asked me to dance. And then another. I was kept very busy and I never again had occasion to listen to the arrogant old dowager. But it didn't matter, her scathing comment had not bothered me somehow. I was completely taken up with flirting outrageously with the men I danced with, pressing my body against theirs as we danced, watching them sneaking glances at my low neckline where my firm breasts bulged upwards, compressed by the tight corset, offering themselves almost in their entirety to the eye.

I saw Betheny occasionally. She seemed to be very preoccupied with the young man who had originally asked her to dance and he seemed rather smitten with her, too. I saw Alex often, but always Antonia was with him and neither of them spoke to me. The first time she noticed me she looked quite shocked, and I knew she was wondering where on earth I had acquired the dress I was wearing. It certainly wasn't the ugly gown she had intended for me to wear.

As for Alex, he watched me carefully, his expression surprised and perplexed.

Kit returned to dance with me several times. We spoke casually of various things, but neither of us mentioned his recent proposal.

At 10:00 everyone went into the dining room where small tables with five or six chairs around them had been set up. Kit led me to the one where Betheny and her partner were sitting, then left to get us each a plate of food.

Betheny greeted me happily, then guiltily apologized for not talking to me all evening.

"It's perfectly all right," I said easily. "It looks like you've been having a good time."

She blushed, glancing shyly at her friend whom she introduced as Roderick Alan Christie, or Roddie as she called him.

Suddenly Alex and Antonia walked up. Betheny greeted her uncle warmly, but gave Antonia a curt, "Hello." When they sat down, I avoided Alex's gaze, though I could feel him staring at me intently.

"I'm certainly surrounded by beauty tonight," he observed expansively, leaning back in his chair and surveying all of us.

Betheny giggled and Antonia smiled coquettishly. Then Antonia said coolly, "That's a striking gown, Carissa. But don't you think it's a bit . . . bold?"

"I think it suits her," Alex broke in curtly, his words carrying a sharp undertone.

I met his look for the first time, staring into his black eyes without flinching . . . defying the anger I found there.

Kit returned then with the food, his arrival cutting the tension that was in the air. But though the food was delicious, I ate little of it, having inexplicably lost my appetite. There was something in the air—I had the vague feeling that a sequence of events had been set in motion . . . by me.

After a few minutes, people began drifting back into the ballroom and I took my leave of the small group at the table.

To my surprise, Alex followed me, and as the orchestra struck up a waltz, he led me onto the dance floor. I did not want to go with him, but his hand held my wrist tightly as he pulled me forcibly into the middle of the room. One arm went around my waist, drawing me close to him, while the other held my hand tightly.

As he whirled me around the room, I was silent, trying not to think about the way his arm felt around my waist. When Kit held me, it meant nothing. Now, in Alex's arms, my body felt weak and my breath came in short, nervous gasps. Dream-like erotic images of the night in the cottage filled my mind.

"You know, I actually felt guilty about what happened that night in the crofter's cottage," Alex spoke suddenly. "I was afraid that I had somehow taken advantage of an innocent young girl. But after seeing you tonight, I can see how laughable that really is. If anything, you're less innocent than Antonia. You've got every man here sniffing around you like a pack of hounds after a bitch in heat."

"Are you jealous?" I asked icily, feeling inexplicably compelled to hurt him, to bait him into taking some sort of action.

But he said nothing, his black eyes merely narrowing in silent fury, his mouth grim and taut. I knew that he was barely keeping his explosive temper in check.

When the dance ended, he left abruptly, and spent the rest of the evening at Antonia's side, ignoring me.

At midnight the bonfires were lit and everyone walked out onto the back lawn to watch them. Standing in front of the window in the ballroom, alone, watching the flames leap high into the black sky, I remembered what Morag had said . . . "Stay inside where 'tis safe. Dinna' go outside, there is evil about."

Suddenly I felt someone behind me and whirling around I came face to face with Alex. He looked down at me, those familiar black eyes as inscrutable as ever. I stared up at him defiantly, determined not to back off. Somehow I sensed that this confrontation was inevitable. I had felt it coming all evening, had been compelled to bring the situation to a climax that was both inevitable and unknown.

And then with one hand, he pulled me against him hard, and with the other hand held my face still while he bent down to kiss me, his lips pressing roughly against mine, his tongue probing my mouth.

I struggled, but he was so much stronger

than I. Finally I managed to free one hand and with it I scratched his cheek savagely, raking my nails across it. He let go of me, his hand flying to his face, where blood was beginning to flow.

I ran . . . out of the ballroom and into the drawing room, where I stopped to catch my breath. I had no idea where to go or what to do.

"Chrissa!" Alex's voice rang out harsh and loud and I saw him standing in the doorway of the drawing room, his cheek bleeding and his face contorted in rage. I ran through the door nearest me . . . the door leading to the storeroom and the dungeon. When I entered the narrow stairwell, I realized the fatal mistake I had made but I couldn't go back.

Running through the ancient kitchen, I descended the rough stone stairway leading to the dungeon. It was completely dark and I could see nothing. Running my hands along the cold, dirty wall beside me, I tried to feel my way. When I suddenly stumbled over a box, I knew there was nowhere else to go. I lay on the damp stone floor, staring into the blackness, waiting for him to come, as he surely would.

In a moment I saw a pale light and I realized that he had stopped to light a candle. The light came down the stone stairway, flickering uncertainly. When Alex reached the bottom of the stairway I saw his face, contorted with rage and passion. I gasped and he heard me, immediately turning and walking straight toward where I lay. When he found me huddled on the floor, he set down the candle on a nearby trunk.

288

As I looked up at him, I knew . . . he wasn't Alex, he was . . .

"Harlot!" The word came out like the hiss of a snake.

Then he bent down and pulled me roughly up to him. Savagely he tore my gown until it hung in ragged strips around my waist. I couldn't fight him. I couldn't move. I just stood there silently, accepting his abuse, feeling somehow that I deserved it.

As I stood half-naked and shivering in front of him I whispered "Please . . ." But it was no use. What was happening was preordained. I had felt it building all evening.

He pushed me to the floor and I felt the rough stone cutting through my corset into my back. Alex kissed me again hard, with hate-filled passion, while I lay on the floor impassively, not resisting. And then as he held me tightly, he looked into my eyes and suddenly his arms went limp.

"What am I doing?" The words were anguished, confused. Slowly, he rose and then turned and walked away, stumbling back up the stairs, leaving the candle burning softly in the distance. I lay there, unable to move, and then I began to tremble. I was cold . . . so cold . . .

"Chrissa! My God, what's happened?"

It was Kit, standing at the bottom of the stairs, holding a candle, staring at me, horrified. I said nothing. He came toward me, looked at me carefully for a brief moment, then said slowly, "Was it . . . Alex?"

"Yes." My voice was flat and emotionless.

"I knew something was wrong," Kit said

harshly. "When I couldn't find either of you ... somehow I knew."

Taking off his coat, he covered my bare shoulders and said gently, "Come with me."

He helped me stand, then led me up the stairway to the drawing room. I heard people in the ballroom, but I saw no one. Kit led me to the servants' stairway and through there up to my room.

In my room he stood me in front of the small fire, then threw more wood on it until it was blazing hot. Gratefully I felt the heat gradually dispel the intense cold that had come over me in the dungeon.

"You must leave here," Kit said firmly. "God only knows what Alex will do with you if you stay."

I nodded dully.

"Stay in your room until everyone has left," Kit continued. "Then quietly make your way out to the bonfires. I'll be waiting for you there and I'll take you in to the hotel at Portree. You'll be safe there. I won't compromise your reputation by taking you to MacKenzie House.

I started to laugh hysterically . . . he was actually worried about ruining my reputation. If he only knew the truth ...

Looking at me worriedly, he asked, "Do you understand?"

"Yes . . . I'll meet you by the bonfires."

"Good."

Kit walked to the door, then stopped as he reached it. Turning back toward me, he finished, "Remember, as soon as all the guests have left, you *must* leave, too. Alex will come for you then."

I nodded and he left, carefully locking the door behind him. I lay down on my bed, staring listlessly at the ceiling. An hour passed. The sounds of carriages drawing up in front of the castle, and people leaving, drifted up to my window. Finally all was silent and I knew that the last guests must have left. Quietly I got up and walked to my door. Putting an ear against it, I listened but there was no sound outside. Slipping on my old black cloak, I walked out into the dark hallway. Softly I walked past the rows of portraits, no longer afraid of them but afraid of the very real person I might encounter at any moment.

When I reached the bottom of the stairs, I looked into the ballroom. It was empty, not even the servants were about.

A moment later I had descended the stairway to the Great Hall and was hurrying out the front door. Rushing to the rear of the castle, I stopped short when I saw one bonfire still blazing, next to two others that had died down. "Dinna' go outside," Morag had warned. And now here I was, outside on this terrible night, alone and vulnerable to whatever evil was loose.

As I looked at the tall, brightly burning bonfire, I knew Morag was right . . . there was evil out here somewhere, waiting for me . . . I could sense it.

Suddenly a dark figure outlined against the backdrop of the bonfire moved toward me and I jumped, startled.

"Chrissa!" It was Kit's voice, firm and reassuring.

I hurried to him.

"We must leave here at once," he said quickly. "I have to get you away from Alex forever."

His pale blue eyes were burning brightly with a strange excitement, as they had when I rejected his offer of marriage. Suddenly I felt ill at ease with him. But he seemed to notice nothing, taking my arm and guiding me away from the castle.

It was then that I saw Alex. He had come up from the seagate, apparently having gone for a walk along the beach, and stood only a few yards from us. Looking surprised, he stared at me helplessly for a long moment, then said hesitantly, "Chrissa, what are you doing?"

But before I could speak, Kit began harshly, "I'm taking her away from you, Alex. You'll never see her again."

Reaching into his coat pocket, Kit pulled out a long, gleaming knife. In the light of the bonfire, the curved blade shone brightly. Kit's hold on my arm tightened until he was hurting me.

"Kit, please, don't," I began, but he ignored me, staring fiercely at Alex.

"You'll lose her as ye've lost everyone else," he said queerly, his eyes grim and determined.

Still Alex just stood there looking at me, making no move to stop us, looking unbearably hurt and ashamed. When he finally spoke, his voice was desperate.

"Chrissa, please, stay with me . . . I'm sorry . . ."

"It's no good, Alex. You've lost," Kit interrupted coldly.

"No!" I shouted, sobbing. "Kit, I don't want to leave him, let me go"

But he continued to hold my wrist tightly, anger and disappointment on his face.

"It isn't your choice," Kit spoke slowly. "I've got to take you away from Alex, as I did the others."

There was a stunned silence, then Alex said softly, "You killed them, didn't you, Kit . . . my father and Jonathan. And you tried to kill Betheny, too."

"Yes," Kit admitted simply, without a hint of remorse. I felt my stomach tighten and my throat constrict with the horror of the sudden, unexpected confession made so coolly.

"For Marianne?" Alex asked calmly.

"For Marianne . . . all for Marianne," Kit answered quickly. "She was part of me. When you killed her, you destroyed my life."

"But I was not responsible for her death!" Alex insisted.

"You were!" Kit exploded, his carefully controlled rage unmasked now. I was shocked to see his gentle, handsome face distorted by madness, his ice-blue eyes alight with an unholy fire, his mouth quivering nervously.

"I swore I'd make you pay for it," Kit continued, "through the same loneliness and isolation you brought to my life. I've seen to it that you inherited Castle Stalker, but lost everything else."

"Kit . . . let Chrissa go. She has nothing to do with this," Alex asked calmly.

"She does! She's the one you love the most,

293

and I've got to take her away from you forever!"

Before Kit could continue, Alex rushed at him, surprising him. Kit threw me aside, and I fell on the hard ground, scraping my cheek and hands. Looking up, I saw Kit and Alex silhouetted against the fire, circling each other warily like two wild animals. Kit's face was contorted with hatred and something more . . . madness. He had the same mad look that Marianne had worn in her portrait, and I realized suddenly that the family must have been tainted with insanity.

And then, as Kit rushed at Alex, I remembered . . . Lorn had held me back until the battle was over, making me watch from the hill with him and his men . . . I looked desperately for Conal afterwards, but I couldn't find him . . . I was filled with an overwhelming guilt for I had betrayed him . . . there was a hailstorm, and smoke from the cannon . . . through the smoke and hail I saw the men move forward to suicide on the English bayonets until that bleak heath was covered with the corpses of chief and clansman . . . but not the MacLarens, for Lorn would not let them fight . . .

When it was over, Lorn let me go, saying, "Find yer lover an' bury him. Then come back to me for ye're mine now."

I ran onto the field, winding my way among the mutilated bodies . . . over all was the stench of death . . . and then I came to the well of the dead, and there I finally found Conal . . .

A scream tore through the night, bringing

me back to the present. I looked up at the two dark figures fighting in front of the fire, and saw that Kit had plunged his knife deep into Alex's arm. When he pulled it out, blood spurted out onto Alex, covering his white shirt. And then I knew . . . long ago Kit had been Lorn MacLaren, treacherous and mad, and Alex had been Conal, the lover I betrayed . . .

And it was all happening again. Kit would send Alex to his grave, through my betrayal.

Kit was holding the knife above Alex's chest, pushing it down slowly, inexorably, while Alex struggled desperately with his one good arm, trying to hold him back.

Moving quickly, I flung my cloak over Kit's head, blinding him for a moment. And in that moment, Alex managed to turn the knife against Kit, plunging it into his chest.

Kit fell back, a stunned look on his face, then sprawled on the ground, barely breathing.

I knelt over him . . . gentle, mad Kit . . . knowing that he was dying. He looked up at me, then at Alex standing shakily behind me, and said in a hoarse whisper, "Brenna . . ."

And then he was dead.

Brenna
April, 1746

In the darkness of my cold, grim cell I sit silently. Tentatively I touch my belly which has already begun to swell slightly from the life within it.

If only Conal had lived . . .

I hear footsteps approaching above. It must be Lorn, come to ask the same question, but to-

day my answer will be different. I will say what he wants to hear and he will gladly release me from this horrible dungeon. He will think I have finally lost my defiance and will triumphantly take me to his bed . . .

Later, when he is sleeping, I will leave Castle Stalker and make my way to Loch Coruisk, the dead place where the grim and awful giants keep their eternal watch. For I have realized what I must do . . . the penance I must pay for my betrayal.

CHAPTER 15

And Love, howe'er the maiden strive,
Must with reviving hope revive!
                    LORD OF THE ISLES
                    Canto Sixth, IX

I awoke late in the afternoon of May 2nd, lying in my own soft, warm bed. Betheny was sitting in a chair next to me and when she saw me open my eyes, she smiled broadly. In a voice that sounded far too mature for the Betheny I had known, she said softly, "Hello, sleepyhead. You've been asleep all day, but everything is all right. How do you feel?"

I answered in a shaky voice, "Fine, I think ... what happened?"

"Dr. Ross gave you a sedative. He said that

you needed to rest for a long while to give your mind time to get over . . . what happened."

And then I remembered . . . the fight in front of the bonfire, Alex wounded . . .

"Alex! Is he all right?" I asked desperately.

"Yes, he's fine," Betheny reassured me quickly. "The wound on his arm was painful but not terribly serious. Dr. Ross took care of it."

Then she added soberly, "Kit is dead, Chrissa."

I must have grown pale for she added immediately, "Perhaps we shouldn't talk about it just yet."

"No, it's all right," I responded firmly. "It's over now . . . it's all over now." Then, "Poor Kit. He was completely insane."

"I know," Betheny said with a shudder. "Uncle Alex explained everything to the constable when he came last night. How horrible to think that Kit had been planning it all this time. Murdering one person after another, and all the while appearing as sane as you or I. I can't begin to imagine the depth of the hatred he must have held toward Uncle Alex. Because of that hatred, grandfather is dead, and Jonathan. And I almost died. Then last night, you . . .

"Well, as you said, it's all over now. Kit has joined Marianne, and I'm sure that's where he really wanted to be. How horribly ironic to think it was all a mistake. Today they found proof that Uncle Alex wasn't to blame for Marianne's death."

"They did?"

"Yes. The constable searched MacKenzie

298

House this morning. Apparently that's the normal procedure. In a secret drawer in the writing desk in Marianne's room, they found her diary. In it she told of her affair with a man in Kyle of Lochalsh. He was married, and she knew Kit would never approve of such a thing, so she pretended to be involved with Uncle Alex. When she told her lover that she was pregnant, he refused to leave his wife and marry her. That was when she decided to kill herself."

"Poor, sad Marianne. She must have felt completely abandoned and utterly without hope."

"Yes," Betheny responded softly. "When I heard what was in the diary, I cried. Marianne was always such a timid, gentle sort of person. How strange to think that in a way it was she who caused the horrors of the past year."

After a moment, Betheny continued slowly, "You know, I'll never forget the way Uncle Alex looked when he carried you in last night. You fainted, you see. I had gone looking for you after the ball, excited and happy and wanting to talk. But I couldn't find you anywhere. Then Uncle Alex came through the French windows into the library, carrying you in his arms. Blood was all over your dress and his shirt. For a horrible moment I thought you had been killed."

Smiling wryly, Betheny finished, "Even Antonia seemed concerned about you. But despite her one moment of kindness I'm still glad she's gone."

"Gone? You mean forever?" I asked, surprised.

"Yes. Uncle Alex decided that everyone would be happier if she moved to London. So he increased her allowance and she left immediately. She barely took time to pack."

I laughed, as relieved as Betheny was that the hateful Antonia would no longer be around.

Then Betheny continued hesitantly, suddenly very nervous, "Chrissa, there's s-something else. Last night, after Dr. Ross left, Uncle Alex took me into the library and we had a long talk. He told me . . ."

She couldn't finish, so I concluded for her, "You are his daughter."

Betheny looked shocked. "How on earth did you know?"

"You look so much alike," I said simply. "How do you feel about it?"

"Well, at first I couldn't believe it. And I felt embarrassed and ashamed. But Uncle Alex, I mean Father, loves me so much, it doesn't really matter that I am . . . illegitimate. That's why he was rather distant all these years. He was afraid to get too close to me for fear that people would guess, as you did. You know, I think that somehow I always suspected the truth. For as long as I can remember, it was he I cared about—not the man I thought was my father."

Betheny had grown up a great deal, I realized. Though the past few months had been a horrible ordeal, she had come through it a much stronger person. For a fleeting moment I almost missed the stammering, insecure little girl I had first met nearly a year ago.

Then Betheny said brightly, "Here we are talking away, and you must be starving."

She pulled the bellpull and a few minutes later Lucy entered, carrying a tray with a teapot and a bowl of soup.

"Morag thought ye might be wantin' somethin' to eat, miss," Lucy said easily. "She made some o' her special Dulce soup, a medicinal brew, ye see, made o' seaweed."

I grimaced and Betheny and Lucy laughed.

"I ken how it sounds, but Morag will kill me for sure if I dinna' make ye eat it."

"Very well, Lucy, I know Morag well enough to believe you. But I may have to hold my nose while I eat it."

Forcing myself to swallow a tiny mouthful, I was surprised to find it rather good, if a bit bland. After emptying the bowl, and drinking a cup of strong, hot tea, I felt perfectly well and restless.

"I can't lie in bed any longer," I insisted to Betheny after Lucy had left.

"But Dr. Ross left strict orders for you to rest in bed through the night."

"I'm not the sort of person who can just lie around when I feel perfectly fine," I insisted stubbornly, throwing back the blankets and sitting up.

Betheny continued to protest, but finally, seeing that I was determined, she gave in. A few minutes later I was dressed.

As I sat at the vanity table, brushing my hair, I looked at my reflection in the mirror. I saw the same black hair, grey eyes and freckled nose—but something was changed. My eyes looked older, wiser, reflecting the new woman who had been born in blood and death and love during the night. Instead of pulling

301

my hair back with a ribbon, or braiding it as I usually did, I styled it in a simple chignon as Lucy had done the previous evening. After all, I was a woman now, not a child . . . a woman who was finally at peace with herself, no longer beset by demons from the past.

"Chrissa . . ." Betheny began hesitantly, "I think you should know. Uncle Alex, I mean Father, is leaving tomorrow morning."

"What?" I cried, dropping the brush. "Why? Where is he going? Is it Antonia?"

"Oh, no, he made that clear enough. He even said he didn't know what he'd ever seen in her. No, he's not going to join her. But I don't know exactly where he's going. In fact, I'm not even sure he has a destination. And as for why . . . well, I think it has to do with *you*."

Betheny was clearly embarrassed, but she plunged ahead anyway, "Last night when he brought you in, he was afraid you were dying. And he said it was all his fault, that he had been horrible to you."

"But that's not true! None of it was his fault!" I shouted frantically.

"Well, *he* thinks so. And he's going away. Oh, Chrissa, I may as well say what I think, even though it's really none of my business. It was obvious from the way he was looking at you last night that he loves you. And I think you love him. No, I *know* you love him! But there's something wrong between you, there always has been from the very beginning. Oh, whatever it is, it should be resolved."

Yes, I thought, it should be resolved. It was time. The terrible events of last night had broken the spell, and now it was time for Alex and me to make our own future. *Our* future. It must be so!

All of the determination I had ever felt to survive, must now be brought to bear on my love for Alex.

"Where is he?" I asked.

"In the library," Betheny answered quickly, her black eyes brightening.

Leaving my room, I quickly walked down the hallway, stopping for a moment in front of the half-finished portrait of Brenna Breac. I knew her name now . . . I knew everything about her, for I had once *been* her. Her sin of betraying the man she loved had been my sin, but I finally atoned for it. And I knew now that she would never haunt me again.

"You failed, Brenna, but I will not," I said softly, with quiet determination. And then I continued on to the library.

I knocked tentatively on the door, feeling terribly nervous, and when a familiar rough voice called "Come in," I entered slowly.

Alex was standing by the window, looking out to the sea in the distance, calm and azure blue today. As I entered, he turned to face me, and when he saw who it was he looked surprised and awkward, his dark eyes holding none of the hard arrogance they once had. I noticed that under his shirt on his left arm he wore a thick bandage, and his face was pale and haggard. I knew that he was unutterably weary from battling raging emotions that he didn't really understand. We stood quietly staring at each other for a long moment.

"You should be in bed," he began firmly.

"No, I shouldn't," I answered just as firmly.

303

"You suffered a great deal more from last night than I did."

"About last night . . ." he began hesitantly, his eyes looking away, unable to meet mine. "I believe that I owe you an apology. I don't know why I behaved the way I did in the dungeon. It was inexcusable. I shall never be able to forgive myself."

"It doesn't matter now," I interrupted him quickly. "It's all over and we can begin again."

"It *does* matter," Alex insisted harshly, and I knew that his anger was for himself, not me. "However, it won't happen again. I'm riding into Portree shortly to arrange things with our solicitor. You and Betheny shall share Castle Stalker. I will go away and you'll never have reason to fear me again."

"Fear you!" I exploded. "I'm in *love* with you, Alex MacLaren, and you're in love with me!"

I went to him then, touching his shoulder, looking up tenderly into his black eyes, so wounded and unhappy.

"The past is dead, Alex, the future is ours."

"I've had such strange feelings about ye, Chrissa. I knew ye were special, not like any woman I had ever known. Not just beautiful, but proud and bright and good. And yet, I felt such anger toward ye at times. And then, last night, when ye refused to go with Kit and stood by me . . . somehow the anger was gone."

"I . . . I owed you that," I said simply.

Alex hesitated, then shook his head, saying heavily in the grim tone of a man completely without hope, "It's no good. I'm fifteen years older than you. You're still a child, an' I've abused you past forgiveness."

"I'm woman enough to be carrying your child, Alex."

This announcement, delivered so calmly, stunned him. I felt rather surprised and a little disappointed that he hadn't somehow guessed.

"You're carrying my child?" he repeated dumbly. It was not really a question but a statement that he could not quite accept.

I nodded, torn between laughter and tears at the sight of the imperious Alex MacLaren for once completely at a loss for words. I had never seen him look so open, unguarded, vulnerable, and I had never loved him more.

But to my dismay this announcement didn't have the effect I had assumed it would. He said grimly, "Then I have wronged ye even more terribly than I thought. And I am truly unworthy of you. I shall make arrangements with the solicitor so that you and the child will be taken care of completely. But I will not add to your burden by forcing you to spend your life with me."

He strode out, slamming the door behind him as I had once done when leaving him. So, there was to be no chance for us after all, because of his stubborn MacLaren sense of honor.

I stood motionless in the center of the room, knowing it would do no good to run after him, to talk further. Words would have no effect. He had decided that he had wronged me, that I deserved better, and words could not shake that conviction. I knew it was entirely possible that he would try to arrange a marriage with

305

some willing man, someone he would feel deserving of me, in order to clear my reputation. And in the middle of this tangle of honor and duty, our love would be lost forever as Brenna's and Conal's was so long ago.

But I was not like Brenna, I reminded myself forcefully. I would *not* lose the only love I would ever know. There must be something I could do, some way I could persuade Alex that his logic was perverse, that his mistakes were forgiven, and all that mattered was our love.

And then I realized what I must do.

I sat in the large, overstuffed chair, waiting patiently. The room was in shadows, lit only by the pale glow of the fire in the grate. The door opened and Alex walked in, not seeing me in the corner. He began to undress, and I watched him silently, holding my breath, filled with the desperate knowledge that this would be my last chance to set right what was so wrong. Then he turned and saw me, sucking in his breath in surprise.

"Chrissa!"

I rose and walked slowly over to him until I stood inches from him.

"I love you, Alex MacLaren, as I shall never love any other man. You took nothing from me. I gave you what I wanted to give, willingly, freely. If you won't marry me, I'll be your mistress, but I *will* love you. Wherever you go, I shall follow, and make it abundantly clear that all I am I offer to you, and to you alone."

Untying the sash on the robe, I slipped out of the thin garment, letting it fall to the floor around my bare feet. I stood there naked, unashamed, relieved at the look of surprise and then undisguised pleasure that filled Alex's eyes. Putting my arms around him, pressing my breasts against his bare chest, I looked up at him and finished softly, "I'm not a child but a woman in love, and if you weren't such a fool you would see that."

There was a moment's hesitation as he stared at me, unable to keep the hunger from his eyes. Then that familiar wry smile crossed his face and he picked me up lightly, as if I were a feather.

"I am not such a fool," he said huskily, "and I can see quite clearly now that you are, indeed, a woman, a most irresistible one. I suppose I shall have to marry you, or my reputation, so recently restored, will be as black as before."

And then he carried me to the waiting bed.

Another tumultuous romantic novel
by Patricia Matthews,
author of the multi-million
copy national bestseller,
LOVE'S AVENGING HEART

Love's Wildest Promise

P40-047 $1.95

Sarah Moody was a lady's maid in a wealthy London home. But suddenly her quiet sheltered world was turned upside down when she was abducted and smuggled aboard a ship bound for the colonies. Its cargo—whores to satisfy the appetites of King George's soldiers in New York. Was Sarah destined to become one of these women? Or would she find the man she was searching for, the man who would help her to fulfill Love's Wildest Promise.

If you can't find this book at your local bookstore, simply send the cover price, plus 25¢ for postage and handling to:

Pinnacle Books
Reader Mailing Service, P.O. Box 1050,
Rockville Centre, N.Y. 11571